THE NIX OLYMPICA

They had climbed for four days. Past the tree-lined ridges, past the snow and ice, to the meteor-scarred rock at the windless summit. They were still on Mars, but they were in space . . .

Michael and Snow lay side by side on the rim of the Nix Olympica. Within the crater, far below, they saw a strange ochre plain, like the deserts of pre-terraformed Mars; and at the center of the plain, a cluster of unbelievable blue shapes.

They started down. For there, in that City of Blue, was to be conceived the Conqueror, the scourge of Mars whose tragic destiny it was to begin the new age . . .

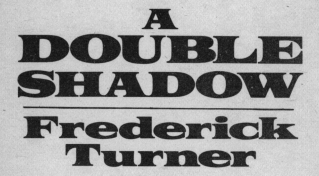

A DOUBLE SHADOW

Frederick Turner

A BERKLEY BOOK
published by
BERKLEY PUBLISHING CORPORATION

for Mei Lin and Daniel

for Benjamin

Berkley Publishing Corporation
200 Madison Avenue
New York, New York 10016

SBN 425-03951-X

BERKLEY MEDALLION BOOKS are published by
Berkley Publishing Corporation
200 Madison Avenue
New York, N.Y. 10016

BERKLEY MEDALLION BOOK ® TM 757,375

Printed in the United States of America

Berkley Edition, FEBRUARY, 1979

Contents

Book III

Foreword:
The Flaws of Raphael Mendel

As I WRITE these words I hear through my feet the bellowing of the three volcanies of the Tharsis Ridge as they spew out the gases and vapor that will one day flow in the sap of the very trees I am about to describe. I live nine hundred years before the events depicted in this novel, and two hundred years after the death of the novel as a viable artistic form; and what I attempt here is a charter-myth of Martian civilization. The planet is even now in the process of Terraforming: through my viewscreen (we live a hundred meters underground) I can see the steaming slopes of the volcano dotted with the tiny, toiling figures of those heroes who are preparing the scenario which I shall here inhabit. Thus at the planet's dawn I provide it with a future history.

All true works of art are ultimately concerned with how they came to exist: they are the history of their own gestation, or, to put it another way, their subject and theme *are* the very problems raised and confronted by their composition. Works of art are selfish and self-concerned: they have to be in a universe where everything but themselves is guaranteed existence and has the advantage of several billion years of mindless, painless and automatic evolution.

This week what I had suspected turned out to be true. Perhaps I should backtrack a little. I occupy the artistically enviable and humanly impossible position of the only poet on a world that is even now being created. This novel is the process of bringing myself to face the human impossibility of my existence: if you like, I am going mad.

Raphael Mendel is the leader of that band of heroic creatures who are now shaping the planet into a fit place for human beings to live. The team is half women and half men. I think of their relationships as one thinks of the archetypal sexual encounters of one's parents: with awe, fear, and jealous anger. They are all tall and muscular, with fine wrinkles around their eyes: those who work on the Phobos crew have flash-burns on their cheeks and foreheads, having elected to look unprotected at the kindling of that new sun; several needed retinal transplants. The ones who worked on the Ring Project (the importation of raw materials from the asteroid belt and the rings of Saturn) have the curious dancelike grace and balance of those who have become accustomed to zero-gravity. Others, whose labors have been confined to Mars, have suffered frostbite, terrible falls, lung damage from inhaling air that was not yet ready to breathe. They all have a dignity of carriage that I can only envy: the morale and unself-consciousness of those who are fulfilling their human purpose.

Meanwhile I live underground near the Tharsis volcanoes and must watch the transformation of the planet through viewscreens. My wife has become cold to me, for what reason I did not know for sure until the last few days. She is very beautiful; we were students together at the University of Oceania in New Zealand.

Some months ago I made an expedition to the Coprates Canyon in order to gather material for this novel. It was my first such expedition (and my last, for I have since been forbidden to leave our comfortable cavern—the Creators are too busy to wetnurse a mere "Earthie").

I took a crawler southeastward across the tumbled

wastes at the western end of the Canyon. It was slow business. I had to find a way across the enormous cracks, that crisscrossed the surface, and the controls of the vehicle were unfamiliar. The weather, as it always is these days, was frightening: hurricans, deluges, immense purple clouds that changed their shape in moments. There is an odd beauty about Mars in the throes of its metamorphosis. Everything is raw and livid. Bolts of lightning burn patterns in your eyes. There is a steady fall of volcanic ash. I played Beethoven's *Spring* sonata and turned off the outside audio, so as to move in a light cocoon of music in the center of the silent violence of the new world.

That was my undoing. I did not hear the warning rumble of the avalanche until it was too late, for the sound insulation is almost perfect. It was a mass of soft mud, in billows and fans like Thoreau's melting clay. In seconds the crawler was immobilized in the soft chaos. Soon afterward, as I desperately threw the motor into reverse and forward, the glass bubble of the tractor was covered with pink and bluish mud, veined like the inside of some monstrous animal's belly.

At this time the matter-transmitters are still in the experimental stage, and the tractor was not equipped with one. There was no escape that way. I tried the radio. Nothing. Beside the radio switches, however, I found a button marked "Emergency antenna extension." I pressed it. There was a grinding hum, then something seemed to free itself. A faint crackle came through the receiver. Evidently the tip of the aerial was now out in the open air.

I tried the emergency wavebands, but without success: I was deep in one of the subsidence fissures, and the signal would not get through. However, I was only a hundred-odd kilometers from home. I tried it. To my mild relief I heard the pilot signal. I pressed the alert button, got a reply.

"Hello Eva, this is me. I've got stuck. The crawler is under an avalanche."

Oh my God. Hang on, I'll get Raphael."

This was odd, but I didn't think about it at the time.

"Hullo, Earthie. You've got yourself into trouble, I hear. Where are you?"

"What are *you* doing there? Oh, never mind, don't answer that, just get me out of here. I'm about a hundred kilometers to the southeast of you, in the . . ."—I looked at the map—". . . Ceres fissure."

"You sound very calm. Good. Perhaps you don't know how much danger you're in. Check the pumps."

I did so, and found they were operating.

"How much air have you got?"

My heart sank, for I knew that the crawler was equipped with a new air system which used Martian air and purified it so that it would be breathable. There was only a small emergency supply: by now, about five hours' worth.

"About five hours."

"O Jesus. It'll take me all that time to get to you. Lie down and breathe as little as you can. And don't panic. Wait a minute—before you do that, check the bubble. There must be tons of pressure on it."

I did so, and indeed there was already some fine cracks, around the seams.

"Just a few cracks."

"Great. The canopy could collapse before you choke to death. I don't suppose you could *dig* your way out? You should have a digger in the tractor."

"Yes, there's a digger."

"Try to open the airlock. Put on your pressure suit first—Oh, by the way, that may save air, it has its own emergency supply—twenty minutes I think—and then be ready with the digger."

The digger is a device which pulverizes sand, rock, and mud, and compacts it into a hard dense spherical shell. It is used for tunneling and mining, and virtually transforms a man into a mole. As he moves forward, the digger hollows out a space before him; the dense material of its walls acts as a buttress to shore up the roof. I put on the pressure suit, hauled the digger out of its locker, and carried it to the air-lock. I had to be ready as soon as the outer door opened, for otherwise the mud would come oozing in and fill the lock in minutes.

The inner door opened and closed without difficulty. I stepped through into the small space within.

Suddenly I felt as if I were being crushed by the weight of the whole world. I gasped and gasped. Nothing seemed to be wrong, but I had never felt a sensation so horrible. I looked around in panic. Everything was still. Suddenly I realized that the force that was oppressing me came from within myself. The whole episode had triggered in me a deep and hidden claustrophobia, accumulated over the years of living underground. I fought for air, breathing so rapidly that my head spun, and groped for the button that would reopen the inner door. I tumbled into the tractor and tore off my facemask. The panic gradually subsided.

I do not know where I found the courage unless it was an incipient sexual shame, but I tried the airlock twice more before giving up. Then I called home again. Mendel had already set off in the other tractor (a flier was impossible in this weather) but Eva put me through to him.

"The lock won't open," I lied.

"Damn. And a digger won't work on tractor metal." I had forgotten that; it was just as well. "I'll just have to dig you out. Try not to breathe."

I lay there for hours. The whole business was a horrible and banal adventure, out of a thousand space thrillers. I was embarrassed: the more so because I had so neatly fitted into the role of the cowardly intellectual. Now Mendel, whom I already hated, would come and risk his life rescuing me; according to the laws of melodrama I would have to redeem myself somehow, probably at the cost of my own. Not a chance. I composed a poem in my head about it: it would look on the surface like a blood-and-guts celebration of Reality, but the discerning reader would perceive in it the glimmerings of a breathtaking cynicism. I called Eva a couple of times but couldn't keep my mind on what she was saying, because of an acute sense of tedium.

And save me he did, in the nick of time of course and at great risk to his life. Just as he arived the canopy began to collapse; he dragged me weeping and fighting through his

newly made tunnel into the open air; at the last moment a
new avalanche began slowly to descend; he pulled me
clear as a blood-red and purple mass of slime engulfed the
whole area; in his crawler he forced a flask of brandy
between my teeth. I was in a complete panic, but had to
fight back a desperate urge to laugh hysterically—not out
of "reaction" but out of a sense of sheer farce. Mendel did
not understand my mood at all; he was a little daunted
himself by my odd behavior.

In the next few weeks I became more and more
fascinated with Mendel. It was his masculinity that
attracted and disgusted me. I rigged up the vision screens
cunningly and illegally so as to follow everything he did. I
concealed what I was doing from Eva because of some
instinct about it.

Yes, he was and is a great hero. I watched him: he never
made faces in the mirror, he never masturbated, he was
always amazingly decent to the women with whom he
expertly and heroically made love. But I wish to leave one
dubious observation to posterity.

I noticed that one of the returned Ring men, whose
name was Marlowe Steele (!), was stealing some of
Mendel's thunder. If possible Steele was even more modest than his rival; his achievements, though in conditions
of lesser responsibility, were almost as remarkable; and
his curly beard and skill on the samisen made him a
favorite among the big-breasted heroines of the planet. I
never actually saw Mendel *brood* about this; but a
shadow sometimes crossed his face when he saw Steele in
the corridors of Central Headquarters or bringing in a
flyer against a full gale.

Eventually Mendel got his chance, if I do not misinter-
pret. He sent Steele off on an assignment, drilling cores in
the Nix Olympica region, which though tedious was
highly dangerous if one did not keep exactly to the rules
(in which case it was quite safe). Sure enough, Steele, in an
attempt to cut corners and complete his work in record
time, was transfixed by a spinning thirty-meter drill
section and sprayed over a good-sized area of the
mountain. Mendel was heartbroken and stood like a

stricken tree at the foot of his friend's grave as the words of the funeral were pronounced; but I noticed that he was a trifle less oppressed in manner afterwards.

I do not mean by this to devalue heroism. God knows, planets are not created without it. And who am I to sneer at the hero? If I want to be a Homer, I must have my Achilles, even my guileful Odysseus.

I come now to the revelation of the last week. Eva is pregnant—her child will be the first to be born on Mars, since the Terraformer women have not wished up to now to be burdened with maternity. And the child is Mendel's. Eva told me the other day, matter-of-factly. I wept. I'm still sighing painfully, with a catch in my diaphragm, though forty-eight hours have gone by. The first human native of the planet, and it will be Mendel's, not mine. It was begotten shortly before I called home to be rescued. I used to love my wife. I hate this planet and everything in it. Nevertheless I have something to leave to it: this novel, which, with all its faults, and at least in intention, is the first work of art in this world.

But there is no reason why the reader should be interested in these motivations. "On with the tale"—it has become my only release, and for me it now holds the only prospect of beauty in my life.

Book I

1.

Narcissus at the Theatre

SUDDENLY THERE IS silence in the auditorium. Ten beats on a light drum. The houselights fade, leaving the faintest heart-tapping of a small orange strobe. Music begins, a slow, brawling cacophony, punctuated by the tremors of an electronic tambourine. A suggestion of the Arabic, surely appropriate to a performance of *The Stranger,* Albert Camus' ancient masterpiece.

The lights slowly come up, the strobe now barely a flicker whose rhythm is taken up by the music. The Stranger and the Narrator are discovered on opposite sides of the audience. (The classical Martian theatre has a stage which runs round four sides of an absolutely square room. The audience sits in the middle.) The Stranger is kneeling in the stylized posture denoting loss of face. The Narrator has his back to the audience.

At once six figures appear around the Stranger. Their heavy pancake makeup, reminiscent of the terrible faces of Rouault, and their costume, a parody of that of the twentieth century, make it clear who they are: the Mother, Raymond, Marie, the Arab, the Judge, and the Priest. In a slow, somnambulatory mime the Stranger rises and acts out with them the chief phases of his story. When the

11

dumb-show is finished, there is a sigh from the instruments, silence, darkness. After a few moments the music begins again, faster, restless, in a different key. The small drum, oboe, lute, and cheng, a long zither with seven strings, are predominant. The theme is from the classical Chinese, the Metamorphosis of the Solitary Female Phoenix. After the opening chords, the Narrator begins to tell the story in the lovely late French of the original, speaking in a slow expressionless scream competing with the music. Sometimes the Stranger himself takes over the narration.

The classical story goes through its heartless repetitions, its elegant and vapid dance; in two hours it has reached the closing cadences, which are accompanied by the hysterical banging of a little gong.

According to the program notes: "This moral pioneer, with his discovery of the artificiality of nature, and his comic final loss of face and descent into madness, still captures an audience over thirteen centuries after his story was written. As the comic diversion Mersault should not indeed distract so much attention from the hero, the unnamed Arab, but this is the complaint of the critic, not the verdict of the audience. Camus wrought better than he knew . . .

"What Camus realized was of course that freedom is identical to arbitrariness, four hundred years before that arbitrariness became fact and the last natural frontier, of physical time, yielded to scientific inquiry and technological manipulation . . ."

Narcissus is at the play because his sister-lover, Cleopatra, is playing the part of Marie. This is her first performance as a full member of the troupe: as an apprentice she has played to enthusiastic audiences all over the planet, and is an accomplished and hypnotic dancer.

In the dressing-room she peels off her makeup, speaking the words that relax her concentration, revealing the ironic, light-boned face; and now she strips her golden body and steps under the impalpable tingle of a molecular shower. For the flight home she wears only a skirt of feathers and a mask, both eggshell blue.

As Narcissus leaves the theatre in the sallow evening light he is surrounded by admirers. His art is technically the ancient discipline of swordsmanship, Kendo, but what gives him his unlucky popularity is the fact that he is an art in himself—or it might be said *herself,* for Narcissus is a freemartin, a hermaphrodite. He/she is one of the small Martian aristocracy, the Bloods or Cocks of Mars. He (the masculine pronoun will be used to translate the Martian neuter personal pronoun) is tall, even taller than his sister, but with the same light bones. Like most Martians he is brown-skinned and black-eyed; he has the Martian depth of chest and slimness of calf and ankle. His face is small and graceful, with almond eyes, a tiny, elliptical mouth with small, spaced teeth that are almost pointed, and very white. His nose is also small, hawklike and slightly hooked, the skin stretched tightly over the bridge and cheekbones. He has muscular shoulders and graceful pointed breasts, revealed fashionably and embellished with makeup of gold and blue.

Narcissus finds himself trapped by the crowd, which fawns on him and seems to crave his characteristic sudden anger. He is about to strike a persistent courtier across the face to make him fall back, when Cleopatra appears, and the crowd is momentarily silent. In that silence Michael and his wife Snow, both Bloods, come out of the theatre talking idly about the performance. They are not aware of being overheard:

Michael: . . . I don't agree. Narcissus must have been embarrassed. She was taking the easy way, not something the groundlings would notice, but really it's a mild form of madness. She was inventing conventions as she went on, glorifying the casual.

Snow: Yes, but wasn't that a reinterpretation of her part?

Michael: Beauty is achieved only in the pure submission to convention—not by arbitrariness, which is a concession to the random.

Snow: You're being a little pompous, Michael. Aren't conventions themselves arbitrary? . . .

She breaks off, realizing that something terrible has happened. The crowd has parted, to reveal Cleopatra by the corner of the theatre, in the pathetic and hostile pose of one who has lost face. Suddenly the sun, a golden pin-head, vanishes under the close horizon of the ocean. Phobos only, incandescent, lights the piazza with its milky blue.

Narcissus, free of the attentions of the crowd and oddly comfortable, speaks quietly in a clear contralto:

"My lady Snow, I am desolated that we must meet under these circumstances, where respects must be curtailed. My apologies." He turns to Michael. "It is to my loss of face that I overheard your unacceptable remarks. Nevertheless it is said that 'what is done to a thing can be undone; but what is done to a person is a fact forever.' Therefore, my lord, to my regret, we are now in a condition of status-war. In addition, you are in my way."

With that he smiles and, with a frightening strangeness, walks swiftly toward his enemy. Michael must either step aside, or, if he is there in solido only, must dissolve his tangibility. Narcissus is risking face-loss and demotion, for if he is responsible for crude contact with another Blood he forfeits his status. However, Michael will also be defiled implicitly by the encounter. At the last moment Michael dematerializes and Narcissus passes through him. Narcissus spins on his brown heel, and picks up Cleopatra's wings from the rack. Snow, shaking and alone, cannot take her eyes from him. Cleopatra edged past her as she stands there stricken, and allows Narcissus to help her into her wings.

The audience questions the art and strategy of this play. Mars has not had a status-war for some years, and Narcissus is known for the boldness of his existential conceptions and a vigorous cleanness of execution. Still, the affair seems to be in dubious taste and shows all the signs of having been initiated on the spur of the moment, without allowing its aesthetic nuances to mature. But "Bloods are Bloods because of boldness and surprise," and "a Cock cannot be constrained." There is an art in shock; by his actions Narcissus has declared that he is a rival with Michael for the possession of Snow, and perhaps even vice-versa: in rivalry with Snow for the soul of Michael.

When Cleopatra is comfortable in her wings, she assists Narcissus into his. A man weighing 160 pounds on Earth is only sixty-four pounds on Mars, but a sixty-four pound Martian would be very rare, for the low gravity encourages small bones and ectomorphism. A Martian two meters tall (they are often taller) would weigh 120 pounds on Earth and only forty-eight on Mars. Thus a trained man with a good set of wings can easily fly in the near-terrestrial artificial atmosphere.

An ordinary set of wings is usually handmade of permaplastic. Wingsmiths require long training, as each set of wings must be tailored precisely to the musculature and bone structure of its owner. The wings of Narcissus and Cleopatra are far from ordinary. Fashioned of a titanium alloy, each feather tapering to rigid foil and anodized in barbaric colors, the "bones" fluted and internally stressed, with tendons of invisible unimolecular fiber, and pivots sheathed in precious stone, these wings are masterpieces of the wingsmith's art. A tyro in these wings would find himself aloft almost without effort, and Narcissus and Cleopatra are not tyros.

The silhouette of a man flying is a rorschach combining elements of the butterfly and the hawk. The relatively rigid forward pair of wings is used for gliding and control, and are not moved except when taking off or in an emergency. The rear pair supply the main propulsive force. Spring-loaded so as to cooperate with human muscles, they are also hinged to allow a man to walk while wearing his wings—an ungainly waddle, quite unlike his quiet grace in the air.

An experienced flyer can attain bursts of speed in excess of a hundred kilometers per hour, or even more in a dive. Range is determined by the flyer's endurance and by the presence of thermals, updrafts, sinking air; if he is skillful he can travel long distances without losing height and without effort. The large lungs and deep chest of the Martian physique are well adapted to flying.

Brother and sister fasten the silky leather thongs of their equipment, shrug with a comically similar gesture, and adjust their headbands. They run a few yards, and with an ear-numbing clap of wings, swoop from the summit of the theatre's steps. Many Martian buldings are constructed upon a low stepped pyramid for the convenience of those who fly, as well as for aesthetic reasons. With a few vigorous strokes Narcissus and Cleopatra are rising in flattish circles, feeling under their wings the warm pressure of air rising from the pavement as it cools in the evening stillness.

The landscape spreads: the theatre, with its severe square roof covered with restrained designs in black and ochre, falls away in odd perspective; the city of Hellas can be seen now in its entirety. It is a small seaport, a crescent of moon-lanterns around the bay, with the waters of the Hellene Sea beyond, mobile as alcohol and glittering in the noon twilight. It is a seascape by Hiroshige, with an orange line at the horizon where the sun set fifteen minutes ago. They smell the perfumes of the town: molten wax, cinnamon and orange groves, warmed stucco and lime.

Hellas is situated on the north coast of the Hellene Sea, backed by a range of ancient mountains, part of the ring-wall of a primeval crater. Narcissus' home is on an island twenty kilometers offshore. They must hurry, for Phobos is past its zenith already and the true night of Mars will fall, when neither the sun nor the artificial star will be in the sky.

Nine centuries ago men kindled the inner moon of Mars, to be a nuclear furnace for the cold planet. Today the range of temperatures at the planet's surface is not much greater than Earth's, the permafrost is melted, and a blue point of light, swifter than any cloud driven by the wind, speckles the ocean under the wings of Cleopatra and Narcissus.

Sometimes they soar a thousand meters over the water, sometimes they skim the waves like seabirds. At length the island of Eleuthera looms up, a mass of darkness casting a huge shadow from the setting moon; the shadow is haloed with scales of light. The fresh, metallic smell of the sea gives way to a waft of forest scents: resins, blossom, and sweet black leaf-mould. It is spring in this southern hemisphere of the planet, a spring of a hundred and fifty Martian days out of a year of six hundred and sixty-four.

Once Hellas was a bowl of dust, the source and store of the great dust-storms that often veiled the planet completely. In this gentler age it is an ocean, but the dust, washed up on islands and shores, proved, like the loess that blew in the late ice age from the retreating glaciers of China and formed the North China Basin, to be a fabulously fertile soil.

Earthly species of trees thrive here, mixed and fantastically mutated. The island is a dense forest of cedars, chestnuts, elms, and beeches, most of them over two hundred meters high because of the low gravity. Their roots are fed with little ocean storms, and their branches are dense with secondary growth: lianas, orchids, mutated mosses, symbiotic and parasitic ferns.

The chestnuts are in flower; huge stingless bees and hummingbirds, thirsty for nectar, prod their fragile cones of pink and white. Now Narcissus and Cleopatra are grazing the treetops: lights show in the green depths beneath; they settle on the landing-perch with a last rush of air. In moonset now, for Phobos, swiftest and closest of all moons, has completed its journey, they shrug off their wings. They are assisted by a beast-servant who has been awaiting them: an elegant white ape, artificially mutated for intelligence and dexterity. He serves them from a tray with flying-cups of sweet, hot liquor to warm them this cool spring night, and retires to squat in the shadows.

Cleopatra and Narcissus now descend the swaying ladder, almost smothered by masses of cultivated parasitic blossoms, among them several artificial species, the work of genetic artists. The ladder deposits them on a polished wooden courtyard in the center of the house. They are still a hundred and fifty meters above the ground; through the *flet* or platform on which the house is built shoot the trunks of the supporting trees, lit brightly here with lanterns, darkening above into a canopy hissing with insects, and heavy with flowers.

2.

Michael and Snow

"I HAVE NEVER liked the hologram transmitter," says Michael's father. "It has destroyed our sense of identity. One can no longer tell appearance from reality. I am sure you would not have become involved if you had been there in person."

"Yes, Father." The imputation is unjust.

"Your case demonstrates the dangers of forsaking the Rule of Less. You have placed yourself in a state of artistic ambiguity, which, to escape, may require further concessions to vulgarity."

Michael looks at Snow for a glance of support but her eyes are lowered, and she seems to be hardly attending to the old man's words.

"Bloods are not born, but recognized. Your family has built its reputation on the purity of its exigence. I will not lightly have this tradition changed."

"Do not be too hard on them, Tak," says his wife Shelley. "Using the solido is not a crime. They have never touched the Vision, after all. It was the fault of those terrible children, Cleopatra and her brother."

"I resent the association of our names with theirs," says

18

Takahashi, "though indeed, I see no way that an accusation of madness can be brought against them. But they are addicts of the Vision, I am told, and infringe the prerogatives of the goddesses. They are admired for their audacity, but it is not a style that can be sustained. They are very dangerous."

"That is my concern," says Michael quickly. "Mother and you need not be involved. We have not insisted on family solidarity, it is not part of our style. We are not like cousin Shadrach, who keeps statues of his ancestors in his courtyards. I expect no help from you."

Takahashi is unbending. "It is well you do not."

At this Snow rises to leave, out of embarrassment or stubbornness, but Shelley restrains her. There is a tense silence as Snow subsides. Takahashi looks into space.

They sit, legs crossed, in the peristyle of Takahashi's villa in the Southern foothills of the great volcano. The low couches are covered with dull brown and yellow satin. A fountain tinkles among earthern pots of flowers.

The day is at its height; both suns are in the sky. The light is brilliant white, like the light of a Tiepolo, but every object casts a sharply defined double shadow, one pale yellow from the artificial star, one a darker blue from old Sol. The light, coming from two sources, surrounds and bathes material reality: stone satyrs and *putti* glow as if haloed.

Above, the immense plumed cone of Nix Olympica, a hundred kilometers away and twenty-five kilometers in altitude, floats in a haze of deeper air and its snows glitter with yellow and blue. Below the villa, from the lower slopes of the hillside, comes an afternoon buzz of conversations, domestic animals, and music. The slope is densely covered with aromatic shrubs, rosemary, juniper, and olives, with occasional tall cedars marking a whitewashed house covered with bougainvillaeas. Further on there are vineyards, and at the bottom, in the meadow, fruit trees heavy with the mutated fruits of this northern-hemisphere Martian autumn.

The walls of the peristyle are decorated with frescoes, depicting in dry ochres and terra-cottas and sky-blue the imaginary lives of the prehistoric indigenous Martians (who never existed) from the works of Burroughs and Bradbury. Further on there are heroic, perspectiveless renderings of the terraforming of Mars; of the cannibalizing of the rings of Saturn for ice and frozen air; of the nuclear kindling of Phobos; of the terrifying eruptions of the Martian volcanoes, including the one that rises so peacefully above the tiles, that were triggered by human geologists to help create a biosphere; of the blooming of the Martian deserts.

Takahashi looks down at last. "It seems your mother has taken your part, for which you should be grateful. I do not like your talk of styles. The support of our House will make such shifts unnecessary."

"So you will help them. What is to be done?" asks Shelley, with the relief of setting to work on a defined task.

"First they must consult one of the goddesses," says the old man.

Michael and Snow retire to the small dark temple under the house, where beams of different sunlights strike through slanted embrasures. There they make the mental signs and mumble the prayers that are prescribed for the summoning of a deity.

The goddesses are the heart of the tiny bureaucracy that rules Mars, to the extent that it can be said to be ruled at all. They act as umpires, constitute a final court of appeal in aesthetic disputes, and officiate at the various festivals that are held at leaf-fall and cherry blossom time in different parts of the planet.

Mars is a femarchy, and its rulers' authority is religious, which means it has no physical sanctions. Tyranny is impossible, for every human being has at his disposal the infinite resources of the Vision, which include an Idiot Guardian who warns him against inadvertent harm. Rulers govern with the consent of the governed, for that is the only power they possess; though it is a rare and disturbed individual who would risk the stigma of madness and social oblivion by an act of rebellion.

Goddesses are permitted under the aesthetic laws of the

planet to use the Vision within broader limits than even Cocks or Bloods. Their rule is sanctified by their infinite motherliness and tender but austere compassion and mediation.

A soft chime of tiny bells and a scent of incense signify the presence of the goddess. Michael and Snow do not at first look up. She is in the form of Our Lady of Remedios, with a great blue-green cape, trimmed in dull red and gold; on her left side, hanging in a featureless ether, is a crescent moon of gold, and on her right, a snake. She turns upon her servants her gentle eyes, and, with a sweet pout, asks:

"What is your trouble, my children, that you call upon one of the queens of heaven?"

"My lady, Narcissus and Cleopatra of Eleuthera have declared status-war upon the House of Herculanaeum."

"For what reason did they do this?"

"To avenge an imagined insult; but chiefly, I conjecture, to test the strength of their aesthetic against ours."

"What do you wish of me?"

"Eternal lady of Olympus, we desire a judgment on the harmony and propriety of this whole venture. Narcissus has begun a fiction which involves us and our names: can there be honor in it for us?"

There is a brief silence, as the goddess dims slightly and appears to look into a space that is not present to her supplicants.

"The fiction is weak in its beginning," she says, "but the signs are good for its future. You will earn great honor and also great sorrow." She looks sharply at Snow. "There are depths in this case that cannot be seen on the surface, and mysteries that time must unfold."

Snow blushes and falls to her knees. Michael, puzzled, turns to her but she will not meet his eyes. He turns back to Our Lady of Remedios.

"I do not understand. Is not the future always dark?"

"Yes, child; but it is dark not because we cannot predict it, but because what we predict must always be the future of a world in which we had not predicted it. Prediction is a great destroyer of futures. Let the event remain in the womb of time, that it may be delivered.

"Do you have any more requests?"

"Yes, Lady," says Snow, speaking at last. "What must we do? Narcissus and Cleopatra have left us no path back to them; no challenge, no redress. How can we continue the fiction with no foundation for action? What must our motives be?"

"Indeed, child, your faith in the Protectresses of Grace is very great. These questions are beyond my authority. I must consult my superiors."

She vanishes, and there is a few minutes' silence. When she reappears, the shadowy form of another goddess has appeared beside her, too indistinct to be recognized, but with burning grey eyes. When Remedios speaks again, it is as if another spirit were sharing her voice, with a curious drone in the questions.

"What is the Rule of the House of Herculanaeum?"

"The Rule of Less," Michael replies.

"Which means?"

"We sacrifice power for the sake of power. We do not use the Vision. We eschew the easy path of immortality. We are fertile, and beget children; we are respected, for no trace of madness is found in us. We have chosen the ancient way of the hero, who is ignorant and therefore wise, and who is wanton and therefore never out of control."

"A commendable liturgy. What is the argument for the Rule?"

"The ancient arbiter Fyodor Dostoyevsky said that if there were no God, everything would be permitted. Since the Vision was constructed, every man has the power to be God—which is to say, there is no God.

"Exigence and limit are essential to beauty, and beauty is the whole reason of our world. Other worlds have other reasons—goodness, truth—but for us our choice is our being.

"That is why my father and mother have chosen not to augment their intelligence by the Vision, nor to lengthen their lives. Death is the proof of beauty."

"Then what is your difference with Narcissus and

Cleopatra?"

"Pardon me, Goddess, but what is your purpose in questioning me?"

"We are bound to be impartial. If there is an answer to your wife's question, you yourselves must find it. We can only assist you. Do not answer questions with questions."

Michael bows deeply. "Narcissus and Cleopatra have chosen what to us is the path of madness."

"To them your path might be that of dullness."

"Yes, my Lady. But—saving your reverence—or reverences—" he looks at the shadowy figure beside Remedios, "Godhead in the full sense of the term is uninteresting. To know everything is to know nothing. To do everything is to do nothing. Narcissus, as you must surely know, treads on the limits of propriety. He infringes your prerogatives—and more, for he claims only humanity. He is immortal, a golem, a living monster."

"But his mind is clear and his will is constant," puts in the goddess. "Do not forget that."

"That is what I do not understand. If the life is formless, what shape can the self take on?"

"That is the problem you must solve. Go on with your description: we interrupted you."

"He is a freemartin and is not bound by the rules of either of the classical sexes. And he is infertile, which is why it is permitted for him to be his sister's lover."

"Let us change the direction of our questions. In the game of Go, do you attack your enemy's strengths?"

"No, you exploit his weaknesses until his strength becomes heavy and he wishes he could throw off the burden."

"Is the best strategy, then, to emphasize what you and your opponent have in common, or to emphasize the differences?"

"The latter, my Lady. His power is power only on his own ground. Shift the ground and the power is weakness."

"What could you do that would most point out the cost of your enemy's strength, that would most clearly demonstrate your difference, and draw the conflict onto alien ground?"

Michael is mystified; and before he can answer he hears a sigh beside him, and Snow collapses to the ground in a dead faint. The next moment she revives; and a new look of bleak ironic endurance comes into her face as she rises to her knees and confronts the goddesses.

"Then we must bear a child. Is that what you mean? That the only way we can throw off the curse is by feeding to the jaws of this monster whatever is most private, most personal, most our own?"

Michael is still confused. The goddesses are silent, their eyes lowered; after a moment they begin to fade away.

Without limitations, even perverse limitations, the human race would go mad with boredom. A status-war is the equivalent, in a society without morality, of a tragic moral struggle, and possesses all its excitement and invigorating psychic refreshment. A status-war is between styles, not principles, and its rules are aesthetic and psychological, not moral. But even psychology is a relative affair. One of the most prized coups in a status-war is the invention of a novel psychological condition, a new kind of motivation for a traditional action, what in a moral society would be termed an ethical depravity. Thus the birth of a child to Michael and Snow will underline the fact that despite, and because of, Narcissus' brilliant energy and originality, he is sterile, and that his sterility is the result of his use of the Vision—an indulgence that is at the heart of his aesthetic style. This new decision will constitute a powerful accusation of insanity against Narcissus.

In the first hours of their decision Michael and Snow are lit by an unnatural optimism and lightness of heart. But soon they are overwhelmed by a sense of disaster. Their defeat at the hands of a stranger, Narcissus' terrifying confidence, the arbitrariness of the challenge, and their individual fears of failing each other leave them exhausted and listless. They sit together in the airy rooms that smell of lime, silent, or sleep for sixteen to twenty hours at a stretch. Michael's scholarly pursuits languish.

The weather is hot for autumn, the chaparral burned brown. They live at a slight fever in this heat, yet lack the morale to arouse themselves to a change of scene. Whenever Michael appears to be making a sexual invitation, even when he is not in fact doing so, Snow shrinks away. Michael's parents are pleased for purely dynastic reasons that they will be grandparents, though they wish that this eventuality might have come about through their offspring's desire to please them, rather than in these unhappy circumstances. They sense the unease of their children, however, and approach them with neither censure nor unwelcome support. This scene must be acted by Michael and Snow alone.

3.

Chrysanthemum

As SOON AS Narcissus and Cleopatra step down onto the courtyard they are greeted by their beloved Uncle Chrysanthemum. Chrysanthemum is not really their uncle, but he is their favorite person and they claim to be helpless without him. He is a magnificent old homophile and pederast, with fat fingers and elaborate makeup, weighing even on Mars over two hundred pounds. Perhaps it is for this reason that he refers to himself in the plural; or it may be a tribute to his own royal inclusiveness, or even because he is unimaginable without an entourage. Usually he is surrounded by some pretty out-of-work actors, an addict or two, students cutting classes, male models, and so on. He comes out of the loggia, in a splended silver and silk dressing-gown.

"Enter Chrysanthemum, distraught. My loves, where have you been all this time?"

"We've hurt your feelings," says Narcissus penitently.

"How sharper than a serpent's tooth it is to have a thankless child. Our old eyes are dimmed with tears."

"It's your birthday. We remembered. But you *know* it's Callie's opening night."

"When we arose from our bed of rest this afternoon, you had already left on your adventures. Why can't you keep civilized hours? You had the best possible training—personal tutorials from ourself."

"Look, Callie has a present for you." Cleopatra produces a gift from the air, chosen that afternoon in the Hellas agora. It is a lacquer makeup case.

"After two hundred of them," says Cleopatra, "even you should be a little less excited when the great day comes round."

"Puer Aeternus, my dear, Puer Aeternus. It's lovely, you darlings. Come to my arms." He folds them to his ample bosom. His perfume is stifling; by the moiled flesh of his face they know he is already tipsy. "Dionysus welcomes his own. My, what big girls you are," he says, feeling their breasts.

"What interest do *you* have in girls?" says Cleopatra, escaping easily.

"It depends on the girl," Chrysanthemum eyes Narcissus lecherously, at arm's length.

"No you don't," says Cleopatra.

Suddenly Chrysanthemum notices a certain pallor and seriousness in his young friend. "What's the matter?"

"I've declared status-war on Michael. I'd better consult the Vision."

Chrysanthemum is shocked. "How tedious. You'll have endless red tape. It makes us feel quite hungry. In fact, now we come to think of it, we feel definitely faint." He peers at his belly dolefully.

At once several beast-servants, mostly apes and bears, appear with a trestle-table, which they cover with damask and delicious food. There are little tree-pigs, roasted with almonds, their fatty skins gored into strips and rubbed with garlic; a sharp curd flavored with mutated lemons; junket and pineapple. Chrysanthemum and Cleopatra set to enthusiastically, but Narcissus will have nothing but a bowl of junket. Soon he retires to his room.

There, over the solido, he records before one of the goddesses his third major artistic venture, the status-game with Michael and Snow. By excluding Snow from the contest he signals his intention to include a possible sexual element in the conflict.

Next Narcissus flashes all over the globe, informing

friends and family of what he has done, reminding them obliquely of feud debts and duties, calling in century-old obligations.

At length he allows himself to fall into the strange, familiar spaces and depths of the Vision. He avoids the superficial problem-solving and address-finding functions of the great computer; instead he seeks out that dreamlike region which deals with future probabilities, and allows himself to bathe in its imagery.

The builders of the Vision feared that an omniscient artificial intelligence might render Man obsolete, and knowing what they knew, the notion was not so unreasonable. Its memory-cores were forged out of the probability-states of all the matter in the universe; its logic circuits were spun from an artificial patterning of all exchanges of energy. To create God, which in effect the builders were doing, seemed to invite a fate more terrible than that of Frankenstein. Nevertheless, in their spirit of experimental hubris they pressed on with this, the last of all possible scientific endeavors.

And it turned out that all was well, that omniscience was a kind of divine paralysis, and to know all is to be capable of doing nothing. The Vision was a celestial putty in the hands of whoever chose to use it. We can only know or do something at the expense of knowing and doing something else, for it is the singling-out of attention that gives knowledge and action their specific character. Not only was the new god a cripple, he was also an idiot.

Following the implications of this discovery, the arbiters of Mars chose a culture of renunciation, dedicated to the pursuit of grace and severe art. The gifts of man's control over the universe were rejected. Sanctions were imposed against the violation of the strict conventions of Martian society: if in tribunal a violation cannot be justified as artistic daring or organic growth, or if the culprit dedicates himself totally to the Vision and takes on its amorphousness, he is defined as insane and society withdraws itself from him. This is Narcissus' problem—for he is perhaps the most cavalier of all the Cocks of Mars, tempting the adverse judgment of his peers at every moment.

Behind Narcissus' pineal gland at the base of the brain is the tiny computer of unbelievable complexity that all human beings are engrafted with: it is his link with the Vision. To use the implant, as he does now, automatically induces a series of massive glandular changes throughout the body, under the controlling influence of the pineal, the master-clock of fleshly time. The pineal was once a third eye in man's therapsid past; but in man himself it sees not the light of space but the inner light of time. The mystics knew it as the seat of the soul; and now it has become the fountain of immortality. The Vision brakes and reverses the aging of the body: thus immortality is the price of knowledge, Godhead is eternal youth.

But the builders were clever: there was a biological price to be paid. To interfere with the process of maturation is to betray the desire of every living cell, to die. Only cancer is immortal: Narcissus, who has been a drunk and a glutton of the Vision since the first forming of his brainstem in the womb, is nothing more than a collection of deathless cancer cells. And maturation, as Plato knew, also brings about that sexual difference that makes us fertile. Narcissus' sexuality is both the yolk and the white of the same shell, he is a freemartin, an androgyne, incapable either of natural death or natural reproduction.

The predicament Narcissus must avoid is classification as a social cancer, and his questioning of the Vision is designed to elicit a course of action that will avoid a merely arbitrary fiction while cleaving still to his sweet style of boldness and apparent carelessness. He needs a sure guide to the future. But to enter the deeps of the Vision, to penetrate its inner brilliancies, is to commit himself to a greater and more irreversible biological alteration than he can afford. Unwilling to go deeper, he floats among superficial and disconnected images: a seagull, with a sense of wind and rain; a teddy-bear soaked with water, an infinite pathos; repulsion and pity, and a purple flower, that merges into a sense of high excitement, and the flower changes to red; a terrible blaze of light; and at last a clear vision of an old hermaphrodite with a huge, gaunt face.

He recognizes this last apparition: it is Gabriel the Seer,

whose skill in the Vision is known far and wide. He is an outcast, a pariah, but he seems to Narcissus to carry the answer to all his questions. Perhaps he can venture where Narcissus cannot go. The tension in Narcissus' body, unfelt until now, and partly the result of the continuous effort to hold back from a deeper plunge into the Vision, suddenly finds relief. As he withdraws from his reverie he feels completely exhausted.

He rejoins his sister and Chrysanthemum in the Brown Room, pausing at the door to support himself in a fit of faintness. The Brown Room is the largest and most comfortable room in the house: square, but with two recesses in the floor surrounded by simple brocaded cushions and carpeted with tatami-mats. On one side there is a veranda separated from the room by a force-field to keep out insects while allowing the clean night air to come through. It has become quite cool outside, and the forest noises are silent. The great trees, lit by lanterns like colored drums, are motionless.

In the center of one of the recesses there is a little hot brazier burning charcoal flamelessly and giving off an odor of hot cinders and sandalwood. Around it Cleopatra and Chrysanthemum are lying at ease on silks and furs, drinking a fine Martian brandy. The faint notes of the classical piece used for *The Stranger* can be heard from one corner of the room. Chrysanthemum is telling art forgery stories, those interminable sagas of logical paradox and aesthetic pitfall. Cleopatra is apparently asleep, but there is something light and steely in her pose that belies appearances. She has changed into a white kimono with five stylized Janet-flowers embroidered on it. Janets are a favorite synthetic species created three hundred years ago: they are pale blue and dark blue, with double centers, and winged like a butterfly.

Cleopatra never speaks much, except on stage; indeed, women on Mars are rather strong and silent in personality, more competent and sensible than their emotional and mercurial menfolk and the rather vain and fanciful androgynes, who are given to hysteria and self-display. This is a sexist society: the relative absence of racial differences has made some other form of social discrimination necessary to exhibit the basic distinctions, dialectics, and tensions of the culture. Undoubtedly members of all sexes are exploited on Mars, as they have always been, sensually and psychologically; but exploitation is one of the most interesting, if limited, forms of human interaction, and when it is entered into willingly (and there is now no other way) it can be at least piquant, and sometimes ennobling. One of the burdens of the male, and of freemartins in their masculine orientation, is the sustaining of *Machismo,* a phallic conceit and heroism which is both uplifting and richly comic.

When Narcissus comes in Cleopatra opens her brown eyes startlingly, as if they had never been closed. Seeing his expression, she rises at once and takes him in her arms. For a moment Chrysanthemum, who is among other things a poet, sees both their faces, turning blindly toward each other, like a face and its reflection in a mirror; they both have the same small elliptical mouth, the white pointed teeth, the triangular flat cheeks, high cheekbones, long neck with a tall tendon in it, the same highlight on the brow, glossy black hair with peacock diffraction colors. They kiss, the mouths still open. Chrysanthemum giggles, breaks the silence:

"I suppose an old pederast should leave you lovebirds to your billing. We shall take ourself to some slut for the night." With that he girds himself, and helping himself to a handful of dried fruit from a yellow glazed dish as he passes, disappears.

Cleopatra notices that Narcissus is shaking: surprised by his laughter, she backs off, discovers that he is not laughing at all, but weeping. He has spent his resources, and is momentarily as weak as a baby. Cleopatra settles him down by the fire. Taking upon herself the office of servant, she strips him of his clothing, to reveal the small breasts, the flat muscular belly, the silky phallus over the maidenly fold beneath. Sprinkling the aromatic contents of a tiny ceramic bottle of volatile oil on her hand, she rubs her brother-sister's shoulders and back with it.

They have a game they played as children—and they are always children in a sense, or fetuses that have got free to find their own peculiar growth—a game of pretense that they have never met before and must introduce themselves. Cleopatra says softly: "I'm Callie, a person of Hellas: who are you?"

"I'm Cissie," he says in a whisper. They kiss again, and now Cleopatra is naked too; their brown breasts, Cleopatra's slightly larger and closer together than her sister's, are pressed out as they embrace. Narcissus, the younger sister, strokes Cleopatra's hair, and Cleopatra brushes the hair out of Narcissus' eyes.

Now their clasps become stronger; each allows a little of the Vision to touch the mind, so that they share a communion of feeling, interanimation of two souls. There is a pit of intimacy into which they fall with hearts in their mouths and butterflies in the stomach; the sight would melt even calloused old Chrysanthemum, had he been there to see.

—For they are really lost, in a world that is always on the sheer edge of the past. They have become the protagonists and exemplars of all human beings in their culture; but doomed by their peculiar beauty to bear the brunt of the continuous discovery of the proper style of the present. They are the art that life imitates; next year people in New Bristol and Heliopolis will kiss as they do; they are at war with knowledge yet reducing always the lonely darkness of the future to the light of the past. Where they have gone, others can follow; but it is too late for them to become followers, for they are addicted to the vertigo of inventing their own lives.

The author, the voyeur, apologizes at this point for the violation of privacy. He has attempted to cover the breach in manners by a speech about Man in general, and Life, and Art. He realizes that the attempt is transparent, but nevertheless will let both the offence and the retraction stand. What is done to a thing can be undone, but what is done to a person is a fact forever. Still, it is evident that reticence will not answer: the author therefore relinquishes it from now on.

In this world anything can be undone but the experience of a person. For a person is his history, is the focus of all his relationships, which are in turn nothing more than their own history. A fact exists only in its statement, and by virtue of being stated. In this universe all other facts can be altered or erased—even retroactively, so that they never existed at all. On Mars there is a philosophical school devoted to the literal elimination of all facts inessential to human experience. With the assistance of the Vision they have destroyed whole galaxies, classes of subatomic particles, and even a half-dozen mathematical relationships. Indeed, from our new perspective, it might be more accurate to say that they never existed in the first place except as illusions, daydreams, or inventions. Technology is philosophy, because the universe can now be altered to fit any sufficiently coherent, and sufficiently incoherent, philosophical position. The ancient method of deciding whether something is real or not—that is, by distinguishing those sensations which cannot be altered by wishing them changed—is no longer viable. There is no hard reality against which human desires and aspirations can test and refine themselves, with the exception of other human aspirations and desires, and finally in the stubborn but indeterminate austerity of art.

It has even proved necessary to re-educate the human sensorium not to automatically transform curves produced by perspective into straight lines: the ratio of transformation on Mars is subtly different from Earth's, because of the tighter planetary curvature, as subtly different as the columns and architraves of the Parthenon from mere cylinders and blocks. Similarly, the reflex that usually eliminates the retinal diffraction fringes of orange and blue has been reformed to deal with the double shadows of the Martian day. Even motions of the visual field due to movements of the head, buzzes and tingles and sournesses that the nervous system normally filters out—a useful habit on Earth, as habits usually are, but most useful in its breach and denial—have taken on new significance in the new world.

Naked, then, philosophically as well as physically, we must imagine these pretty lovers in the pathos of their loving plight. Denied the warmth of their contact, we console ourselves with the erotic and aesthetic point of the scene, which is that we must be bystanders and look on.

4.

The Inn at Valdorno

DESPITE, OR RATHER because of, their resolve to conceive a child, Michael and Snow find it impossible to approach each other with desire. The determinateness of the human future they have decided to create has apparently stifled it before it has begun. Michael has been shaken by what his mother calls "those terrible children," Narcissus and Cleopatra; he relives over and over again the moment when Narcissus spun on his heel, and imagines that he remembers a careless laugh as his enemy turned his back: he knows that he himself does not possess the irresponsibility, the trust in the predictable weakness of others, that he has seen in Narcissus. And he remembers Cleopatra, in the terrifying rigidity of the posture of the insulted. He had not meant to hurt her so, and is afraid of her rage in being so hurt. Snow pities him, but cannot support him, for she is damaged in a way that she cannot share with her husband; and he would reject any offer of emotional help in any case.

So the days pass: they occasionally smile at each other across the dinner table; Takahashi and Shelley serve them silently; they even joke about subjects unrelated to the feud. At parties and gatherings there is an aura of ill luck about them, but they ignore it and keep up appearances heroically, giving themselves to their friends and taking an interest in the proceedings as if nothing had happened to absorb them in themselves.

Nevertheless this is not enough. They cannot constrain their flesh by the same discipline as the spirit. They sleep in separate rooms and avoid each other's touch as they pass in doorways. Snow has lost weight, and her pale beauty has the desolation of a glacial waste. By contrast Michael does not change physically—he is well built and handsome, but in no way physically remarkable, and his body's health is not affected by his ordeal. If anything, he has a slight flush, a tension ·that resembles excellent muscle tone and differs from it only subjectively: a pain of shame, a tremulousness.

Upon a broad and repeated hint from Shelley, their best friend Gunther takes Michael aside one evening after a party. Gunther is a man of Science, which today is a kind of scholasticism, devoted to explaining a universe that is entirely the result of human intention, in a fashion that does not require the invocation of the intentional. Science is one of the odder perversions of thought and is highly regarded, though there are only a few dozen real scientists on the planet. Gunther has a blocklike head, is rather imperceptive, but possesses an endearing willingness to help others. With his usual lack of tact he plunges in:

"Look here, Michael, you're running yourself into the ground. This kind of heroism is foolishness. You ought to use a psychomorphic and cheer yourself up."

Michael at first denies any knowledge of what his friend is talking about; but Gunther has struck home. He *is* running himself into the ground: there is nothing he can do that is both graceful and emotionally possible. He is in a double bind—one of Gunther's special interests—paralyzed if he does not admit the effect the challenge has had upon him, and forced into further loss of face if he does admit it. Of course a drug or psychomorphic could provide precisely the mood he requires. Narcissus himself

would not scruple to use one: but then Narcissus' aesthetic
style is not predicated, as is Michael's, on absolute
authenticity of feeling. Indeed, the advice of the goddess is
part of his problem, for it has added the fear of sexual
impotence to his difficulties: a self-fulfilling fear, self-
fulfilling indeed partly because of his fear that it is self-
fulfilling. Finally Michael pretends no longer.

"I can't take a psychomorphic. That would be playing
Narcissus' game. He challenged me on the basis of my
personal integrity and I must fight tied to the stake."

"I thought you'd say that." Gunther likes to lecture, and
he draws himself up now to do so. "There's only one thing
to do: something completely irrelevant. The way you deal
with a double bind is to start behaving as if it didn't exist . . ."

"But I've been doing that."

"No, you haven't . . . An animal will often find that its
behavioral repertoire is so arranged that two sets of
automatic responses are evoked by the same event—
responses that contradict each other. For instance, a
female appears in the domain of a territorial male of the
same species. He is motivated simultaneously to kill, and
to mate with, the female. What does he do? He starts to
build a nest. The reaction is quite inappropriate. But it has
staved off the problem, and over time his species will
evolve so that this behavior becomes biologically
institutionalized, forming the core of a set of mating
rituals—a dance, if you will—which is designed to bring
about the happy event. And the possiblilty of a
breakdown of the spacing-system of the species, that
ensures sufficient forage for each individual, is still
filtered out, because the dance is a code which only
operates in mating situations."

Gunther is right—this kind of ritualization acts as a
selective pressure to bring about the evolution of the
complex and beautiful games of nature: the colors of the
peacock, the antlers of the stag, the brain of man. What
Gunther does not see is that this is the mystery of nature,
to create games, dances, play, where the forces of *ananke,*
of fate, are neutralized and the fanciful, the irrelevant, are

given their head.

"Very well explained," says Michael, smiling, "but how does that help *me*? I can't very well build a nest."

"Do something equally absurd. You've often talked about getting up an expedition to climb Nix Olympica. Do it now. It'd be good for you. I'll come too if you like."

"But that makes no sense."

"You know, Michael, you're the most sensible of all of us, but you're not very bright sometimes. Of *course* it makes no sense. Everyone on Mars will wonder what you're up to. It's unpredictable, which means it must be right."

"But *you* predicted it."

"Only because I know about this sort of thing, and I know you."

"But it's not consistent with my character."

"Yes, it is. You would have climbed that mountain anyway one day if you hadn't been upset by the challenge. And you need a retreat to plan your strategy."

It dawns on Michael that perhaps this is just what he needs. Gunther's analogy of the mating beasts is a lucky shot, for it is closer to Michael's predicament that Gunther knows. Reasoning along that line, if the expedition is to bring the beasts together, they had better be alone.

"You're right, Gunther, but let us do this by ourselves, all right? You've already done more than enough for us."

* * *

During the Terraforming of Mars the volcano Nix Olympica was climbed several times. In that period, when for two hundred years the planet groaned with eruptions and climatic changes, huge glaciers crawled down the slopes of the mountain, interspersed with periodic lava-flows and episodes of extensive wind and water erosion. Gradually the planet settled into the gentle rhythms that it displays today, leaving Nix Olympica a complex of deep valleys and gorges, ridges, domes, and saddles two hundred kilometers across, culminating in a single

immense mutilated cone. Slow cascades, half-dissolved
into mist because of the weak Martian gravity, inch their
way down thousand-meter precipices. Forests of gigantic
conifers march over the blue ridges toward the distant
treeline. And the summit has not been conquered for
nearly a thousand years.

Into this world of stasis and violence enter Michael and
Snow, on foot. They are lighter in heart than for many
weeks, in big boots and coarse socks, shorts and shirts
with pockets full of raisins and chocolate, a compass,
maps, and a flask of whisky distilled from the hardy
barley that rolls over the peripheral plains of the North
Polar Region in summer. Within their rucksacks are tiny
oxygen, water, and protein synthesizers, filmy pressure
suits, two molecular-polymer ropes, pitons, crampons,
ice-axes, and an ancient storm tent.

As they leave the sunny foothills behind them the
weather changes; at first a warm, pearly haze veils the
ridges and isolates the great plane trees strung along the
river—they are taking the old road that follows the valley
of the Orno—but as the vale narrows, fluffy clouds
appear in the golden light. It begins to darken; and by the
afternoon of the third day, at an altitude of three
thousand meters, it has started to rain. At first there is
only a fine drizzle, with occasional gouts of fog blowing
slowly around a rocky buttress; later the lower levels clear
and there is a spectacular thunderstorm among the lesser
peaks of the region.

They reach the southern end of Lake Chiasso in the
evening, and hurry to gain the hospice at Valdorno before
nightfall. At this time of the year the inn holds only a
handful of visitors; the skiing season will not begin for
some months. The hospice is situated in a sheltered
meadow a little below the Cascades of Chiasso where a
hanging valley discharges its bridal vapors into the huge
trough of the Vale. The sound of water cannot be escaped:
here on Mars a thinner and finer, more variable sound
than earthly waters, a hiss rather than a boom.

The inn is simply built of brightly painted pine, like its
rivals in the neighboring resorts of Auzat and Scharmitz.

Inside it is quiet and polished, with rice-paper screens, mats, and cushions on the beautifully laid wood floors, vases of mountain flowers and dried fronds, and raw silk lamps. The place has a reputation for its hospitality and its taste. As Michael and Snow enter they hear the sound of a string quartet in an inner room, and smell the wholesome fragrance of lavender.

Like most commercial ventures in the crazy global economy of Mars, there is no question of profit or loss in the hospice at Valdorno. Any Martian, if it took his fancy, could be a millionaire—in purely material terms—just for the desiring. Economic value, if it has any real meaning now, describes either the quality inherent in an original artistic creation, or a relationship between the provider and the appreciator of a service—a relationship which is entirely reciprocal and needs no compensation for either partner.

A Blood is a person whose life is a conscious work of high art and who is therefore best capable of appreciating a service. Being served, he in turn renders the ultimate service in return, by making the excellence of that service public. A Blood calls forth the utmost virtuosity from those whose services he employs.

As soon as they enter the Inn, Michael and Snow are surrounded by small tittering maids in combs and kimonos who lead them into the huge bath-house behind the main building. There they are stripped of their damp garments and left in a hissing twilight where the slightly sulphurous water is turned to steam by red-hot pumice stones. They relax in a great stone tank of blood-hot greenish water—water only lately on its long way down the cliff-face behind the Inn.

There are three other people in the tank. One of them recognizes Michael and Snow and approaches them, bowing politely so that his beard touches the water. He asks them if they will share his table that evening. They agree, and after a massage they join him, wearing clean linen kimonos, in the indoor garden where they will eat their evening meal. The garden is a tiny representation in raked gravel, dwarf cedar, rocks and moss, of the islands of the Hellene Sea. Seeing this, a cloud passes over Michael's face and the strain of the last weeks reappears, for he is reminded of his enemies.

Their new acquaintance is a rather rare specimen on Mars: a physical throwback to a more differentiated racial type. He is very stocky for a Martian; rather pale, with auburn freckles, brown hair, and a red beard. One of his front teeth has been cracked into two pegs, and he has not had the defect corrected. He has piercing hazel eyes and is something of an anachronism in his manners.

It turns out that he is a painter by the name of Frederick Remington, in memory of the ancient artist of the American frontier. He is gathering material here for a work embodying the spirit and history of Nix Olympica. He seems, indeed, to have a mysterious connection with the mountain, for he knows a great deal about its summit.

"Above the treeline is a zone of rock and tundra," he tells them, when he has ascertained their intentions; "until you get to the snow, which goes up to about fifteen thousand meters. From then on, you're going backward in time, back through the Terraforming to the old Mars.

"At twenty thousand meters the air is as thin as it was at the surface in the old days, and you'll even find some ancient Martian lichens; and above twenty-three thousand you're really in outer space. So you might say the journey upward is also a journey inward, into the secrets of the past . . . as the bulk of the mountain diminishes, you pass through the concentric layers of the planet's history."

"How do you know all this?" asks Snow. "Nobody's set foot on the summit for centuries."

"I don't know, do I?" Remington suddenly looks over Snow's shoulder in an oddly quizzical way, as if he had caught sight of his reflection in a mirror. "There are old geological and climatic studies about. In fact the Inn here has quite a lot of them up in the attic. One could dig them out of the Vision, but it's much more fun this way."

He pauses. "You know, if you do reach the top, most of your problems will be over." He looks at them sharply. "But don't tell anyone about what you find in the crater."

They press him for what he means, but he changes the

subject, and they do not insist. For an hour or so they discuss conceptual art (it is this genre in which Remington proposes to treat the mountain). Soon they begin to feel the soporific effects of the warm sake they have been drinking with their delicious mountain trout (cooked in ginger, shallots, almonds, and soysauce, a specialty of the house). Snow and Michael take leave of their new friend and retire to their tiny bedroom in the eaves.

Snow, restless, in her nightgown, goes to the dormer window. It looks out on the lake, bathed now with the bluish sheen of Phobos, and marked here and there at its margins with the tiny orange lights of fishing villages. The clouds have cleared; it will be fine tomorrow.

Michael, slightly drunk and feeling a sense of wellbeing, is impatient for Snow to come to him. "What are you looking at?" he asks lazily. She does not reply. Something in the way she is standing gives him a faint chill of sadness.

"It's my period," she says at last. It is a lie. Something in the light outside, and the garden downstairs, has reminded her of the scene at the theatre in Hellas. Before she returns to the bed Michael has fallen asleep.

5.

Nix Olympica

NEXT MORNING THEY set off early. The air is pure and soft, the lake a dreamy blue. At its head they can see the gorge of the upper Orno, and above the gorge, hanging like an apparition, tilted back from the observer by the curvature of the small planet, the grotesque cone of the mountain, ringed with perpetual snow, now green, now white in the shifting lights of Mars; trailing a twenty-kilometer banner of cloudy ice-crystals in the jetstreams of the stratosphere.

Michael and Snow have had a lunch packed, of paté, bread, and wine, which they eat at noon near the entrance to the gorge, after a brisk hike along the shore. They finish with some little pears. It would be an insult to the mountain cuisine to use the protein synthesizer without need.

In the afternoon they begin the difficult climb up the flank of the valley. By nightfall they have reached a hostel nestled on a grassy alp about halfway up. This time at Snow's desire they sleep separately. Next day they take the crest of the ridge and by evening have reached a mountain shelter at the foot of a steep, hook-shaped glacier. Both are tired and cold; they light a fire in the hearth and settle down before it in their sleeping-bags. They are now nearly seven thousand meters up; their breath is becoming short and labored.

They wake early, and watch the morning come up over the hills and plains of Mars. By now they can even see the deserts that fringe the fertile complex of Nix Olympica, an ancient, dull copper color that first caused this world to be named the Red Planet. They turn back to the peak, their objective.

"I wonder why Remington told us not to say what was in the crater?" asks Michael, partly to make conversation.

"There's an old story, which nobody has bothered to check, that there are people living up there who don't like to be disturbed. They've set a privacy override on the Computer, I suppose," Snow replied. "How far have we come?"

"About a quarter of the way up," says Michael.

"I don't know how long I'll last."

"Once we get used to it, it won't be so hard."

"The mountain's very frightening."

"But beautiful."

"Yes, beautiful."

That day they encounter the first real climbing of their excursion, mostly fairly simple crevasse work, and then later in the afternoon a scramble up a broken rockface. By evening they have reached the crest of a new ridge, a knife-edge pointing at the heart of the main peak. On the leeward side of the ridge there is shelter from the now persistent wind, and here they pitch their companionable but unnecessary tent. They break out, for the first time, the warmsuits they will wear for the rest of the climb, filmy, skintight garments that are capable of maintaining the correct temperature and pressure for the human body for a variety of conditions up to the rigors of outer space. These garments make a tent unnecessary, but the psychological need to be enclosed in a human space has not been bred out of the line of Man, and Michael and Snow, munching the tasty cubes from the synthesizer and drinking coffee made from melted snow, are grateful for its comfort.

Now for the first time Michael broaches the subject of Narcissus' challenge.

"Why haven't you said anything about what happened at the theatre?" he asks bluntly.

"I didn't want to interfere with you, I think," she says. "You were fighting something out with yourself."

"How do you know I'm strong enough to do it alone?" He has relinquished his pride, is opening up in order to invite a reciprocal gesture.

"You *are* strong. I wish *I* knew how to survive the way you do. You still have the trick of hope."

"This is absurd. I'm the one that's been moping about."

"Well, this is new for you."

"What do you mean?"

She is lying on her side, facing him, the glow of the tiny light on her long cheek, her pale body masked in the shimmer of the warmsuit. Her breath makes plumes in the air. She is like a ghost. He sees a darkness about the corners of her mouth and eyes that he has seen before, and been troubled by without understanding.

"Don't you see, Michael? It's all rather pointless. When we were lovers it seemed there was some direction or reference in our lives. But it's all just a game, really, isn't it?"

"What is?"

"Everything. The feud, our lives, the whole world."

She is right in a sense, of course, though someone like Chrysanthemum would be able instantly to see the flaws in her analysis. Let me put it this way: the conventions of naturalistic narrative and dialogue to which we have adhered in the last few pages are indeed merely conventions, and having seen that, we should by rights lose interest in the story. Snow has in a sense done just this: she has seen the narrative machinery at work, and the illusion of reality is destroyed. But even if life is a fantasy, cannot a fantasy be enjoyed for its own sake, even if it has no chance of being "real"? On the other hand, is not the fantastic also a kind of reality? How, in a world under the complete control of the human will, can the illusory be distinguised from the real? Does it make any sense to accuse the real of being merely a game, when it makes no pretence to be otherwise? In one system the prime value might be truth; but in another, it might be interest, or expressibility, or consistency, or beauty, or joy. Can one legitimately import the values of one system into another? And even if we can "see through" the values of a system, does this matter? Naturalism or realism could indeed be artistic strait jackets; but they could also be a charming and antique eccentricity, part of the flavor and mood of a story.

Snow, with all her strength of personality, has been misled by a certain seriousness of character to mistake the ludic for the trivial, the arbitrary for the meaningless. She comes of an ancient world, and is much more like Michael's parents than Michael is—a phenomenon common in marriage, it may be noted apophthegmatically.

But her slow, unnoticed pain is nevertheless impressive and even terrifying. Michael's heart sinks. He had thought the challenge to be the worst thing that could happen; but this revelation of his wife's despair, of a sense of darkness and disaster gallently withstood year after year, of a defeat not temporary and external like his own but basic and given, is almost more than he can bear. He is *angry* with it, helplessly and painfully.

Next day, like ghosts in their warmsuits, they set out along the ridge, roped together. They are soon forced to leave it, however, and the morning and afternoon are spent crossing an enormous waste of snow. At midday they pause to eat; and they don their oxygen converters, for both have become short of breath and dizzy.

Around midafternoon they have an odd adventure: a speck detaches itself from a crag and wheels above them, plunging periodically into colored shadow and bursting out again into the light. It is only when one of its shadows passes them that they realize how huge this bird is—forty feet from wingtip to wingtip, eaglelike, but oddly humped and pure white in color: a Roc, once a legend in a bestiary but now a substantial if rare reality, a product of the genetic wizardry of the life-artists of Mars. Like many synthetic beasts, the Roc is adapted only to a very specific environment; it preys on the hypertrophied mountain cattle of the region, that batten in summer on the luxuriant alp-grass, and hibernate in winter. The Roc, too, hibernates, feeding on the accumulated layers of fat it builds up in summer, and picking, in its rare periods of winter wakefulness, at the frozen carcasses of the wild cattle that it stores outside its eyrie. Rocs do not attack human beings, but this one is beginning to stock up food for the winter and is curious about the two tiny figures, so far above the level of the grass, toiling across the snowfield. After an hour it disappears.

They spend the night on a ledge they have dug and flattened out of the steep snow. Over the last day Michael has recovered a little from the shock of his wife's revelation; or rather, the feeling has become purer and less turbulent. He sees back into the years of their marriage, the thought of her despair putting out one by one the lights of his favorite memories. They are both very tired. He treats her very gently and she, in pity, shows good cheer and hope for the success of their climb.

The next day is a plodding ascent up the interminable snow. At about midmorning they both feel the screaming of a psychic alarm inside their heads: their Idiot Guardians have apparently decided that their charges' lives are now at risk and are warning them to turn back or to allow themselves to be automatically protected from harm. Without qualms Michael and Snow override their Guardians and press on.

That evening Michael again feels a helpless anger with his wife, or rather an anger at that part of her that he wishes he could think is a cancer in her, something he can mentally detach from her, and so he probes further.

"Why didn't you tell me before?"

"I did, but you thought it was just a mood. You'd never felt that way yourself, so you didn't understand."

"But sometimes you're very happy. What about the paté in the gorge?" They had enjoyed that lunch, four days ago.

"Yes, I'm happy sometimes."

"Even though you can never forget your basic pessimism about life?"

"Yes. I'm sorry."

"So all those happy times were just on the surface, just distractions? It makes me feel as if you've been fooling me . . . even as if you were being unfaithful."

Snow begins to speak, changes her mind, looks at him tenderly; then: "I've never been unfaithful to you."

"That's not what I meant.—But how do you bear it? You're the strong one, not me. What keeps you going?"

"I don't know."

In the next five days the air gradually thins out. The sky darkens from blue to indigo to black. To prevent snow-blindness from the dazzling albedo effects of the two suns they wear masklike snow goggles. The days merge into each other; fatigue and a stunned tedium become the accepted state of mind; every inch of exposed skin is burned black by the unshielded ultraviolet. It is like an endless ritual. Occasionally they turn and look back at their planet, the view spectacular yet unstartling because of its constant presence. The weather remains fine, but for a few flurries of snow one night. And soon they approach the region where there is no more weather, and the stars are visible at noonday, and the snow thins to frost and finally to naked rock: tumbled raw lava; basalt, pumice, ash. Some of the rocks are marked with the intricate and two-dimensional designs of the indigenous Martian vegetation, an odd carbon-iron-silicon-based life molecule, here maintaining a last tenacious foothold against the encroachments of Terran ecology.

The day before they intend to make an assault on the summit they pass on their left a subsidiary cone, belching a cloud of gases into the sky. Around it an illusion of air is preserved, the sun dims and the sky is almost blue. This fumarole, like others elsewhere on the planet, is kept in operation by the invisible Guardians of Mars, to replace some of the air lost to the planet's weak gravitational field. The expedient isn't really necessary, since a relativistic matter synthesizer, big brother of the units with which Michael and Snow are now breathing, could easily be set up to supply sufficient oxygen if it were desired. The mountain is emitting carbon dioxide, water vapor, hydrochloric acid gas, hydrogen sulphide, ammonia, and other poisonous compounds; but one of the rules of Martian aesthetics is to use as primitive a technology as possible to achieve a given end. Because of the inconvenience of the volcanically maintained atmosphere, the planetary ecologists have been forced into unprecedented flights of virtuosity, such as the invention of an aerial phytoplankton that feeds on ammonia and CO_2 and excretes pure nitrogen and molecular oxygen. The phytoplankton uses as its energy source the broad-spectrum radiation of Mars' two suns, and shields the Martian biosphere from the worst effects of cosmic-ray bombardment; Mars lacks a magnetic field which would otherwise afford some protection. It is the aerial plankton that is in turn responsible for the yellowish tinge of the sun, and the brilliant Martian sunsets.

One of the effects of the ascent is indeed the thinning and intensifying of those same sunsets. On the last evening Snow and Michael watch the sun go down, eyes carefully shielded. Below them a huge storm is raging round the mountain, but it does not affect them up here, any more than a hurricane is felt ten meters below the surface of the sea. They stand in a waste riddled and cratered with meteor impacts, windless and gloomy. They do not speak, for now in order to be heard they must place their heads together; there is no air to conduct the sound. They are now entirely under the protection of their sealed warmsuits and oxygen masks. They have encountered that day several difficult rock climbs, and their muscles ache and quiver.

Next day is harder still; slow rope-and-piton climbs up sheer faces of basalt, traverses over falls so terrible the mind cannot comprehend them, gasping claustrophic adventures in chimneys and cracks. Both are beginning to run a fever because of the radiation. The shielding afforded by their warmsuits is adequate for a few days, but their skins are sore and their heads swim with the beating solar wind of charged high-energy particles.

At last, stunned by a burst of sunlight as she reaches the neck of a chimney, Snow loses her balance; Michael braces himself against the rope and holds her, but as she falls her left foot catches in a crevice and her leg breaks with an audible snap. She dangles, screaming silently with sickness and vertigo.

Hand over hand he pulls her to the summit, for to Michael's surprise it is indeed the last stretch and they are now lying side by side on the enormous circular rim, distorted by distance and the planet's curvature, of the main crater of Nix Olympica.

The brown bone of Snow's tibia has broken through the skin and is stretching the sturdy fabric of her warmsuit. She moans and faints several times in quick succession as Michael, sobbing with empathy, forces open the outer airlock of her facemask, places a painkiller in it, closes it and struggles to make her come out of her daze long enough to open the inner lock and take the pill.

At last she swallows it; in a few moments the pain has subsided enough for her to get hold of her faculties and calm herself. Forehead to forehead they discuss what is to be done.

At this point, Michael and Snow have reached an aesthetic crisis, the test of their style that this entire venture has invited. The problem is that in a moment Snow could be healed and off the mountain, were they to desire it; the quandary is reminiscent of that of the novelist, who can at any point invoke a *deus ex machina* to bring about a desired twist of the plot, and who is therefore stifled with freedom. But the problem here is knottier still, for unlike the novelist's public, which can be relied on in most cases to accept as inevitable the actual course of the plot, and will not trouble with alternatives except by an extraordinary effort, Michael and Snow, as the only, and most important, audience of their own actions, are fully aware of the alternatives.

To attempt with their ordinary mountaineering equipment to descend the mountain would be dilettantism, an unnecessary invitation of pain, false heroics. On the other hand, to use the Vision and escape their predicament would be an admission of the aesthetic unsoundness of their expedition from the start. The aesthetic stakes of mountaineering are danger, fear, and pain; to refuse to pay when one has bad luck is to deprive the game of the necessary element of risk.

To compound the problem, the great storm they have noticed the previous day has intensified, and is swirling in slow whorls around the base of the mountain. Unprotected descent would be suicide. This seems for a moment to be the only viable course.

However, as if by a stroke of the pen, an expedient suggests itself. Snow remembers the words of Remington at the Inn, about the crater and what they may find there. Michael seizes the opportunity; leaving Snow lying against a rock and as comfortable as he can make her, he sets off across the barren lip of the crater. When he has advanced perhaps a hundred meters Snow suddenly wishes to call him back and tell him something important; but she thinks better of it and refrains from the direct mind contact which is the only method of doing so.

After about a kilometer Michael is able to see what lies within the crater. It is a strange ochre plain, like the old deserts of pre-Terraformed Mars, blotched with the indigenous vegetation. In the center there is a cluster of unbelievable blue shapes—crinoids, cusps, cycloids, and paraboloids; something like a group of complex and wind-blown tents or sails that have been frozen forever in the commotion of their flapping. What is unbelievable is their size. Martian architecture is usually quite modest in dimensions—the opportunities for gigantism offered by low-gravity design are too tempting, and are thus foregone—but here there are buildings two and three kilometers high, with unsupported horizontal structures that puzzle the eye like a gestalt illusion. Everything is totally still and quiet, but for the subtle motion of the crater lip's pale yellow shadow past and through its dark blue shadow, as Phobos rides with unnatural speed over the immense caldera.

Michael estimates that with a supreme effort he can carry Snow to this city of blue and demand of its inhabitants the help and shelter they need.

6.

The Voyage of the *Nausicaa*

NARCISSUS IS PRACTICING *kendo,* the art of swordsman-ship, with a crude dummy on the wooden platform among the trees. He is waiting for Chrysanthemum to get up, so that he can inquire about the seer Gabriel, who is Chrysanthemum's old friend. Narcissus is still tired from the passions of the previous night, and the swift strokes of the sword, blinding in their speed and grace to an onlooker, feel to the swordsman himself forced, clumsy, and uncomfortably ahead of his breathing. He has noticed a general staleness in his form these last weeks: oppressed with turbulent feelings about his sister's success in the theatre, he has forgotten the Zen of the sword, which is detachment and personal uninvolvement. He, not the inertia of the sword, is doing the work—which has become *work* in the process.

"When should we leave, then?" says Cleopatra to Chrysanthemum. They have entered the courtyard from the breakfast room behind. Narcissus, caught by surprise, and doubly vexed by this and by the coincidence with his train of thought, finds himself in a awkward pose; and in a most unZenlike pique he whirls and slashes the bamboo dummy in two, before Chrysanthemum can answer.

"I was under the impression you weren't supposed to do that," Chrysanthemum says instead, rather tactlessly.

Narcissus ignores him, sheathes the sword, and observes to Cleopatra: "I thought you would be at the theatre already."

"No, there's no rehearsal today. Is something the matter?"

Rudely again, he brushes the question aside and turns to Chrysanthemum.

"Leave for where?"

Cleopatra replies: "Chrysanthemum has been asked to exhibit at the capital. We're invited to the reception. I thought we might all go."

"Cleopolis *would* be the right place to follow up your dramatic triumphs," says Narcissus rather nastily. "But don't you have to finish your run here?"

"Yes, but it's only two weeks more. You *are* in a bad mood."

Again he ignores her. "I wanted to talk to you, Uncle Chrysanthemum, about seeing your friend Gabriel. Where does he live?"

"I'm not saying, until you kiss and make up. Tell your sister what's on your mind."

"He's just jealous of my acting," says the object of his remark.

Narcissus snorts and turns away.

"Don't sulk."

"Children, children," says Chrysanthemum flutily. "Birds in their little nests agree."

Narcissus collapses and sinks to a cross-legged position on the platform.

"The whole thing is spoilt. Here we are in a mess of banal motivations, just like a wretched psychological novel."

"The trick, my boy, is to make them part of the high endeavor," says Chrysanthemum. "Fuse them in the crucible of Art."

"Aren't you serious about anything?" asks Cleopatra.

"I *am* serious. Accuse us not of flippancy. Wise old

Chrysanthemum knows his aesthetics."

"But I don't even *want* to go on with the feud."

"You're just like your Mother Salammbo. Always committing suicide." Salammbo was one of Chrysanthemum's many mistresses at various times in the last century and a half. "Perpend. The invitation is for the thirty-fifth of Chalcedony. It's September now—that gives us four months. We could go by ship; *Nausicaa* needs to get the barnacles rubbed off. Wait—" he waves Narcissus to silence. "Gabriel lives in the Sporades with the pariahs. It's not strictly legal, but if we're taking a trip past there anyway, it'd be natural to drop in and see him. And so we'll kill four birds with one stone."

Mars is covered with a network of canals, constructed about six hundred years ago partly for irrigation, partly for pleasure-craft, but mainly because the sheer poetry of Schiaparelli's optical illusions has appealed as much to the builders of Mars as to its early fictioneers. So fiction tends to become truth. From the Hellene Sea the Inter-Oceanic canal links up with the Hellespontic Ocean to the southwest; another, the Great Southern Canal, connects the Hellespontic with the misnamed Mare Erythraeum, which is not actually a sea but the subtropical mountain area, south of the huge equational canyons of Coprates, where Cleopolis is situated. The Martian Sporades are a group of Hellene islands lying on the direct route to the entrance of the Inter-Oceanic canal.

"*Four* birds?" asks Narcissus, cheering up a little. "Callie wants to go to Cleopolis and I want to go to see Gabriel. What's in it for you?"

"Well," says Chrysanthemum, "selfish interests were not entirely uninfluential. There's a young lad I know, cooped up with only his pretty pink hormones for company, in a baron's mansion on the Great Southern. I was thinking that we might take the occasion to drop in on his father the baron and see how the dear young fellow is shaping up."

"Lecher. What's the fourth bird."

"Michael and Snow will be in Cleopolis in the coming solstice. They always do the season. You may feel glum now but you need this war. It'll liven you up."

Narcissus rises to his feet, a new look of dancing excitement in his eyes. "Yes, we'll go, won't we, Callie? Dear uncle, where would we be without you?"

So a few weeks later they gather in the Brown Room on a fresh Melody day, both suns in the sky, the light pouring through the tree leaves and dazzling them with whitish green and tender pink, the whole verandaside a knotted and cascading fabric of light. The brown walls glow. They drink a pewter cup of port, standing in the bright air, isolated, looking at each other. Cleopatra blazes, golden in blue duck slacks and a thin white sweater, a sexual object of the twentieth century, with waved hair, lipsticked and brassiered. She has the gift of great actresses, to change even the shape and profile of her body for the part she plays. She drains her cup, and sets it down as a signal that she is ready to leave.

They climb down a series of ladders, carrying ocean-going gear, Chrysanthemum puffing and complaining. It gets darker and greener; the forest floor is brown and still, and in the quietness there is a strange bumping under the leaf mould. They take a little path that winds down the slope between colossal boles. The bumping gets louder, is combined with a whine, and finally, as light starts to come through the forest, a hissing roar. They come out onto a rocky headland bathed in blinding light and a fresh wind. Below, the Hellene Sea is in incredible motion, a crawling at the close horizon deepening into a steep, serried confusion of waves. They are higher and apparently shorter than Earthly waves, rising as the bottom shallows into thin, fine, perfectly intact breakers that float against the rocks and burst with a heavy boom!, shaking the ground under their feet and sending a sunlit mist, infested with rainbows, into their faces.

They turn away and descend the carved stone steps to the boathouse in the cove on their left. The noise hollows, diminshes. They cross a tiny beach of white sand, high-water-marked with a delicate fawn sample of Mars' new shells. Mars has no tides, as its moons are too small, but the low gravity allows large random shifts within bodies of water, depending on the force and direction of the wind. Rapid ripples hiss up toward the travelers' feet.

The boathouse is constructed of painted wood and is built out on stilts over the sea. Inside is the graceful and rigid form of the *Nausicaa,* bounding almost imperceptibly in the submarine light. The building is as big as a barn, and echoes the slappings and business of the water. Spokes of light, with shoals of tiny fish, wheel in the green depths.

The space is almost entirely taken up with the floating docks and the big ship. She is a catamaran, with deep, rounded hulls bent like a bow toward prow and stern, terminating in stylized papyrus flowers five feet above the deck. She is nearly fifty feet long, built of polished mahogany and teak, painted with barbaric insignia at the prows. She has a higher freeboard than an Earthly vessel, but is designed to hydroplane over the water's surface in the right conditions. Her mast is not stepped at present, but it can carry an extraordinary breadth of filmy unimolecular sail. The sails are stiffened, slackened, or rendered permeable by electronic impulses controlled by a minute computer in the mast, depending on the strength and direction of the wind. Despite her size, the ship has the liveliness and responsiveness of a racing dinghy.

They board the *Nausicaa* and stow their gear in lockers below decks. Narcissus starts the tiny fusion engine; the huge doors of the boathouse swing open; Cleopatra casts off, Chrysanthemum gestures helplessly with a boathook and the big boat slides out into open water with a boiling of foam at her heels. Standing on the broad deck, they step the titanium mast and spars. A few moments later Cleopatra runs up the jib. It opens with a pop!, and with Chrysanthemum at the helm the catamaran comes around and heads for the harbormouth, with a burble under its twin prows. Narcissus runs up the mainsail as they pass the headland, and there is a sudden strain and lift as the starboard hull almost leaves the water, and the ship gathers speed abruptly, huge fans of spray bursting from her port prow. They can now see the whole island behind them, a steep and blessed mound of trees above trees, in various blossom. . . "Nature's little handiwork," observes Chrysanthemum soulfully.

Having gained searoom, Chrysanthemum lets the wheel spin and Narcissus allows the mainsheet to pass out freely until the mainsail is goosewinged out to port. The wind is now almost directly astern, and Narcissus and his sister set the spinnaker, like a gigantic bubble crawling with rainbow diffraction patterns. The mast bends and the ship leaps forward, the huge concave of the sail pulling her up out of the water until the whole feel of the ship alters and in a curious rushing gait, outpacing the swells, the *Nausicaa* is hydroplaning westward at over thirty knots.

They set the autopilot and join in the main cabin. Chrysanthemum busies himself in the galley, and soon reappears, preceded by the delicious odor of steak and hot biscuits. They eat a hearty lunch, for the spray and exertion have given them an appetite.

The cabin is comfortably furnished in wood and brass; windowseats upholstered in canvas conceal lockers containing old games of Scrabble, Snakes and Ladders, Monopoly, incomplete decks of conventional and Tarot cards, a chess set with an agate button instead of a missing pawn, a Go board (Narcissus is an expert) and numerous works of problematic pornography (the equivalent of the twentieth-century detective novel). Toward the stern is the hatch leading to the cockpit, which is surrounded on three sides with shockproof glass, and which contains the automatic pilot, the wheel, and the binnacle. In the absence of a planetary magnetic field, an inertial compass, steadied by gas-floating gyroscopes, points toward whatever North the planet can be said to possess.

Freighted, then, with games of chance, and guided by her own inertial history alone, *Nausicaa* sets out on her voyage. An odd mood comes over her crew—even odder for any age before this: a rather delicious sense of arbitrariness, of being capable of anything. For Chrysanthemum it is a sensual feeling, inasmuch as that ancient and subtle creature's feelings can be guessed: a reptilian sense of exhilaration, such as can be seen in the faces of the great Martian seagulls when Cleopatra comes out to feed them scraps. Cleopatra herself feels dreamy and tense, as before a performance. Narcissus has a fine and exciting sense of foreboding, of a danger of being irrevocably changed.

Brother and sister go out on the foredeck. There is the unsettling absence of wind that one sometimes notices on a racing yacht when the vessel is virtually keeping pace with the moving air; though the *Nausicaa* is bursting through the waves, and her sails are stretched to quivering, there is a warm stillness. The sun (for it is almost in the tropics here) beats down hotly, and soon Narcissus and Cleopatra take off their sweaters, to lie like bosomed matelots, figureheads, on the white planking, rolled slightly to and fro by the motion of the ship, sweaters folded under their heads for pillows. Narcissus allows himself to slip into the Vision, while preserving all his immediate sensations; a shudder goes over him, and he passes into that oddest of all states, sleep under the Vision, where dreams take on the force of reality in their own universe.

Cleopatra, who feels ignored by her lover, spitefully edges up to him and with her lipstick paints him obscenely all over with organs even he does not possess. When Chrysanthemum appears a few moments later he is shocked. Narcissus wakes up, and perceiving his state, blushes furiously.

"Cat!"

He jumps her, and they fight viciously, covering each other with lipstick, as Chrysanthemum chuckles and offers advice. The battle becomes more tender; as the lovers do not seem to mind and indeed encourage him to stay, the old lecher settles down to watch their pretty encounter. Their long bodies slow like fighting-fishes, glowing with color, and slide over each other with a restless shaking.

When it is over Chrysanthemum applauds. We must not imagine that there is much in common between ancient and present decorum.

That night Chrysanthemum serves a magnificent souf-
flé. They eat it out on deck; the wind has become hotter
and drier, and the sails give off little bright shocks of static
electricity. It is a Fohn wind blowing over the mountains
to the northeast, heated by compression, and redolent of
the deserts beyond. The sunset is fantastic; the sun and
moon are very close, one orange, sinking, the other white
and on the rise, both haloed together with a caul of red;
for Phobos rises in the west and sets in the east, outpacing
its primary's rotation. Above, reddish brown streamers
stretch from horizon to horizon in the pink-green air. The
sea has calmed, and moves like a volatile oil, salmon pink
and deepest blue in the shadows of the waves: colors from
the ancient seascapist J.M.W. Turner. Far to the
northeast they can see the jagged crests of the mountains
that ring this ocean (probably an old meteor crater); they
are lit with a bronze glow.

After a nightcap of brandy they decide to sleep on deck,
rather than in the staterooms in the hulls on either side of
the main cabin. They fetch up pressor-field mattresses,
programmed to keep them comfortably in place while
they sleep, alert their Idiot Guardians, give instructions to
the autopilot, and covered with light maroon silks, they
fall asleep.

At two o'clock in the morning Narcissus wakes to see
Phobos, almost as bright as day, at its zenith; it is very
hot; he has a sense of sadness and loss, and then falls
asleep again.

Next morning they sight a series of small, rocky islands
covered with aromatic scrub. These are the Martian
Sporades, where dwell some of the planet's strangest
inhabitants, most of them officially mad, having committed some breach of taste or misuse of the Vision:
addicts, psychospiritual cancer cases, mystics, prophets.

One island is populated with Solipsists; the whole place
shimmers and transmutes, and monsters can be found in
inshore waters. The island is whatever the closest of its
inhabitants desires it to be, sometimes a ship, sometimes a
furnace, sometimes a populous city. Odd strains of music,
bellowings, laughter, are blown to the *Nausicaa* with the

wind, and sweet and nauseating smells. They pass the island by: it is an unlucky place.

Another island is empty but for a two-headed giant called Uther. Uther is two persons who agreed to become one person; they were great friends; now he is addicted to himself but full of fear and loathing; he wanders about pounding his flattened heads with his fists.

On another island are the Forgetters. They have used the Vision so unwisely that their bodies and brains have ceased to record any change except for the processes of metabolism. Many of these were very witty and nervous people before their change. Now they are no longer nervous, for they cannot remember anything. They are like happy, happy children, and they live in the present without clocks or calendars.

The Rememberers, who live on a larger island nearby, are almost exactly the same. They remember everything, and are therefore in a perpetual waking dream, incapable of selecting a single action or thought to dwell on for the moment, since their whole lives are present to them. Thus human time is the line between memory and forget-fulness.

Nearby is an island densely populated with one person, who has replicated himself thousands of times, because he cannot bear other people and loves company; and the island of the Mother, who, going backward in time, gave birth to herself by parthenogenesis.

On a big island called Skiros live the Technological People. They have devoted themselves to living comfor-tably without the use of artificial intelligence. One of their jet aircraft swoops low over the ship and hails them loudly. The Eleutherans ignore this provocation, and soon the island is left behind with its airfields, factories, do-it-yourself workshops, and bustle of traffic.

At last they make landfall on the endmost island of the chain. Chrysanthemum knows the place; he has a friend there he wants Narcissus and Cleopatra to meet. Quietly the *Nausicaa* slips through the blue waters of a deep cove fringed with sea caves which belch and boom with the slow swell. At the head of the gulf there is a beach of black volcanic sand and a huge old willow tree where a stream rushes through pebbles to the sea. Here live certain nymphs, the lovely, almost mindless products of genetic engineering, who possess the capacity to change shape into water creatures and who are almost irresistibly attractive to humans of all three sexes.

On the highest point of the island there is a temple, covered with splendid sculptures and rotted frescoes. Its only human inhabitant is a crippled old hermaphrodite who has been given the gift of prophecy at his own request. He is crippled by a purely psychic disease, producing an inability on the part of his nervous system to tell left from right. This ailment began when he became able to foresee the future: handedness is intimately connected with our perception of time, in fact in one sense it *is* our perception of time. Thus he is unable to move without great concentration, cannot write consistently in one direction or with one mirror-image orientation, and finds difficulty speaking in a correct word order. His name is Gabriel, after the ancient Colombian writer Gabriel Garcia Marquez.

The three Eleutherans climb the steep path in the quiet of the evening, leaving the *Nausicaa* anchored and their dinghy beached. The temple's golden roof can be seen at times through the clefts. At last they come out on a sweet meadow covered with daisies and acanthuses, with the stream bubbling through it and olive groves on the gentle slopes on both sides. There is a smell in the air of lavender or rosemary. Behind they can see a scatter of islands lit brown by the falling sun. Phobos is rising in the west, casting a track of bluish glitter on the dark sea. They turn back to the temple; it is enormous, in the classical Doric mode but expressing in its proportions a totally different meaning: not harmony and balance, but a kind of ambiguous and stony tension, a sense of weight borne patiently but in pain.

Gabriel can be seen squatting on the temple steps before a small woodfire. He rises to wave goodbye, corrects himself, and changes the gesture to one of welcome. He wears nothing but a loose, dirty cloth wrapped about his body, that does not conceal his withered female breasts. As they come up to him, his eyes have trouble tracking them, and his body jerks with barely controlled epileptic feedback from one side of the brain to the other. Despite his handicap, he is an awesome figure, with a huge spade-shaped and vermin-infested black beard, an enormous suffering face, a big hooked nose, and a tic in his bleared right eye. He is smoking a cigarette, which has burnt down to the fingers of his left hand, and periodically he shakes his right hand with the pain dolefully and absentmindedly. Cleopatra finds him oddly attractive, coughing and concave though he is, with his small thin body, hanging hollow face, and sun-blackened skin.

They exchange polite expressions, and Gabriel invites them to share his evening meal, which he provides by direct invocation of the Vision. A banqueting table appears, groaning with boars' heads in aspic, peacock, lobster, flagons of wine, and heaped fruit. As they approach the meal there is a raucous screaming, and half a dozen winged females descend, horribly emaciated and vilely covered with ordure, to upset the trestles and defile the food. Gabriel makes no attempt to stop them, but, swaying to and fro and wringing his hands, he wails and weeps. Narcissus draws his sword, the long razor-sharp blade of the Samurai, forged on Earth many centuries ago, with its blue shot-silk glitter, and the harpies disappear, screaming and flapping wildly.

These apparitions are in fact Gabriel's many wives and lovers, who, when his gift of prophecy was still under his control, had been won to him forever by his ability to guess their actions in advance. Addicted to him for his understanding, and maddened by his faithlessness (subjectively he was enjoying their rivals as he enjoyed each one, for past and future were present to him), they have accompanied him to this island, followers he cannot dismiss, a reminder of the human costs of his talent. Indeed, if the stupid and beautiful nymphs of the island did not feed and protect him, he would long since have fallen victim to the harpies' attacks.

They make a light meal on the provisions Chrysanthemum has thoughtfully brought up from the ship, and settle themselves around the fire to talk. Chrysanthemum finally asks his old friend to tell them something about their futures. Gabriel begins with a series of strange and hollow noises:

"Erwowlf a foh snugele kitethap uth, dirb a foh zidolem uth, urbmun foh nushcartsba uth . . . utni . . . metamorphosed . . ."

He begins again:

"Poems and songs many of subject the . . ."

After other false starts he finally settles into comprehensibility.

There is a sense in which the rest of this novel is a garbled and expanded version of his account, but there are also massive differences, impossible to point out, caused by the infinite regresses involved in a future enacted by free knowers of their own fate. The great computer, source of Gabriel's power, can calculate on the basis of all information to date, but even those formidable resources are taxed by the difficulties of playing a game against what is simultananeously a piece in the game and another player. It can indeed calculate the outcome of such a game, but the speed of its calculation is identical to the speed at which the events it predicts actually take place. The future is not invariable; indeed, it does not exist—or rather, any future which does exist is not in fact the future at all, but the past. By "exist" is meant "can be known for sure," for there is no other sense of "exist." The way we tell the difference between the past and the future (and this difference is the only definition of both) is that we can know the past but not the future; or—and this is the same thing—we cannot act in the past, but we can in the future. To a knower of the "future" those persons whose actions he can predict become nonsentient objects, like the participants in eclipses, for their actions are part of his past. However, if those persons discover the nature of the prediction, it ceases to apply to them. Thus whenever a prediction is made, on one hand it alters the four-dimensional geometry of the universe, so that it becomes topologically a torus rather than a sphere; on the other, it instantly renders itself inaccurate. One interesting corollary is that predictions made on the basis of all present information are accurate only to the extent that they are misunderstood. Narcissus, Cleopatra, and Chrysanthemum, then, will enact to the letter the text of Gabriel's prophecy, to the extent that they fail to comprehend it. They are participants in a drama (or novel) only on the condition that they are not aware that they are. Indeed, part of the art of their performance is the heroic naiveté with which they play their parts, a naiveté which is also the acme of aesthetic sophistication—decadent pastoralism, existential slumming.

7.

The House of the Goddesses

FOR HOURS MICHAEL has plodded across the barren plain of the crater floor, Snow unconscious in his arms. The descent of the ringwall has been an ordeal almost beyond endurance; but this last stretch is inhuman. Michael cannot get a certain rather dull tune out of his head; he keeps humming the same few bars over and over, unable to find the melodic line out of them and into the rest of the song, or out of the tune altogether.

The hugh blue structures do not seem to get any closer. Without the perspective provided by an atmosphere, distant objects have a crystalline and obsessive clarity; there is no rest for the eye, for everything is in perfect detail. He is transfixed. The stars, the sun, and the moon beat down. Even tiny Diemos can occasionally be seen, when it passes close to its incandescent sister, and becomes brilliant in turn.

Snow is in a state of shock. From time to time she wakes and smiles distantly. Michael, seeing this, forces himself onward in despair.

The last few kilometers are accomplished in a state of mind that Michael will not afterward be able to remember. He recalls beating with his fists on the utterly solid and unidentifiable material of the closest of the buildings, but cannot recall the mood in which he did so. When in a trice he finds himself inside, with Snow lying on the floor beside him, and then they are suddenly surrounded by women of odd complexion and clothing, he has no awareness of his own attitude.

He wakes in a little gold-mosaic room like a chapel, with Byzantine figures of sages and holy men in a dense forest of arabesques. He is lying on a pallet on an apparently marble floor; he feels marvelously rested, cheerful, and prosaic; and he is ravenously hungry. He rises, pushes open a wrought bronze door, and shouts.

"Hello! Is anyone there?"

At the end of a corridor he sees a figure pass quickly, in another corridor at right angles to the first. The figure seems to be a woman in a pink silk sari. She has a small, voluptuous brown face, large-featured with a caste mark on the brow; and with more than the usual number of arms. A moment later another woman turns the corner of the corridor and comes toward him. She is tall and statuesque, with a classical nose whose bridge is level with her brow, and keen intelligent grey eyes; she is dressed in a flowing white robe with many folds, her hair is done up in a graceful coiffure. On her shoulder is a small, sleepy-looking owl which blinks suddenly and ferociously, and mutters quickly into its mistress' ear.

"My name is Pallas Athene. It is my desire to serve you," she says formally.

Michael, who is a pious rather than a religious man, and who has never had occasion to traffic with the law, is suddenly abashed with the realization that he is in the presence of the goddess. He falls to his knees; she approaches and raises him up, saying:

"You have done well, child, very well. Do not be afriad. You are in the Mansion of the Mosaics, which is one of the Divine Mansions." Indeed, the corridor, like the room he has just left, glows with dimly lit azure, pink, and gold.

"Where is Snow, my Lady?" he asks.

"Safe and sound, and quite healed. She has been telling us about your adventures."

The goddess takes his hand and leads him down the corridor. When they reach the end they turn right, and as they do so another goddess passes them. She is keen-faced, dressed in a coarse grey material, with white-gold braided hair. She smells faintly of pine forests, and crackles with electricity. Her light blue eyes have tiny pupils; there are runes embroidered on her hems and sleeves.

"Who was that, my Lady?" asks Michael when she is gone.

"The Goddess Frey."

"And who was that other one I saw, with many arms?"

"The Goddess Kali, of creation and destruction."

They pass through the doorway and enter an enormous room, whose great curved lightscreens and curtain-walls of glass look out on the landscape of old Mars. Michael shudders with vertigo at the sight. The gigantic arches, vaults, and shell of the room are covered with a dense filigree of mosaic, lit from beneath in gold flushes where it catches the light. The mosaic style is here less Byzantine in character, more Persian.

In the center of the room is a round table of the same blue substance as the outer walls of the Mansion. Around it are over a hundred tall chairs or thrones constructed in various different fashions and materials. Nearly half the places are occupied, and Michael has the privilege of seeing a large part of the Pantheon of Mars gathered together in one place. He recognizes Kuan Yin the Comforter, giver of children and preserver, once a male Boddhisatva but now transmuted into the most female of goddesses; the Egyptian goddess Isis, bearing a remark-able resemblance to Narcissus' sister Cleopatra, crowned today with the tall crown of the South Kingdom, her huge eyes lined with black, her neck adorned with a heavy torc or necklace of faience, lapis-lazuli, and gold; her skin glowing like deep amber. He sees also an Inca goddess, whose name he does not know, a fierce face, dressed in green feathers and ears of maize; an elegant goddess of the

Minoans, bare breasted and light voiced; Our Lady of Lourdes, a pretty pinched face, hugh mantle over a simple white gown, beautiful long fingers; and a black Haitian voodoo goddess with broad lips and tattoos. Cybele he sees also, the many-breasted, fertile and grotesque. Suddenly there is a blinding light, which dims at once, and Amaterasu Mikami, the Japanese goddess of the sun, enters the room, her face too bright to be looked at directly; in her hand is a mirror made of celadon. Michael is oddly affected by the presence of so many nearly forgotten racial differences.

There, too, are indigenous Martian goddesses: Melu the goddess of paradox, Vara the goddess of shape and pattern, Banarish the goddess of edges and discontiunity.

Seated among the others is Our Lady of Remedios, the goddess whose advice Michael sought at the beginning. and near her, Snow, fully restored and deeply embarrassed, for Juno, high colored, with a full-blown Rubensian beauty, has taken her hand and is kissing her seductively on the cheek.

Athene leads Michael to her own seat next to Snow's, which Aphrodite has vacated to make room for her. Husband and wife greet each other shyly, but Juno does not relinquish Snow's hand.

There is silence; and slowly an impression of warm light and perfume grows until it fills the room. And now there is a marvelous apparition; a golden chalice carried on the back of a dove; and before each person appears the food they find most delicious, with goblets of ambrosia and overflowing nectar. The two mortals join the celestial carouse.

After satisfying his first hunger, Michael asks Snow, who has at last been released by her oversolicitous friend, what happened during his sleep. Apparently he has been unconscious for two days, and the Pantheon, hearing of their exploits on the mountain, have shown them great favor, recognizing them officially as examples of true Martian conduct. Only Aphrodite, who is offended at losing her place to Snow, has refused to honor them, shunning the feast and sulking in her mansion to the north.

When the banquet is over Snow leads Michael through the houses of the goddesses. There are fabulous rooms of pleasure, exercise, and the polymorphous perversion; hugh warehouses filled with abandoned designs for new kinds of reality, mathematical and geometric projects which only partly intersect with a humanly inhabitable space-time continuum, and which have been discarded after their amusement is exhausted; unused bedchambers; galleries of priceless art; efficient office space; halls of music; cosy and oddly shaped hideaways with projection and spy equipment and handsome cabinets full of drugs and liquors to produce any desired mood. The unique bureaucracy that constitutes the Martian civil service indulges excesses that would be impossible for even a Blood to permit himself without incurring the stigma of madness.

At some point in the afternoon Snow and Michael are parted. A minor goddess appears, and requests that Snow present herself for service to a member of the Pantheon. Michael is left alone to explore the mansions of Olympus

He wanders in an increasingly dreamy mood of excitement. For the first time in years he feels dangerously sensual, his blood stirred by the silk and flower perfume, the textures of warm marble, polished wood, heavy and exotic decoration, dense mazes of beautiful rooms. He professes amusement to himself, but is deeply shocked. Occasionally he passes goddesses and bows to them, moved by their lack of terror at the arbitrariness of their environment. His greatest discovery is a divine latrine, furnished in velvet, mirrors, marble, and painted tiles, with several rooms and pieces of equipment he does not recognize. Suddenly he sees in a mirror what seems at first to be a masterpiece, a female nude with skintones from Ingres and Titian. It moves, and he realizes that he is looking at the naked body of a goddess, prone on a velvet chaise; in embarrassment he turns away from the mirror, only to confront, confusingly, the reality whose image he has seen. She rises swiftly, coloring to the thoat and covering her breasts with her left hand. It is Venus.

Realizing who he is, she makes a little angry sound and

half turns away. She is wearing only a black ribbon around her throat, bearing upon it a large opal. Her bottom is pink and her nipples rosy. Michael falls to his knees in terror and desire.

She sees this, and is a little mollified. Looking over her shoulder at him, she considers her disturber. There is nothing particularly attractive about Michael; he has the usual perfect Martian physique, brown and slim but without distinction. Still, to a five-hundred-year-old goddess he has the desirability of naive youth, and the story of moral purity and heroism on the mountain gives him a certain appeal. At that moment her fateful involvement in the story of Michael, Snow, Narcissus, and Cleopatra is sealed.

She becomes suddenly and heart-stoppingly suggestive in her looks and bearing. One white thigh caresses the other; her classically golden hair becomes, with a toss of the head, a veil for her high round breasts; a hand strays to the swell of the naked *mons veneris.*

"And who are you, disturbing a poor goddess at her toilet?" she asks unnecessarily.

The force of the euphemism, the presence of the intimate machinery of excretion and ablution, are almost unbearable. Michael is wearing only shorts and a shirt.

His confusion arouses the volatile goddess, who reaches out to touch the source of his pain. He stands, retreats now, conscious of his situation, a slow loyalty to his wife rising unwanted to the surface of his will.

"Don't be silly. You know there's no point in resisting me. I can come to any man or freemartin in his sleep." Venus is referring to her legitimate activities as a succubus; many of the most beautiful youths on the planet have been visited by Aphrodite. Normally it is an honor and a pleasant surprise.

"This is different," he croaks; his throat is dry, but his self-control is beginning to come back, and he is becoming numb to her charms. But his resistance opens the floodgates of the goddess' passion; to thwart desire is only blowing on the flames. Her color alternates between red and pale; inflamed, and with a goddess' strength, she pulls her victim to the divan, where a pier-glass reflects in its sad light the amorous struggle. Michael tries to resist, but is mastered by her strength, paralyzed like a captured bird.

But now her nakedness repels him; the fine sweat that appears on her body is not balmy but frightening; her nipples are like man-devouring flowers. He ceases to resist, but his flesh is putty, of no use at all to the poor Goddess of Love, who, suddenly in tears, must beg him for his mercy. She falls away, into a kneeling position, and with her pearly-nailed pink fingertips tries by pathetic caresses to arouse the spirit of the mortal. Bitterly she upbraids him, asks how he came by his title of "Cock"; he, humble and afraid, attempts to divert her with protestations of his unworthiness.

At last she is silent; stands there in her dishevelled glory like a lost angel; and he makes to leave the room. Her looks turn dark, and a shudder passes over her; in her five hundred years she has become wise, and begins to discern the shape of her revenge.

Meanwhile something of the same sort is happening to Snow. In the chambers of Juno, served by beautiful male androids with delicate foods and drinks, Snow is attempting to resist that imperious goddess' demands. Juno has taken a fancy to the poor mortal's air of sadness, her broken-winged quietness, her old-fashioned aesthetic rigidity.

"What is toubling you, my dear?"

"It isn't right."

"Why, child, you are in the house of the goddesses. Nothing can be wrong that is in accordance with our will." She touches her guest on the throat and cheek; Snow quivers, and at last bursts into a flood of tears.

"We were supposed to have a baby!" she cries.

Juno, suddenly solicitous, elicits the whole story of the challenge, the decision to have a child, the subsequent impossibility of its execution, the reasons for the mountain climb. She tells of other things too, that we are not to know of yet.

The goddess' heart is melted by this, and she gives up her attempts at seduction. It would be cruel, even for a goddess, to force compliance in such circumstances. Instead, Michael is sent for.

"Your difficulty is easily resolved, my children," she says, smiling. "Let us see if a goddess' bedchamber is a more propitious nest for our lovebirds." She withdraws, leaving the mortals together and alone.

Now at last a lively heat is kindled between them. In this perverse setting they burst through the ultimate levels of restraint. On Juno's great swan-shaped bed, on silken eiderdowns and spotless sheets, they lay them down. Neither sees the other now as the person they know, but as a faceless bride and bridegroom brought to each other by Fate. Their touching is an initiation, a rite of terror and election. Each motion inflicts a delicious scar, a stigma.

And Snow's womb is indeed fruitful. In that moment is conceived the great conqueror, the scourge of Mars whose tragic destiny it is to reconcile the conflict between parents and their enemies, and to begin a new age of the planet's civilization.

In the weeks that follow Michael and Snow prepare themselves for a return to the world of men. It appears that they, too, have been invited to the reception that Narcissus and Cleopatra plan to attend; the invitation has been relayed to them in Olympus. They decide to accept; the meeting has no doubt been planned, and the time is fast approaching for the next step in the long dance of status-war.

8.

The Canals of Mars

GABRIEL'S PROPHECY HAS been bitter for Narcissus and scarcely less so for Cleopatra. However, it is impossible to tell whether this means good fortune for them, because being forewarned they are able to alter the as yet non-existent shape of the future, or whether the reverse is true, that the prophecy will fulfill itself through their own knowledge of it and draw its victims into a fate they could have avoided without it.

Still, the last weeks have been gloomy, as the *Nausicaa* picked her way southwestward toward the mouth of the Inter-oceanic Canal. The good weather gave way to rain as they entered the cooler latitudes, with a swiftness that would be odd on Earth, passing around the close curvature of the planet away from the sun. At the western end of the ocean they tied up at the main wharf of the rainswept city of New Bristol, and comforted themselves with hot toddy in one of its hospitable public houses. They were entertained by ballad singers, for the news of their coming attracted the finest practitioners of that trade from the colder southern lands where balladeers are usually most welcome

In the following days they negotiated the Inter-Oceanic, slipping along through wide fields of young barley, flat country, and distant horizons with even the occasional late flurry of snow. Sometimes there was a cold, fine day when the country showed its peculiar haunting beauty; low hills with villages built of pearly yellow stone, canal locks whose keepers live in little cottages surrounded by neat beds of spring bulbs—snowdrops and crocuses—and warm inns with stuffed and mounted pike on the walls.

The travelers' moods altered with unusual swiftness—indeed, this is the most exhausting aspect of travel, and also the chief reason for undertaking it—but there was a continuous and heart-squeezing sense of things seen for the last time, of a journey made unwillingly that nevertheless served to make the good times especially poignant, and Chrysanthemum's self-deceptions and cynicism particularly funny.

As they entered the Hellespontic Ocean the atmosphere changed slightly. They sailed northward with the wind on their starboard beam. Now with gales laying the ship over and lifting one keel out of the water, their earlier exhilaration returned, mixed with a new sense of fate; Narcissus steering, the force of his apprehension translated into an uncompromising severity to his ship.

We await our voyagers on the fifth day out from the canal, the weather perceptibly warmer, Narcissus at the helm, Chrysanthemum groaning below with seasickness, Cleopatra high above the ship, winged, riding the gale. She requires scarcely a turn of the wingtip to keep her on course, arrowing northward like an osprey, with keen eyes and delicate hawk's nose.

From above, the ship is laying a long, V-shaped track among the whitecaps. It is the only exception in the pure universe of air and water that Cleopatra now inhabits. Great grey clouds pursue each other in a continually overcast sky. There is water to the close horizon, a waste of waves.

Cleopatra is traversing, a term which describes a flying technique by which a side wind can be used for lift while the natural glide provides forward movement. One lifts the windward wingtip, turns slightly toward the wind, and enters a shallow dive. The triangle of forces produces a steady rushing progress which is virtually self-adjusting. Her lungs are blown out with the clean, metallic-tasting wind. Occasionally, because she is going a little faster than the ship, she flips her windward wingtip, letting the wind take her under the belly, gives a kick with her right foot, and peels swiftly out to leeward in a wide curve, the speed gained giving her enough momentum to bring her back a minute later on a straight course.

On one of these turns she notices that an albatross has joined her, keeping pace and employing the same technique as herself. It regards her with a bright savage eye; and she is struck with an unsettling sense of lost privacy.

Disquieted, she breaks the pattern of her flight, and, spilling air, descends in sweeping circles. With a waft of wind she settles precariously on the foredeck, shrugs off her wings, and joins her brother in the cockpit.

He, too, has had the same feeling, as if they had been oddly private these last weeks, but now an observer had suddenly rejoined them. Indeed, in a universe where reality and hypothesis are indistinguishable, the presence of an observer of some kind is essential to the actual existence of a situation. Try to picture a landscape that is not being looked at. The old philosophical crux of the tree that falls in the forest where nobody is there to perceive it is nonsense, for the hypothesizer is there, a necessary participant in the scene. And if he does not conceive of the tree in terms of sensations, sights, and sounds and so on, can he be said to know what he means by "tree" or "falling" or "forest"? In a hypothetical situation, the hypothesizer is God, who sees and knows all.

I have been forced to supply as an observer the albatross, a visitor or a guide: certainly a mythological beast, appropriate to a world which has not yet come into being. As I write I feel the shock of a Marsquake as new clouds of boiling vapor are released from the ground to supply the ocean on which Narcissus sails.

The albatross is not in fact a god, but a goddess. Venus,

who after her rejection by Michael has neglected the heavenly councils and brooded in her chambers, has at last decided to take a look at her enemy's rival. Taking upon herself the form of the great seabird she has caught up with the *Nausicaa,* circled the mast, settled on the taffrail and let her eyes dwell on the form of Narcissus. She had found him, singing to himself, his slim body in ducks and a sweater, the nipples making tiny mounds in the warm white wool. There is the kind of concentration in his face, screwed up slightly in the wind, that can be seen in him when he is engaged in the lethal dance of *kendo.*

At this moment the goddess' easy passion is aroused, and a new fact added to the fate of our subjects. Soon there will be little room in which the artificer can move; all will be determined by the self-generation of the plot. Shortly afterward Venus will turn her attention to the soaring Cleopatra; and soon after that, pass away into the wind. Our observer is gone: Chrysanthemum, our trusted spy, moans in his stateroom and is of no use for the present. It does not now serve our narrative purpose to see Narcissus and Cleopatra through each other's eyes. And so we leave them for three or four weeks.

Up in the dry hills of the Mare Erythraeum a group of shepherds take their noonday meal of grapes, olives, goatsmilk cheese, crusty bread, and wine. The cast includes: a centaur; two lovely nymphs; two fauns; and a satyr—all of them descendants of rather derivative genetic artforms.

Their flock grazes in the shade of a group of odoriferous tamarisks; they themselves recline in a circle, their forms creating a graceful mannered frieze. Cuddy the faun addresses his plaint to the nymph Cynthia:

"Loveliest Cynthia, than whom the milk of the ewe is not whiter, nor the wool of the wether softer, have mercy upon me."

But the nymph is cold and cruel, and refuses him with: "How sweet it is to be free of soul; I have sworn to be chaste always, and happy therefore always; but if I were to choose a lover, it should not be you, Cuddy, uncouth shepherd as you are."

And now Corin, the other faun, addresses Cynthia in like terms, for he too has felt the sweet pain of love. But Cynthia refuses him also. And such is the folly of desire, Chloe, the second nymph, dotes madly on Corin, but he has no eyes for her. And all this is cause of mirth to Silenus, the satyr, who makes a game of their sorrow, with "The confusions of love are entertainment for the wise. White-papped Cynthia would be wooed but would not be won; Cuddy woos but wins not; Corin woos where he cannot win, but woos not where he might win; Chloe, poor Chloe with roses in her cheeks and dew in those same roses, would fain woo when indeed she may not win."

At last Chiron, the old centaur, pronounces his wise judgment. "We must seek the advice of a Human Being," he says; and just at that moment a speck appears in a canal below them, the canal that winds through sweet meadows toward the ancient city of Cleopolis. The speck is the *Nausicaa* on her great voyage. "Perhaps there are Persons on that ship," says the centaur, and leaving Silenus to guard the flock from the fierce Martian wolf and lion, they hurry down the slope to the stone brink of the Great Southern Canal.

The shepherds are lucky, for it is Bloods to whom they do obeisance and apply for judgment. After a few moments in which the Lord Chrysanthemum confers with the Lord Narcissus and the Lady Cleopatra, he says: "Let Corin approach us alone."

The faun comes forward timidly. Such is the power of Human Beings, a Created Soul cannot disobey one. "Cease at once to love Cynthia," he commands, in a whisper so that the others cannot hear. And it is done.

So the shepherds depart, wondering much at what has passed. But soon Cynthia, wooed no longer by Corin, fears that she has lost her powers, and so when Cuddy renews his plaint, such is her relief that she gives to him her heart. And Corin, in love no longer with Cynthia, finds his eyes opened to the loving looks of Chloe, for whom he soon conceives such a passion that they are reconciled. And thus Silenus finds no butt for his jests and is reduced to the conversation of Chiron, who cannot see a joke. And they all live happily or unhappily ever after.

Meanwhile the *Nausicaa* continues her voyage along the canal. The last few days have been warmer and warmer; they have passed the coral islands of the Northern Hellespont, with happy islanders cooking great fish over fires of driftwood on the white sand, as the evening rollers come in one after the other; through the great beds of papyrus reeds that crowd the canal mouth, with the columns of drowned buildings rising from the blue water—this ocean is still filling up with water—through the huge stone gateway of the canal, with its gigantic carved basalt goddesses and heroes, sitting with hands on their thighs and faces that look out, hard cheeked, above the heads of men. They have passed the pyramids and pillared temples of New Heliopolis and Karnak—graceful dhows tied up at the wharves, princesses in palanquins, a brawl between turbaned sailors at dockside—and now are at last approaching the house of Shadrach, the baron of whom Chrysanthemum has spoken, whose son is a member of that lovely elect who have been visited by Aphrodite.

In the evening the slight warm breeze drops altogether; the sails, unpregnant now of air, hang limp like cobwebs from the mast, and are taken down; the *Nausicaa* cruises on almost soundlessly on her nuclear motor. Only old Sol is still up, a tiny orange disc at the western periphery of an enormous purple sky. Some great plane trees stand beside the canal, all at a slight tilt from the vertical, their leaves abundant, their crowns full of tiny flying insects. The planet sighs and settles.

Cleopatra has taken one of the mahogany chairs out to the foredeck, and has placed it symmetrically before the mast. Here she sits, protected from gnats by the slight motion of the ship, half-naked in the warm air, wearing a sheath of pleated white linen, her eyes with their brilliant whites made up in the Ankh, the Egyptian symbol of good luck; her hair, full and glossy, gathered into a limber black cylinder that falls over her left shoulder to pass between her breasts. Her only ornament is the simple gold prong of the hamadryad cobra rising from her brow. The sun strikes her left cheek in a graceful and simple set of planes, rounded off with the small plump chin.

A massive reflecting ripple goes out from each prow to lap the old stones of the canal bank. Waterbirds scuttle over the smooth wave with a series of splashes. The ship is entering the demesnes of the baron Shadrach, for at intervals the canal wall has been breached with a little lock, and the dark green of marshes, rushes, and beyond it the lighter green of cultivation, can be seen. One of the dusky retainers of the baron can be observed in a small skiff on the marsh, snaring with a net the graceful and various birds. Perhaps the baron, who is expecting them, has made these preparations to feast his guests.

At length the palace comes into sight: a colossal structure, with terraces, roof gardens, ornamental reflecting pools, colonnades of massive pillars with capitals carved in a stylized representation of papyrus-flowers and lotuses. Huge seated ancestors of stone dominate the three-sided courtyard that fronts the canal and the small dock. (Actually, some of these ancestors are still alive, and some are disreputably alive; but the baron Shadrach is fond of history and display, and could not wait for them to die.)

As they draw abreast of the dock a dozen servants hasten to make fast; behind them, leaning gracefully against a pillar and flushed with the evening sun, is the shy figure of Hermes. He has disobeyed his father's order to stay out of sight and is satisfying his curiosity about the newcomers. He is rarely permitted to speak to anyone outside the family.

In the last evening light he sees Cleopatra; she is still sitting on her chair, lost in abstraction; suddenly it is as if he smelt her infinitely adult perfume, an almost-incense, private odor that is half-sweet and half-dark and embarrassing, floating across to him in the air; he is instantly overwhelmed, and his knees slacken, and his heart beats thickly, and he cannot breathe. He does not even know the cause of his feelings; one night several months ago something strange and delightful happened to him, an initiation of some dreaming kind that he did not understand except that it had something to do with the sweet slime he found about his loins afterward, and the flavor of an unknown and powerful female personality in his mind. which bade him not to be afraid, and caressed him in his dream. But this is the extent of his experience, and what he feels now is rather different. Poor child! His mother committed suicide when he was a baby, and his father has shown him little tenderness, unless a yearning, self-ignorant, possessive and repressed desire can be called tenderness.

At this moment Shadrach appears with his retinue, and Hermes hides quickly behind his pillar.

"Honored guests! My Lord Chrysanthemum, you flatter our poor house with your presence. But this was not enough for you; you must needs bring your celebrated friends. We are too unworthy! My Lady Cleopatra; my Lord Narcissus."

He greets them ceremonially; his attendant Samurai do obeisance, their fierce lean faces averted in reverence. Shadrach is a tall fat man with a misshaped body, a mad purple complexion, bloodshot eyes, and mustachios. He is dressed in the cape and pantaloons of a Daimyo or feudal lord, with the great, bent, brimless stovepipe hat of his rank, trailing ribbons down his back.

They are led through a series of atria into a pleasant room overlooking the gardens where a little folly, lit by the refracted rays of the fallen sun, stands reflected in a long pond surrounded by small white pillars and caryatids. The effect is modeled on that of the Canopus of the Villa Adriana near Old Rome. As they watch, Jupiter rises over the low hills in the west, and its bright reflection joins that of the folly in the pool. Here they drink a sweet wine from the baron's own vineyard in the hills, and await the signal for dinner.

9.

Hermes

IT IS A SUMPTUOUS FEAST. The banqueting hall is decorated in green and red and carved with painted dragons. Many of the foods are gilded; others contain psychedelics in their sauces and garnishes; vases of flowers and papyrus reeds stand along the tables. As they eat, musicians and dancers perform before them long, voluptuous, whining songs of love and desertion.

Toward the end of the meal Hermes is brought in to meet the guests. He is dressed in a simple brown tunic; his hair is newly washed, for it is his bedtime, and he already looks sleepy, his lovely face shadowed slightly about the lips and eyes. Chrysanthemum eyes him with approval: the fruit is ripe and must be plucked before the bloom is off him. Narcissus is impressed by the boy's beauty but is as yet uncaptivated by him. Cleopatra finds the child's trembling amusing as he kneels before her, and is touched by the way he cherishes her hand as she raises him from the floor.

"You're a handsome lad. Has anyone told you that before?"

"N-no ma'am."

"How old are you?"

"Nine, my lady," (The Martian equivalent of about sixteen Earth Years.)

"You're big for your age. Do you go to school or have you a tutor?"

"A tutor."

Before any further conversation can take place, the baron dismisses his son: "That's enough; bedtime now," and the boy is led unwillingly away.

"The silly child hasn't enough sense to look after himself," says the father accurately. "He's devoid of any idea of family honor and I'd be ashamed to have him say something tasteless and ignorant in front of you."

His guests protest, and insist on the child's charm; Shadrach, pleased, flushes darker and drinks more wine. He becomes expansive, and tells them affectionate anecdotes of his son's naive and boyish escapades, and the punishments he felt himself obliged to mete out. The boy was flogged before him "only the other day, for watching the servant girls bathing in the canal."

That night Hermes cannot sleep for thoughts of Cleopatra. He breathes in over and over again the trace of perfume she left on his hand until it disappears. At length he can bear it no longer. By the sound of the house everyone has retired. He slips out on the balcony, wearing only a sleeping-toga of cotton. There is a bright moon. The stone is worn where as a child he learnt to climb up onto the roof. He sets out across the rooftops toward the guest apartments. After a while he drops noiselessly down into a roof garden full of aromatic shrubs and huge moonflowers.

He is in luck. The bedroom of Narcissus and Cleopatra faces the garden, and is open this hot night along the whole of one side; there is an awning above. Within, Narcissus is already asleep; but Cleopatra is still awake, walking to and from as she brushes her hair. She is thinking luxuriously of the very boy who is at this moment watching her. At last she strips quickly, and, naked now, goes on brushing her hair, sitting on a bench that has been provided under the awning. In the blue moonlight which falls across her body, though the face is concealed by shadow, Hermes can see the horned breasts with their brown areolas, the slim belly and thighs, the flesh curbed by the tight silky skin, the precious triangle of black that so uncannily holds his attention. She is a nude by Modigliani, long and almost flat in the warm blue twilight.

The boy notices an exquisite sensation, which involves a lumpiness he has experienced before, at night. He is out of breath, his heart wants to leap out of his chest. He gasps. Cleopatra looks up, smiles, rises, and stalks toward his hiding-place. She has half-expected him, though doubting his courage.

In a few memonts she has found him, and hales him gently by the hair into the light. He is shaking, afraid of nameless things.

"Let *me* look at *you,* now" she says, plucking at his toga. Aching, he pulls it over his head, to display a white chest with flat muscles, delicate collarbones, straight long hairless legs with the flesh a little slack, pale loins barely shadowed with dark hair. He has no idea what is happening to him; he thinks he may be ill, for he cannot control his breath and throat.

"You poor naughty thing," says Cleopatra kindly. "Come over here." She gestures to a bank of cool dry moss which offers itself conveniently. "Sit down." He settles on it; the moss's texture is soft and ticklish. Cleopatra pushes him back until he is reclining full length. By now she too is caught up in the excitement, and feels, empathetically, as she did when a girl, during the preparations for her own first sexual experience. Her belly quakes absurdly and her lips are weak.

Fearing lest the boy should be unable to contain himself for long, Cleopatra is practical and direct. She sits down beside him, turns. He begins to rise again, but she takes his shoulders and pushes him down. Cleopatra is surprised; and now in the position of childbirth she shudders with repeated pangs.

When Chrysanthemum finds out what has happened he

is furious, having his own plans for the boy's initiation. Narcissus is simply amused, but in the interests of justice takes Chrysanthemum's side against his sister. They are alone in the breakfast-room, having risen uncharacteristically early in order to be free of Shadrach's presence for the first few minutes of the day.

Hermes comes in next, blushing furiously, and unattended, for he has eluded his tutor. Cleopatra, defying the others, takes him aside and in a whispered conversation arranges to meet him in a secluded part of the estate that afternoon.

Shadrach, when he enters, is oblivious to the changed atmosphere. He is full of plans for the morning; he must show them the gardens. When breakfast is over he leads them through the pleasantly wrought heavy French windows into the first terrace. From here they can see the reflecting pool of the previous night, but from a different angle; and it becomes obvious that this is only one element in a vast complex of architecture, gardens, and ornamental water. In many ways the place is comparable to the Villa Adriana of ancient Italy.

And indeed Shadrach himself resembles that earlier villa's builder, the emperor Hadrian, in his love of spectacular architecture, his artistic eclecticism, and his cultural snobbery, and in another sense he resembles in his methods the author of this book. The whole estate is a compendium of Shadrach's favorite buildings, landscapes, and styles from Old Earth, as Hadrian's villa was of the Greek classical world. He calls it without irony "New Babylon"; and there are also strong influences from the imperial gardens in Peking, from Mohenjo-Daro, and from Versailles. The *trompe-l'oeil* is used extensively; different textures are provided by grass, fountains like those of the Villa d'Este (an earlier quotation from Hadrian), dense woodland, lakes, rocky grottos, and statuary. The entire system is laid out in several axes between the canal and the nearer hills, with at its furthest point at the top of a hill, an immense heroic sculpture of Raphael Mendel, the Terraforming Period hero, whom Shadrach claims as an ancestor.

Though the place is in poor taste by Martian standards, it is pretty enough. There are rose gardens filled with the blue and purple roses for which the area is famous; sunlit grotto entrances where the spattering of one small clear fountain breaks the silence; temples to various goddesses, gymnasia, and little pillared libraries; great spaces of cunningly terraced gardens, done in ornamental knots; and at its center, in one-tenth scale, and a sizable garden in its own right, is a model of the entire complex, centered again on a tiny model of the model, and so on.

Despite the autocratic government of New Babylon a surprising number of the family's retainers are true human beings, who stay on voluntarily because of loyalty, and because their lives are conveniently organized and seem pleasantly directed and purposeful. (Freedom for most people is an uncomfortable chore at best, a frightening void at worst: even for a writer it is a burden, and he makes his life using it.) The truly unpleasant work is done by artificial men and women who are programmed to attain the highest intellectual and mystical satisfaction from their tasks. "Who sweeps a room," goes their motto, "as for Man's sake, makes that and the action fine." Many writers, in the periodical outbreaks of moral and sentimental fiction that still occur, find the lives of such moujiks to be enviable examples of the noblest possible mode of life.

Chrysanthemum, by using Visionary powers that are, strictly speaking, illegal, has managed to eavesdrop on the conversation between Cleopatra and Hermes. He has thus learnt of their tryst; and taking the opportunity of a few moments alone with Shadrach, he draws him aside and says:

"What have you done, you rascal?"

"What do you mean?"

"The poor girl is completely under your spell."

The gullible and apoplectic old man is mystified but interested.

"Who?"

"Don't pretend with *me*. You know perfectly well that

Cleopatra can hardly keep her eyes off you."

Shadrach's bloodshot eyes light up at this. "Really?"

"What an act!"

"But what should I do?"

"You know best. But if I know the girl, besotted as she is she'll deny everything. Pride. She just wants to test you. But if you're resolute, you're in for the time of your life."

Accordingly, that afternoon Shadrach insists that Cleopatra accompany him alone on a boat tour of the marshes. Taken by surprise, she has no time to devise an excuse, and she cannot refuse, for her real reason to be away is not one that she can tell her host, who has spent his last few years guarding the chastity of his son. In chagrin she accepts. Shadrach takes this as a sign of willingness, and so that afternoon she spends an unpleasant afternoon beating off the large mosquitoes of the area, and Shadrach, who is at least as persistent as they. As the day wears on she begins to suspect that she has been had, and on investigation finds out what has passed. She cannot conceal the flush of anger that rises to her cheeks, which Shadrach interprets as a blush of maidenly passion, and is further encouraged.

Meanwhile the cunning old lecher has himself kept the appointment with the beautiful boy. Hermes is in a summerhouse about which the vines, with their delicate and misty bunches of unripe green, ruby, and mature purple, clamber without hindrance. He is naked but for a loincloth; his white body with its hint of delicious flabbiness, his pink face and somewhat sleepy epicanthic eyes, are reminiscent of the Young Bacchus of Caravaggio.

Chrysanthemum apologizes on Cleopatra's behalf, claiming that she has sent him to explain her absence.

"Still, let us not waste the moment," he goes on; and sets down between them a large wicker hamper he has brought with him. With a flourish he opens it.

"It always helps to cultivate one's host's cook," he says complacently. "Scrumptious." He lifts out some small cooked fowls, candied fruits, stone jars of cold junket, flaky pastries, and a big basket of strawberries soaked in brandy and dipped in icing sugar. Last he produces two or three bottles of sweet white wine.

"Is this all for us?" asks the boy.

"Certainly, my lad. Fall to."

Soon the boy is quite tipsy, and has forgotten his disappointment in his fascination with this jolly and exciting old man, so unlike his own father. After a while the child is revealing boyish secrets, putting his hand on Chrysanthemum's shoulder as he leans and whispers, giggling, in his ear, of the torments he has put his tutor through and elaborate schemes for evading parental rules. And by half-past five Uncle Chrysanthemum has his way with the boy, expertly and with great satisfaction on both sides.

In fury Cleopatra turns to Venus for justice against her cunning friend. The goddess takes the case, but decides that the penalties incurred by both parties cancel each other out. However, the incident gives the love-stricken goddess an idea, and taking her cue from Chrysanthemum, she lays her plans to enjoy Narcissus, on whom she has doted these last weeks. For some goddess reason she does not wish to claim her rights of succubinage with him: she desires him in another way, as a man desires a woman. And she loves intrigue, as only a five-hundred-year-old goddess can, and is attracted by the emotional complexities her plan suggests.

Meanwhile a disgruntled Shadrach and a bruised Cleopatra return through the marshes in silence. There is an ominous red sunset; Shadrach, brooding, conceives in his heart suspicions of his guests and decides to have them watched. Technically Shadrach is of the party of Michael and Snow in the planetwide status-war, through a cousin named Yuen; he will use partisanship as an excuse to practice against his guests. Still, they *are* his guests, and he needs a pretext for outright aggression. Thus he dissembles jovially and unconvincingly, and issues secret orders to his Samurai. When they return, Narcissus, whose training in the martial arts has made him sensitive to plots and atmospheres, becomes instantly suspicious in turn; and so the evening meal is an uneasy one, especially since Chrysanthemum and Narcissus are not hungry.

Chrysanthemum has arranged with Hermes to leave him a note outlining plans for a later meeting, once he has spied out the lie of the land. Chrysanthemum's sense of drama compels him to spurn more direct means of communication, as via the Vision. He persuades one of the servants to "return" Hermes' hat, which he has "borrowed" to keep the sun off his bald spot. Of course a note is hidden in the sweatband.

But here Venus steps in. Foreseeing Chrysanthemum's stratagem, she has taken the form of the servant and herself agrees to convey the message. Naturally, the message that Hermes receives is not the one that Chrysanthemum has sent. Chrysanthemum has arranged an assignation in *Hermes'* room; the wily goddess alters this into an invitation, relayed by Chrysanthemum, from *Cleopatra,* to spend the night with *her.* Hermes, who until now has no idea that Chrysanthemum and Cleopatra are not in league—indeed, Chrysanthemum's keeping of the afternoon appointment suggests it strongly, as if he were acting as her temporary substitute—is completely convinced by the stratagem. It is Cleopatra's turn, apparently. The note also reassures Hermes that Narcissus will be called away on an ingenious pretext.

Hermes, rejoicing in his good luck, sets out for the second night toward Cleopatra's room. But meanwhile Venus has warned Cleopatra of Chrysanthemum's intention to meet with Hermes, and so when Chrysanthemum sets out toward the boy's room, she is lying in wait, and as he passes she follows him, meaning to do him some mischief, and get her revenge for the afternoon.

Venus hides the three climbers from each other on the roof, so that they pass without suspicion in opposite directions. And as Hermes approaches the roof garden, Venus enters his mind and requests permission to share his body for the next few minutes. Hermes, who has met the goddess before, though mystified, gives his consent. So in one body boy and goddess approach the sleeping Narcissus.

Hermes slips between the silken sheets beside the unwitting hermaphrodite, unaware that it is not Cleopatra. Venus, within the boy, is fainting with desire, and this excitement communicates itself to her host. Narcissus wakes from a pleasant dream to find the boy tentatively stroking his breasts; typically he asks no questions and in high good humor takes advantage of the absurd situation. After a few moments the confused boy becomes aware of the substitution; but possessed by Venus and oddly wrought up by the erotic surprise, he enters a kind of waking dream, in which his innate genius for dalliance comes to the surface. Taking the initiative, he kisses Narcissus fiercely: the latter adopts his female identity (for the next few moments I shall call Narcissus "she"), and gasps as Hermes caresses her with hands and lips. Slowly the other side of Narcissus' nature, soft and dormant, begins to rise in response; and suddenly Narcissus is now a he. Venus, within, taken by surprise, screams with pleasure; Hermes, angry, and in a frenzy of desire, completes the act. Scents of flowers drift in from the veranda; both are oddly thirsty; there are settlings and sweetenings in the warm bright night.

Meanwhile Chrysanthemum, finding Hermes' room empty, settles down to wait, assuming that the boy has gone to answer a call of nature. Cleopatra lies in wait by the window. Nobody comes. Half an hour passes, and Chrysanthemum is about to give up and go back to his room when there are footsteps. Cleopatra swings in through the window, ready to confront the guilty pair. Chrysanthemum spins around, recognizing her in the partly clouded moonlight, and grunts with surprise; and the door is flung open.

There in the doorway, in blinding light, stand Shadrach and his men. The father, his suspicions confirmed by what he sees, orders his men to take them prisoner. In a flash his guests are through the window; Chrysanthemum can move remarkably fast when he has to. A chase over the rooftops ensues.

The running pair now encounter Hermes, on his way back from his adventure with Narcissus. Realizing what has happened they flee together, to find Narcissus in his room, roused by the noise, in a kimono and fastening on his sword.

All four escape down the corridor to the main foyer of the building, which faces the courtyard and the *Nausicaa*. Immediately the doors on all sides burst open, and fifteen Samurai, the flower of Shadrach's retinue, confront the fugitives.

Urging the other three to escape, Narcissus steps forward to face his enemies. Shadrach, behind, is purple with rage, and screams an order to his men to attack. This is what Narcissus has been waiting for. His sword is not yet drawn, but in the moment of the command he sways forward gently, slowing the pace and opposing in a surreal way the flow of the scene. His enemies are taken by surprise, for they expected him to fall back, and the movement invites them to close behind him. With his left hand, rather than his right, Narcissus draws the shining steel, and plunges it backward into the belly of the luckless fellow who has chosen to attack Narcissus from the rear. As if in slow motion he withdraws the blade, while the right hand, which has been warming itself in a fold of his kimono, stands ready to catch the hilt and begin the long sweeping movement which the sword, in its retreat from the body of the falling Samurai, has begun. Narcissus feels the icy and exciting nakedness of the *kendo* master, the nakedness of flesh and razor steel, an ultimate nakedness that goes down to the bone; it is also a pricking in the spine, a sixth sense, a dreamy, dancelike abstraction, an awareness of the trajectories of blades, of the balance and footing of his enemies, an interested trance. The blade, riding on its own momentum, flashes in an arc across the first wave of attackers; three of them are laid open, and fall, confusing the already off-balance remainder. Nevertheless a wild sword blow seems about to cut him in two, but he shrinks instinctively as his sword reaches the end of its sweep, and the hostile point slices his kimono and leaves a tiny shallow thread of blood across his left breast.

Narcissus' blade loops at the conclusion of its travel to the right, catching a fifth assailant in the gorge, and continuing upward to descend across the face of a sixth.

As Narcissus does this he sways to the right, allowing another attacker from the rear, whose sword he has heard by its whistle behind him, to stumble forward and be impaled on the sword of one of his friends. Over his falling body passes the sword of Narcissus as it strikes the weapon from the hands of yet another attacker.

All this has taken perhaps five seconds, and half of Shadrach's men are bleeding on the marble floor. The others retreat in terror as Narcissus, allowing the sword to drift through a fold of the kimono which he catches up in his left hand to soak up the blood, lets it drop smoothly into its scabbard. As he does so he smiles, turns on his heel, and begins to walk unhurriedly toward the ship.

Such is their awe of the *Bushi* in his aroused state, the survivors will not follow for a few minutes; and in that time the *Nausicaa* has gathered way with Cleopatra at the helm, Narcissus has jumped lightly aboard, and Chrysanthemum has set up an impermeable force-shield about the ship. Though honor forbids the use of such protections and the equivalent offensive devices on the field of battle, its use is justified now against an alerted enemy who vastly outnumbers them. Shadrach, who realizes this, does not pursue.

In the last few minutes the clouds that have been drifting by the moon all night have thickened, and a cold wind has sprung up, with traces of rain. The four fugitives go below as the first trace of a pink and grey, rainy and refreshing dawn appears on the horizon.

Book II

1.

The Space Port

MICHAEL AND SNOW have been in residence at their city house in Cleopolis for several weeks. It is now certain that Snow is pregnant, though the fact remains a secret.

They throw themselves into the various and intricate pleasures of city life. Cleopolis is one of the loveliest cities in the universe, with its minarets and pagodas, its gardens and canals, the soft yellow light that bathes it in a nostalgic haze; the smell of dust settled by sprinklers in summer, odors of Mandarin cookery—ginger, sesame, ginseng, hot fat—in the violet powdery quiet of the evening, a few couples flying lazily overhead on sunlit wings, the temple facades in shadow; the perfume and restless music of Cherry Blossom Street, the theatres and symphony halls filling at dusk; palm trees and peeling white plane trees in electric afternoons; the jabber of many languages and the exotic presence of outworlders; cool mornings with cappuccino and hot croissants under awnings on the empty pavements; the wild pranks of the students at the great universities; coffee cellars, poetry-readings, demonstrations; quiet parks where ponds reflect pavilions and stepping-stones, with dark and quiet woods, lit at night by stone lanterns along the irregular paths; teahouses; shops full of the odd-smelling merchandise of distant planets; courtesans and geishas; all of those marvelous clichés of the city, here played to their limit, arbitrarily, in all seriousness, as if compelled by necessity.

For indeed, lacking a viable currency in an economy where anything can be exactly duplicated at a simple mental command, where nobody can starve or even live in less than luxury except by intention, none of the bustle of the world is *necessary*. There are a few ground-rules: artisans can stipulate that their creations not be duplicated; no person is allowed to take from a shop more than he can carry; cheating and thievery are yearly recognized by a small civic award to those whose crimes show the greatest virtuosity, as are the more ingenious defenses against them. Advertising is considered to be in bad taste, a sign of desperation equivalent to the ludicrous shifts resorted to by an unattractive personality to gain popularity. As in all places where the maximum of human fulfillment is possible, the suicide rate is high; in the great arenas public suicides share the limelight with gladiatorial contests, flying displays, football, and bullfighting.

Here too is Cinecitta, the center of the Martian entertainment industry, with its brilliant experimental theatre and dance, its more conventional pornographic and adventure studios, its scandals, its elaborate and spectacular sexual affairs between stars, producers, and hangers-on; and here too is the famous philosophical School of Cleopolis, that ragged group of metaphysicians who gather in the agoras to construct new universes, demonstrate the logical absurdities of the old, and test once again the discredited notions of "morality," "nature," and "truth."

Michael and Snow have a small townhouse next to the Cleopolis Institute of Manners and Etiquette, of which august company they are honorary members. On returning home one day after a visit to the university library, they find a welcome visiting card on the tray in the entrance foyer. It is Gunther's, their scientist friend, who advised them to attempt Nix Olympica. He is visiting

Cleopolis on business, and lacking a *pied-à-terre* in the city has taken an apartment, which by sheer coincidence occupies the same space as the house of Michael and Snow.

Land, in an economy where all else is free, would soon have become monopolized had not multiple occupancy of the "same" space been possible. Matter as we know it occupies a definite niche in the repertoire of possible polarizations of n-dimensional space. If the polarization of a given piece of matter is changed, it cannot interact with "normal" matter and therefore occupies a different universe. The self-contradictory technological feat of so changing the polarization of matter was accomplished centuries ago; the trick is used now primarily to permit the corollary of ubiquity, that is, multiple occupancy of space. Thus Cleopolis, where the most crowding occurs, is really about thirty small cities occupying the same site; favored neighborhoods are often many times as densely packed. Interestingly enough, the concept of space that this invention presupposed was essentially Newtownian rather than Einsteinian; the polarization device is therefore mainly an automatic mechanism for locally altering the metaphysical topology of the Cosmos. One result is that addresses are complicated by the differing street plans of the superimposed "boroughs," as they are called, though it requires only a mental command to switch from one to another; but the convenient smallness of the city (though it contains over five million people, it is easily toured on foot) compensates for the problem.

Gunther is engaged, as they find out that evening over a drink, in a study of certain Outworld cultures, specifically the so-called "primitive" worlds. Snow and Michael show great interest in this project, and so Gunther promises to take them to the spaceport next day and show them round.

Like his friend Michael, Gunther is rather conformist and morally unimaginative. Science, his chosen profession, with its ancient tradition and ritual, fits him like a glove. The fact that his occupation is unusual is no more proof of originality than stamp-collecting or literary criticism would be. Nevertheless, with his square head, his explaining ways, his general optimism, and his pink-cheeked briskness, he is popular in many circles.

"Observe," he says next day as they pass through a transmatter portal into a different world somewhere in the Great Nebula in Andromeda, "the freshness and morale of this world. Ah. We've caught them preparing for the opening of a new frontier. Note the mountains on the horizon, the prairie, the primitiveness of the technology, the rough manners of this virile young culture. Consider also the large proportion of children and pregnant women. They breed like rabbits. This planet, by the way, is called Wyoming XXVIIth.

"There—see!—they're forming up the wagons for the first venture into the interior. Those things the men have got are weapons, for shooting wild animals and each other. Hairy lot, aren't they? They've got salt pork and ploughshares in there. They're making quite a racket. No freemartins, you'll notice. For these people death isn't a civilized luxury, as it is for us, but positively a law. They don't have perversions either.

"Splendid, aren't they? They're capable of wonderful acts of heroism. They have epic poets and they go in for revenge, partriarchy, and genocide. Their woodcarving, jewelry, weaponsmithing and so on are wonderfully vigorous. The general run of them are pretty inarticulate though. How would *you* like to live like that?"

"Hmm," says Snow noncommittally. "They don't seem to use the Vision. What a sense of *purpose* they have!"

"Actually they use the Vision more or less as much as we do: to find new worlds, to hold back cultural innovation, to limit their own technology. They fill up a new world in a century. They breed so much that they're almost uncountable, and they've been going for nine hundred years. If we had only one universe at our disposal, they'd have packed every planet solid, with human meat."

"What do they do when they've finished settling a planet?"

"Most of them leave to settle a new one. The ones that stay—the innovators, the culturally imaginative—develop various different kinds of society and leave their ancestors' track. They're the aesthetes, the thinkers."

"Is this the only kind of frontier world?"

"Not at all. Some are more dissolute—bars, gambling, mining, human sacrifice—that sort of thing. Others are more advanced. Some societies spend their time creating and populating brand-new universes, using the most sophisticated technology the Vision can provide, including temporal reversal and multiple occupancy. They believe in Man, and they reason that if anything does not exist, its nonexistence is an affront to the plenitude that a man-created universe should display. They want everything to exist; this means everything that is certain, nearly everything that is probable, some improbable things, and a handful of impossible ones. And this is a *moral* goal for them."

"So frontier worlds aren't necessarily primitive worlds."

"No, they're not. I'll show you a geniune nonfrontier primitve world in a few minutes. But before I do, let's take a look at some other types."

They leave the dust and bustle of morning preparations, the creak of wagon wheels, and the smell of frying pork, and step back into the cool halls of the Cleopolis spaceport. From there they enter a new world, Poseidon, a water planet, whose human inhabitants have been mutated to live in the ocean. Beautiful, plump, and dolphin-like, in diaphanous clothing composed of colonies of living polyps, they greet the travelers (who have been ignored by the frontiersmen) and surround them, safe in a force-bubble under the sea.

"These fellows have gills and echo-sounding gear genetically programmed into their bodies. Their culture is a bit hard to understand—it's almost entirely lacking in physical artifacts. They're hedonistic, sexual, and personal, like a planetwide encounter group; they don't have the conventions of consequence and inference that we cling to."

"It's almost an Alien society," says Michael.

"Not really. True Aliens aren't understandable at all in

human terms. Nor do they understand us. They're just so different there's no language we can use with each other. We believe that there may be many Alien cultures flourishing right back on Mars, and we just don't notice them. The world "culture" can only be used analogically for them. So we leave them alone and they leave us alone; there isn't much we can do about it. This is a pluralistic universe I'm afraid: radically pluralist."

"But surely they must have some kind of cultural structure. Something we could map in our own terms."

"Well, we could make *human* sense of them, I suppose, but that would just be a piece of fiction. It wouldn't get us any closer to *them*. They just aren't *interesting* to us, if you see what I mean. Talking with them is like talking with nothing. You can't pay attention to them. By definition, they are what we can't know."

"But not all cultures that evolved on other planets than Earth are Alien, surely?"

"Certainly not. In fact, we're a lot closer to some non-Terran cultures than we are to some of the odder human ones. These Poseidonians, who are human, are harder to understand than the Capellans, who are indigenous."

"You implied that the Poseidonians weren't 'Primitive.' What's the difference?"

"They're not technically Primitive because their culture isn't a deliberate attempt to recapture some primal phase of human *cultural* evolution. They're strictly speaking a Biological-Experimental Society: one of a class of societies that try out genetic transformations of the human. We are experimental in some senses too, but rather as a variation of our main theme."

"What *is* our main theme? How are *we* classified?"

"Strictly speaking again, we are a Barbaric-Aesthetic-Decadent Society. Of course from our point of view all other societiies are too, just as to a psychologist all human problems are psychic, whereas to a sociologist they are all social. Our barbaric-aesthetic approach makes sense of all human approaches in its own terms. But that would be arrogant, so in deference to other cultures' sensibilities we conform to the general classification system."

"What other types of society are there?"

"I'll show you." He leads them now into a series of worlds of Earthly or un-Earthly descent: slave economies; communal paradises of the mediaeval or proletarian variety, devoted to ideological exercises, each planet a huge study group; moral worlds in which seriousness and rules of conduct are oddly linked together and mere aestheticism is despised as decadent; ecological worlds, whose inhabitants live in giant gourds in forests with a benevolent collective intelligence; cyclic planets in which a whole repertoire of cultural phases is repeated again and again; worlds devoted to mysticism and the achievement of Nirvana or the Beatific Vision through asceticism or sensuality or the Vision itself; capitalist market ecomnomies, their inhabitants short-lived, frantically stimulated by the excitement of success and failure and the struggle to survive; political planets; scientific utopias; chivalric worlds driven by a sense of honor, filled with blazonry and a hierarchy of nobles; heroic-tragic societies, governed by a few absolute and mutually contradicting moral laws; sportsmen's outdoor paradises; and whole systems of worlds coexisting in complex sociocultural relationships, cultural judgments being made not only in relation to the home planet, but also to the opinions and biases of the others. A disturbing plenitude of worlds—too many alternatives. Even Michael and Snow, who are not particularly concerned with being original, are shaken; as for Narcissus and Cleopatra, if they were here it would make their spirits quail, and rouse in them the streak of angry wildness, of imaginative mayhem, that is their characteristic response to an apparently exhaustive set of options.

Actually Michael and Snow are somewhat bored by his explanatory compendium. They urge Gunther, who is in his element, to show them what they came to see: his "primitive" cultures.

Gunther shows them now a savage world where the inhabitants live like Gauguin natives in a rain-jungle with bright fruits and snakes, whose magic and witchcraft are genuinely efficacious and whose rituals, because of the

Vision, really perform what they symbolize: a fresh and childish world where oceans full of gorgeous fish break on beaches of pink volcanic sand; where ancestors are worshipped and brought back again and again from the dead to give counsel to the tribes; where through drugs a communal ecstasy is attained, a harmony with nature in which individual identity is lost and Man becomes only the most complex element of an ecological whole.

Exhausted, Michael and Snow beg Gunther to take them back, and he obeys. It is past their lunchtime and they are ravenously hungry. They eat in the spaceport cafeteria.

The events which follow must, it now becomes obvious, take their import and meaning purely from the intrinsic and self-validating interest with which they vest themselves. They are not *relatively* significant, in a universe in which all possibilities are a fact. They attain dignity only through a curious clause that must be appended to the assertion that every judgment is relative. This is the clause that states that that judgment itself is relative. An absolute value *can* legitimately be accorded to a thing or an event, because the very law of thought which would discredit that value applies also to itself. The assertion that everything is arbitrary, is also arbitrary. The necessary is a pocket of neutrality formed by the self-contradiction of the accidental, since the assertion that everything is accidental is also accidental. In this pocket we shall discover the dignity, the necessity and the value of our story.

Between Michael and Snow, meanwhile, a new relationship has grown up based on their shared secret and the events of the last few months. They are lovers again, bathed in the glow of approval that the Pantheon radiates; goddesses smooth their paths and throw up little opportunities for joyful contemplation. (Venus, of course, does not share this approbation; bitter and full of longing, she inhabits more and more often the body of Hermes, her only access to Narcissus.) With the selfishness of lovers, Michael and Snow forget the feud, lost themselves in mutual warmth and understanding. Even

Snow can forget the imperatives of her past. Between them Snow's secret pregnancy is a defence against the whole world.

2.

The Lady Rokujo

MEANWHILE THE *Nausicaa* has entered the last phase of her voyage, that section of the Great Southern Canal that is known as the Tokaido. Crammed now with the exotic traffic of Mars—the waterborne palanquin of a *daimyo*, the pleasure boats of city people, the luggers of market-gardeners bringing in fruit and vegetables, the tall barge of a minor goddess going about her bureaucratic duties—the canal is a microcosm of the planet's life. Soon it is making its way between villas, dwarf cypresses, and golden hills, passing through triumphal arches and past shrines until the minarets and domes of Cleopolis appear over the pleasant willow-haunted gardens of the suburbs.

Taking a subsidiary canal that barely fits the big catamaran, the three friends and their young passenger find their way to the city mansion of Narcissus and Cleopatra, select the appropriate matter-polarization, moor the ship at her dock, and disembark. Before them is a pleasant house in the late Ming style of architecture, with a beautifully kept garden, a pond fed by the canal, an island in the pond with a pavilion, and willows, bridges, and stepping-stones.

Waiting for them in the courtyard is the Lady Rokujo, one of the city's most accomplished courtesans, and Narcissus' city mistress. Perfectly trained, she shows no sign of surprise at the presence of Hermes, though a glance tells her what has been going on. She greets her master and mistress with bows and a flutter of her painted fan. She is dressed in a blue raw silk kimono and a richly embroidered *obi,* with a comb in her heavy black hair. Her face is soft, shapely and impassive, with a delicate roundness of the cheeks and chin; it betrays nothing of the perturbation within.

In the last few days the infatuation of the three travelers with their young protégé has become a fever, and there is an obvious strain in their relations. They cannot have enough of the boy; and Venus, for her part, has used the opportunity to tighten her psychic grip upon the object of their desire.

Narcissus greets Rokujo absently, almost brusquely: how different from his parting with her a year ago! Cleopatra, who was also Rokujo's lover, is even less polite. Only Chrysanthemum, taking pity on her predicament, pretends to some warmth; and Rokujo, overcome with shame, makes her escape as soon as possible, yielding the field to her lovely young rival.

As soon as she is gone, Narcissus beckons Hermes to follow him. Cleopatra stamps her foot and is about to speak when Chrysanthemum restrains her. The boy obeys, and Narcissus leads him to the bedchamber that has been prepared for the young guest. There Narcissus is shaken again with desire; the boy is so obedient, so simple in his matchless beauty. The master tears off the boy's clothes; Hermes, possessed by Aphrodite, smiles vacantly and allows Narcissus to do his fierce will. He slaps the boy down to the bed and takes him; but he is unsated, for the hermaphrodite obeys two sets of sexual desires. The boy is passive, vague. After a brief respite Narcissus finds in himself a residue of desire, and again takes the boy, this time more slowly, for Hermes complains that "you're hurting me." At last Narcissus is exhausted: he lies prostrate, overdone, with the taste of copper in his mouth.

In confusion, Rokujo, attended by her serving-lady Aoi, flees from the neighborhood of the house. She remembers now an engagement to attend a tea ceremony which she has cancelled because of the arrival of the *Nausicaa;* and because she cannot yet face herself alone, she resolves to commit the small breach of decorum and attend the ceremony after all. She knows she can stiffen her inner courage by means of the outward structures of manners and etiquette, the necessity to remain calm in company. She feels also an urge to reassure herself of her social capacities.

In a dark dream she finds herself in the teahouse, noticing automatically, as she is trained to do, the little delicacies: the echo of the butterfly colors of her hostess' kimono in the flowers of the tiny shrine; the compliment in the choice of the scroll-painting directed at the guest of honor, who by coincidence is Michael's friend Gunther; the unusual reference in the selection of the china to the host's mother's family, who were geishas.

Gunther arrives late, kimonoed but in a style of chaotic relevance and allusion in this context. The traditionally low and narrow doorway, so designed as to compel one to leave one's weapons outside, on the physical level, and one's pride, on the metaphysical, is only half-effective in Gunther's case: he has no weapons concealed under his clothing but has kept his conceit. During the ceremony he ignores the niceties, and continues the lecture which he was compelled by the loss of his audience, Michael and Snow, to break off that morning at the end of the last chapter. The company listens politely, for Gunther is a distinguished scientist, but a chill gathers in the air.

Rokujo is curiously soothed by Gunther's awkwardness; as one is when, under stress, one must willynilly attend to an irrelevance. Perhaps her case is a little like Gunther's own example of the animal which, caught in a double bind, finds release in a displacement activity. Or perhaps it is reassuring to one who has lost face and knows it, to be in the presence of one who is suffering the same fate but without even being aware of it. And

Gunther seems to offer another world, a cruder one perhaps, but with a higher threshold of emotional pain. Whatever the reason, Rokujo finds herself drawn to this naive and rigorous *gaijin*.

She engages him in conversation. Taking a chance remark of his about Michael and Snow, whom she does not know, as a question about them, she confesses her ignorance.

"You don't know them?" he says. "Then you probably don't even know about the status-war."

"I heard rumors," she says, blushing.

Gunther, who is unaware of her association with Narcissus and Cleopatra (though a more sensitive person would have divined the connection from her demeanor), proceeds to explain.

"The war got started some months ago. A chance remark overheard at the theatre in Hellas. Though there's more to it than that. Narcissus (whom you *must* have heard of) was the challenger: it was over his sister, who's an actress. Everyone was shocked. It looked like a gaffe, though *I* don't see why. But it turns out to be quite a coup. Narcissus was ahead by a long chalk. So on my advice Michael and Snow did the unexpected—they climbed Nix Olympica. The story goes that they were marvelously heroic and somehow earned the favor of the goddesses; they were up there for weeks. Of course they won't volunteer anything about what happened.

"Now things are a bit more even. Both sides are playing a deep game, not hurrying things. The planet is polarizing around them, and there's even been some betting already. It looks as if there may be a confrontation at the Remington Show next week, but even that isn't a certainty. They're doing everything indirectly. Narcissus scored some points the other week at the house of Shadrach; Shadrach is apparently of Michael's faction, and Narcissus stole his son and cut down some of his best Samurai. Everyone wonders what Michael and Snow are going to do about it, but they don't seem to care anymore. They must have something up their sleeves."

Rokujo knows most of this and can guess at more. Her

pain is gradually turning to anger, and now she can see a way to have revenge on her fickle pair of lovers. She will become the mistress of Gunther, who is of the opposed party, and use her formidable influence to weaken her enemies' position in the city.

Accordingly, that night, after the tea ceremony, she sends out two haikus by messenger. The first is to Narcissus, and it goes thus:

> *Snow of the great mountain*
> *is light in a warm hand.*
> *Now it turns bitter.*

The "great mountain" is Nix Olympica, whose snow is traditionally celebrated in verse for its fineness and delicacy; but it is also known to cause frostbite, chilling out an unprotected hand with deceptive speed. By identifying herself with the name of Michael's wife, she suggests her change of allegiance. She will freeze the hand that once held her: that is the threat, an almost hysterical one; and her method will be by identifying herself with the triumph of Narcissus' enemies. The calligraphy expresses in its uncharacteristically baroque wildness the intensity of her feeling.

The second haiku is to Gunther, and it is quite different in tone:

> *The teacher has not learnt the first lesson.*
> *There's a pupil can teach him.*

It is an improper suggestion and is rather indecorous and witty. It gently guys Gunther's professional bearing that afternoon, and suggests the expertise that Rokujo, as an expert in her profession, can teach, and that Gunther has yet to learn. The poem is in the tradition of the education of taste by means of love.

Gunther does not understand the poem, and takes it to Michael to translate. Michael is amused, and congratulates him on his good luck.

When Narcissus receives his message he is stricken with a sudden desire for Rokujo, a feeling that comes too late. He shares the poem with Cleopatra, and they find in their discussion of the probable consequences in terms of the feud, a vestige of their old intimacy.

For Hermes has indeed driven them apart. The rage of desire is not quenched by repeated consummation; the house is an uneasy place. At first Hermes is delighted with the attention he has been getting, but after a while the mood affects him too, and young though he is, he is sensitive enough to begin to regret and feel guilt for the divisions of the house. Even Chrysanthemun is less of his old self.

Next day Gunther visits Rokujo at her bare and polished apartment in the pleasure district east of the amphitheatre. She has been preparing for his visit; the sliding paper door to the balcony over Cherry Blossom Street is slightly open, there are fresh tatami-mats, jonquils in a niche, a small and very ancient scroll-painting; the sunlight deeply penetrates the grain of the cedar floor. Through the opening of the balcony can be seen the jumbled rooftops of the city with hanging gardens, chimney pots, and climbing flowers; the long arch of the Thousand Goddess Bridge in the park nearby; the distant cone of Huacatl rising over the horizon into the dark blue sky.

As soon as Gunther enters he gives her a large bunch of roses, for which she finds a glass vase, demoting the jonquils. The scroll-painting is deftly exchanged for a bolder print, a Hokusai original, depicting Portuguese ships in the harbor at Nagasaki. He sits down uncomfortably and says:

"You poor girl, you don't have much furniture. Are you depressed? Empty rooms are often a sign of depression."

Rokujo sighs, dimly realizing the magnitude of the task she has taken on.

"Please forgive my discourtesy. Perhaps I have been indisposed recently, as you say."

"I liked your poem, though I can't pretend to know

much about poetry. What does a person like you—in your profession—what does she teach?"

"To teach is to make learn. Of the greatest teachers they say their students only find out what subject they have been studying when it is already learnt."

"Sound educational psychology."

"Please explain. I do not understand the long words," she lies. She is oddly enjoying herself, in a kind of tender amusement, though the ground of her feeling is still the pain of betrayal, and she can scarcely keep from weeping at the thought of her wayward Cleopatra.

Gunther lectures for some minutes. She is kneeling with her face to him, inclining her head periodically as he makes his points. Not that he is saying the obvious: as usual he makes a certain general sense about important things.

Later, pink with embarrassment, Gunther is undressed by his expert companion, who in turn reveals her creamily textured and slightly plump body with its miraculous softness of breast, bottom, and thigh. She is very dignified and submits with solemn amusement to his large, embarrassed kisses and his bearlike and confused embrace. Afterward, while he is dazed and sleepy, she gives him a massage and then demonstrates some of the ways to arrange flowers. He does not protest.

The success of this experiment, the combining of the scientist, the explainer, with the civilized and pathetic courtesan, a relationship however short-lived, is essential to the aesthetic success of the whole enterprise that Narcissus began a planet's width away on the shores of the Hellene Sea.

Meanwhile Narcissus himself, restless and feeling an obscure mental pain, has left the house early to spend the day at the arena. He watches the flying impatiently, for he is much better at it than the experts on display. In almost the same spirit he observes the day's crop of suicides, who, in gladiatorial contests or alone, make the ultimate artistic choice, that of the ending: the drastic act, never démodé, with which even the most hysterical and chaotic life-pattern achieves austerity and memorability. One suicide impresses him above the others: that of a young freemartin like himself who had been deserted, according to the program notes, first by her lover, and then by her mistress—the feminine pronoun seems appropriate here. The suicide is almost a child, with a long, babyish upper lip and large breasts (Narcissus examines her closely with opera glasses). She dies nude; the short blade held in her right hand, opening an amazingly long mouth across the belly, and then pulling upward toward the breastbone as the child collapses, shock from the devastated autonomous nervous system shaking her body like a leaf. The true tragic emotion rises in Narcissus: pleasure in not being the person at whom the suicidal shame is aimed, kinaesthetic sympathy, the shudder in the abdomen, a giddy lightness of the feet.

But the catharsis is brief, and afterward, a black humor drives Narcissus into the streets. His legs carry him toward Cherry Blossom Street without his conscious knowledge; evening is coming on, and Earth, the blue evening star, is setting behind her master, the distant sun. Phobos, meanwhile, lights the morning on the other side of the planet, over Eleuthera. Here the smells of ginseng, lacquer, curry, and incense are strong in the warm air. Narcissus cannot put away from him his lust for Hermes, whom he knows has spent the day with Cleopatra, is jealous, and furious with his own jealousy.

And simultaneously he remembers Rokujo, the afternoons of civilized pleasure with her and Cleopatra in the little green and white pavilion of jade, her grace and tact, the sanity and civilization of the arrangement. And he suddenly remembers a snatch of music from *Youth,* the fourth in the great song-cycle *Das Lied von der Erde* by the ancient composer Gustav Mahler. The translation is Chrysanthemum's:

> *In the middle of the pond*
> *stands a small pavilion*
> *green and white, of porcelain.*

Like the backbone of a tiger
made of jade, a little bridge
leads to the pavilion.

—A tiny house. And here sit friends
in lovely clothes; some drink, some scan
their verse; some talk, or do not talk;

upon their arms the sleeves of silk
slip to the elbow; caps of silk
squat halfway on their bobbing necks.

But on the pond, so bright and still
strangely all transforms again
into a mirror's pictured scene:

all are standing on their heads
in the pavilion of green
and white, of porcelain;

the bridge of jade, like a half-moon
arches upended in the pond.—
In lovely clothes friends laugh and drink again.

With unbearable nostalgia Narcissus remembers; and
reflects that the pain he feels now, the disturbance and
uncertainty, were as inherent in that life as the inverted
reflection in the poem's pond.

At that moment he arrives suddenly at Rokujo's door.
He becomes aware of where he is, and just then Gunther
comes out, with a satisfied look on his face. Off his guard,
the frustration too much for him, Narcissus sees only a
coarse enemy. Some element of disdain prevents him
from drawing his sword; instead, he catches Gunther by
the sleeve, spinning him around; as he blinks stupidly
Narcissus slaps him across the face. Gunther does not
change his expression, so, blind with fury, Narcissus
strikes him again with a swift and terrible blow across the
neck. Gunther drops in the gutter as if pole-axed.

The edge of Narcissus' hand is numbed by the impact.

Gunther does not move. In a trice people have gathered around the pair. Narcissus realizes the shame that has come upon him—crude contact with a Blood—which means demotion, loss of face, social ostracism, unless he can make his conduct good in tribunal.

And the predicament is worse yet. One of the onlookers, who has been examining Gunther, cries out that he is dead. Gunther was unprotected by an Idiot Guardian: it is part of his scientific pedantry to avoid the use of the Vision for this purpose, and he has ordered it to take its agents out of his brain.

Realizing that Gunther's death was not voluntary, one of the bystanders resurrects him immediately. He opens his eyes, shakes his head, and rises slowly to his feet, his back to Narcissus. He turns round and discovers his murderer, regards him, puzzled. For once Narcissus is at a loss. His heart sinks. Gradually Gunther begins to realize what has happened; and as he does so his look becomes cold. Gunther has no patience with those who cannot control themselves; it is not exactly an aesthetic feeling, but more closely approximates that ancient mood of certainty and dismissal that was once called a sense of morality.

"What did you do that for?" he says. "I never did anything to you."

Narcissus is silent, wishes he could leave, but Gunther seems about to say something else, and he has a right, it appears to Narcissus, to be heard. But he says nothing; instead, he thinks of all the ways that Narcissus has offended him, ignored him, or belittled him simply through the force and gaiety of his presence. And Gunther is quite unaware of any reason why Narcissus should hate him, and feels mistreated and poisonously hostile and moral.

Above at the balcony Rokujo has seen everything. Realizing that it was Narcissus' very passion for Hermes that caused his distracted behavior, but also sympathetic with the tragic nostalgia he must feel; and in a thin fury at the loss of face she is being forced to suffer, she feels a clamping pressure at the temples, a swimming nausea, and the scene goes black. She faints, wakes at once, and faints again. She is a heap of gold in her gold kimono with its two large blue butterflies. Aoi, her serving woman, bends over her in anxiety.

The tribunal is set for the day following the art show. Narcissus returns home, enters without a word, and, unable to sleep, enters a deep state of concentration, crosslegged and half-entranced, in the small meditation room facing the garden. About two o'clock in the morning Hermes, worried about his master, finds him there, his eyes unseeing, his face older and bereft of a large part of its beauty.

The boy has been profoundly disturbed by his experiences of the previous day. Out shopping with Cleopatra he has been snubbed twice, and, what is worse, he has seen Cleopatra herself ignored and spoken faintly to. The supporters of Rokujo and Michael are powerful and influential.

"Something terrible has happened, I know it," says the boy. "Tell me. Please."

"I killed a man."

"Was it over me?" asks Hermes, with the egotism of youth.

"In a way, darling," says Narcissus, smiling sadly. "But don't worry about it." He strokes the boy's head.

"What will happen to you?"

"I shall be all right. Our family is always at its best under pressure." Narcissus loves the large, rather coarse eyes of the boy, the big lips, the pathetic back of the head, furry and shorn, the childish nape with its two tendons. Passion rises again, and he kisses the boy on his neck.

Hermes is suddenly in great distress, and begins to weep. He loves all three of his friends, and is more and more convinced of the evil he has brought upon them. He shakes with sobs. Narcissus pulls the dark head down to his breast, allows the boy to rest there, mothered, safe. The shaking subsides.

But just at this moment Cleopatra, roused by the

sound, comes in, her brown face hard.

"You've forfeited your right to the boy. Give him to me."

"No."

"Come here, Hermes. I'm going to take you away."

Hermes does not know what to do. Like many orphans, he is unsure about the world's need for him; and now when he is loved at last it seems as if his best friends are being destroyed by his presence.

Luckily Chrysanthemum now makes his entrance. The old pederast has given up his interests in the boy and has philosophically accepted his defeat. He is yawning mightily.

"Fighting again?" he asks drolly. "Let wise old Chrysanthemum be the judge. *I'll* take the boy and you two can fight over each other. As for you, Hermes, my lad, you seem to be in demand. We'll have to have you spayed."

They all laugh at this attempt at humor: the situation would be unbearable otherwise. Venus, observing through the boy's eyes, realizes the impossibility of their predicament, and moves her young host to declare that he is very sleepy. He retires to bed.

The three friends look desperately at each other.

"Look," says Chrysanthemum. "I'll deal with Gunther. He's an utter asshead, and he'll be at the show. When I've finished with him he'll be in no state to press charges."

Reassured a little by this, Narcissus and Cleopatra go to their separate rooms, though Narcissus is still unable to sleep. Hermes, meanwhile, soothed by Venus yet mistrustful of her, at last begins to resist her power. His attempt is not entirely successful, but some of his own feelings surface against the goddess' compulsion: he feels piercingly lonely, and even misses his father Shadrach and the quiet, dreamy life of his home. In his bed he curls up into a ball with his teddy-bear and his coat of many colors, and cries himself to sleep.

3.

Art

"MARTIAN AESTHETICS TODAY," says Chrysanthemum, "is an odd kettle of fish. The fact that we have aesthetics at all is in a sense an historical accident: the first Martian settlers took care to transplant Earthly notions (while changing them, naturally) and so we have 'art.' In fact, it's all we have. All our etiquettes are nothing more than the traditional rules of a behavioral genre of art. And science," he goes on, bowing ironically to Gunther, who is present, "and indeed courtesanship," with another bow to Rokujo, "are also more or less affected forms of art."

They are gathered, a large group of fantastically attired art lovers and guests, in the Zero Gallery on Ninetieth Street. The interior is a series of impossible perspectives, in gradually merging shades of grey and white— impossible because the interior space has been designed according to a multidimensional topological model, and packs more volume into the building than its exterior dimensions can allow.

Into its halls and galleries shines the light of a dozen different suns. These have been carefully picked from the local group of gallaxies to be framed by viewing devices similar to the instantaneous matter-transmitters of the spaceport. Both types of instrument work by so perfectly recording and interpreting all electromagnetic and gravitational information from the "destination" that the precise conditions there can be exactly recreated; there is no difference from the "real thing" or "actually being there." The problem of the time-lag in the propagation of physical events (related to the speed of light) is solved by reversing or advancing the dimensional timeflow of the "image." This form of space travel has always been available to Man in a crude form: there is no event whose nature cannot be completely deduced from its effect at any other point in the universe. This is what the word "universe" means.

They have captured in this fashion a rare pulsar, whose weird violet light casts a stroboscopic flicker on the kinetic artwork it illuminates; a powerful young blue star, filtered by the material of the window, its surface crawling with tight flat relativistic effects of gravitation and magnetism; a slowly pulsating Cepheid, shrinking to an orange point and bellying out to a hugh vague red veil; and a black hole, seen in a visual translation of its gravitic intensity as it shrinks forever into nothing. The charmingly antique modernism of this decor is now in fashion again in the art world. Its camp scientism is a development from the recent intellectual craze for Scholastic theology: a sort of aesthetic-philosophical slumming in the mythical regions of "fact."

"To continue with our theme," Chrysanthemum goes on, "the characteristic motifs of contemporary Martian art are eclecticism, parody, pastoral naivety, the frontier, nihilism, the Emperor's New Clothes, and, of course, forgery.

"Eclecticism.—To avoid becoming strangled by the past productions of genius we have adopted the stratagem of playing them off against each other, allowing their different styles to aesthetically contradict and thus negate each other. This provides for us a space for original action. The guest of honor of this retrospective, Mr. Remington" (and here Chrysanthemum bows to the short, figure in the front row) "is a master of the eclectic. Take, for instance his name itself.

"Instead of creating *modes* of expression by manipulating the *elements* of expression, we manipulate whole modes of expression themselves, thus using *them* as the elements of our creations. A good example is Mr. Remington's masterpiece *The Grand Canyon:* using the basic tones and notions of the nineteenth-century American frontier painter he has depicted our own great canyon in Coprates; but still, there is something stylized, in the ancient Chinese mode, about some of its passages that should alert us to deeper significances: the rendering of the mists on the canyon floor, the cottage on the shoulder of the mountain, the air of permanence in impermanence. The self-portrait it contains is Hogarthian, anecdotal; yet there is something definitely Victorian in its Brunel-like rumpled confidence, its Whitmanesque flamboyance.

"'Mere plagiarism and technical virtuosity!' says the artistic naif. Not so. The painting is united by its irony, its gentleness, its awareness of human fallibility, even a certain quality of hope or artistic conceit. Conceited people are after all the only people worth knowing—though I admit my advocacy is not unbiased—for conceit implies hope, implies that one thinks one has something to give the world, and that one still expects the world to have something to give in return.

"And this brings us to parody. Parody, like eclecticism, protects us from being choked by our own creations, for parody, too, proves to the parodist that there exists a possible point of view outside that of a great past work of art: not in this case the point of view of a different great work, but rather the very point of view that can coolly mimic what it parodies. Parody is that which allows us to use the point of view of a previous work as a protagonist or hero whose actions are dispassionately observed by a new detached observer. Indeed, it is this process which constitutes the only meaningful definition of change in human cultural history, and thus in the evolution of the universe itself. The universe is a continuous parody of itself—that is why events succeed each other.

"The opposite side of the coin from parody is pastoral naivety (though we often combine them, face to face, so to speak). Pastoral naivety, contrary to received opinion, is not merely a pose the worldly-wise artist puts on to gain certain aesthetic ends. Rather, it is profoundly confessional. All great artists are naive persons who, if they stated their corny and embarrassing feelings directly, would be hooted out of face by the cheapest metropolitan sophisticate. Thus they adopt a flimsy subterfuge, which is to appear to be pretending when they are in fact pouring out their hearts. They put their deepest emotions into the mouths of some Doricles or Mopsa, and then join the audience in their superior and mocking laughter. Note, however, that the artist himself must watch the audience in order to know when to laugh. Art is a kind of public suicide or disavowal of oneself. You can tell what an artist believes by looking at what he apparently derides. Part of every great parodist—to return for a moment to the subject of parody—believes quite sincerely in every grotesque position he feigns to counterfeit.

"The frontier.—Of course contemporary art is committed to poiesis, and the various forms of imitation I have mentioned are a means of clearing a space for creation. I say this with a straight face. Originality *is* a virtue, but it is a virtue of the artwork, not of the artist. The artists who most devoutly believe themseleves to be original are slavishly derivative; and those who are sure they are humbly following a master often create art which is profoundly original. Not that we hereby condone self-ignorance. I myself"—says Chrysanthemum, using an unusual pronoun—"believe myself to be derivative, and consequently my art may be original, but this very knowledge, this inference, casts doubt upon the sincerity of my humility. In other words, I am involved in a 'vicious' circle—a predicament I welcome, for all self-consciousness is a vicious circle and art, as opposed to myth, is impossible without self-consciousness.

"What I have just said is not just a statement, but a demonstration (another definition of art, by the way); or, with respect to my learned colleagues of the philosophical persuasion,"—he bows to the two or three tattered members of the School who have bothered to attend—"in analytic terms, a *mention* as well as a *use* of language.

"It is precisely this mechanism, the vicious circle, that, as I previously hinted, is the mainspring of time. We keep the universe going by being aware of previous ways of being aware. Art provides the standpoint from which that 'being aware' becomes possible. Without art, there would be no time, except in the trivial sense of time as a mere dimension, discussable in the same terms as a common or garden spatial dimension. Thus without art, this universe would stop.

"The expansion of the universe in time is the condition, and the business, of art. Art creates the present, by which past and future are distinguished from one another—and past and future are only the distinction—and art makes the present move, by which the past accumulates itself, encroaching on that nonexistence we call the future.

"The point of the accumulation, or 'edge' of the universe, is what we mean by 'frontier.' Art is the frontier of reality's expansion into the unreal. This is to say that art *contains* the unreal, the nonexistent, for us. And art *reflects* us perfectly because it is backed by a more perfect vacuum than could possibly exist; I shall explain this point later. Obviously a volume (of however many dimensions) which is bounded by an edge beyond which nothing exists is topologically identical to a volume that *contains* a boundary which in turns contains a piece of nothingness. Now *nothing,* in itself, is topologically interesting—the pun is intended—in that it can have no size, any more than any other attribute. Therefore, for our purposes, it can be as small or as large as we want it to be—this is what "having no size" means. So you can visualize a big piece of something (the universe) swimming in a bigger medium of nothing, or a small piece of nothing nestled in a large medium of something. The two are the same.

"Every aware human being contains a piece of nothing; it is the arena of his creativity. So also does every work of art, if we conceive of it not as an object, but as a completed act of relationship between artist, artwork, and audience. (Artificial human beings, like Rupert, here,"—and here he pays his respects to a distinguished looking Android in the company—"combine the best of both.) Reality is a system of parentheses containing an absence.

"Of course there *were* ancient schools of philosophy which purported to show that the word "nothing" cannot be used meaningfully as just another noun. They are confuted by the fact that we regularly use the word "hole" as an ordinary noun, discussing, for instance, a hole's dimensions and shape—this is part of the point of Mr. Remington's choice of subject in *The Grand Canyon*— and in science, as Gunther here knows very well, there are perfectly identifiable physical entities which consist entirely in the *absence* of some other entity, and which can be perceived, measured and known by means of instruments. The only criterion we need in order to be able to discuss 'nothing' coherently is a boundary or frontier around it to set it off from 'something'; but this argument cuts both ways: a 'something' which is not bounded by whatever it is not, cannot be coherently discussed either. The philosophers who outlawed 'nothing' were deceived by their ignorance of the *containers* of nothing, that is, human beings or creative situations such as a work of art. Having no containers for nothing, they could not admit it into the world of their deliberations. Of course the more philistine among them, who asserted that there was 'nothing in art' or 'nothing in metaphysics' were asserting something that was perfectly true, a valid intuition which constituted, did they but see it, an implied reproach to their own system, of its lack of inclusiveness.

"Thus art is a boundary which gives size and shape to nothing, which is itself without form and void. This is what 'fiction' means. Art is a hole in the world, a hole that the world requires in order to go on growing and not be smothered by itself—growth whose name is Time. Society, to call the world by another name, also needs its frontier, as the ancient historian Frederick Jackson

Turner well knew. Art is a contradiction (a *logical* void) like the contradiction between the two-dimensional picture of the world given by one eye and that given by the other, that forces the brain into stereoscopic vision. It is the contradiction between three-dimensional entities that forces the universe into its most brilliant illusion—duration, process, time. Art is that expression of the set of all sets, or universe, which demonstrates the essential incompleteness or self-contradiction of all relational systems; the concretization of Cantor's, Russell's, Gödel's ancient paradoxes.

"Let us return, after this dithyramb, to our discourse, and leave the digression in parentheses, so to speak, containing the 'nothing' of which art speaks. 'Nihilism' was our next theme, and we have already more or less covered it: it is entailed by the notion of 'frontier.' Of course, nihil, nothing.

"The topology of this excellently designed Zero Gallery is nihilistic: an inner space, literally surrounded by outer space, separated by a boundary whose inner side bears works of art. My piece, here,"—and he gestures toward the object in the middle of the floor covered by a sheet—"is a sort of reversal of the more general nihilistic topology of the building that contains it, as you will see.

"Art, as I said before, is a kind of suicide, a finishing or negation of the world. It constitutes a velocity, the escape velocity of the universe. It traffics with the unsayable, the imperceptible.

"As such, an artwork is a cultural not a physical entity. There is an old story about the confidence man and the emperor: how the emperor is persuaded that he is wearing a magnificent suit of clothes when in fact he is wearing nothing. He appears to the populace who, like him, for fear of appearing gauche, not *au courant* with fashion, lavishly praise their ruler's new clothes. But one little boy speaks up, the eternal spirit of priggish and philistine skepticism, and declares that the emperor is indeed naked. Now the boy should have been better educated. For what is culture, society, life, the world itself, but an elaborate shared pretence? All is how one thing appears to another. We agree not to doubt the existence, say, of a piece of granite, on condition that it agrees tacitly not to doubt ours. The boy in the story, with his sophisticated and optimistic realism, is more destructive to the universe than the naive nihilists who join in praise of the nothing wherewith the Emperor has so gallantly covered himself.

"Our last topic was forgery. Forgery is the sincerest form of art criticism, for it genuinely extends the creative life of the artist. Back in the twentieth century there was a great forger called Van Meegeren, whose forgeries of Vermeer were accepted as genuine by the art world for decades. For that brief time—imagine it—there were more Vermeers in the world, the world was that much richer with the thought and feeling of the great Dutch master. When at last, through purely scientific, not artistic, evidence, the 'fraud' was detected, and the nasty little boy had seen through the pretence, the world lost a little of its light and promise.

"Nevertheless forgeries should be unmasked: the strain and tension which the negative principle of skepticism provides is a constant spur to the artist. Our guest of honor is a distinguished forger, and he would surely agree.

"My little piece of sculpture, here, is just such a tribute to Frederick Remington himself, the artist whose work so richly surrounds us. It is a forgery, which is itself authentically in the spirit of its master; whether the master himself will agree to acknowledge it as its own progeny, and thereby adopt it as an *objet trouvée* into the body of his own works, is what his humble servant, in respect and emulation, wishes to ascertain. We await your decision."

At that Chrysanthemum, with a twitch of a cord, reveals the sculpture. The sheet drifts to the floor as a chorus of sighs and a patter of applause breaks out among the audience.

"The work is titled *The Suicide of Phryne*. You will observe the classical Greek treatment of the limbs and torso—those Greeks, with their absurd belief in a reality one could artistically imitate, their odd notion of the existence of Truth! A supreme fiction, an illusion that has earned them their distinguished place in cultural history!

Note the limpid simplicity, if I may say so, of the descriptive passages. Something of that Greek skeptical optimism is implied in the work—though the uncharacteristic and highly romantic action of the subject—suicide—denies it.

"But it is the medium of the work to which I chiefly wish to direct your attention. The statue is sculpted out of a piece of nonexistence. Inside it there is nothing at all, believe it or not. Thus the work is a technological as well as an artistic achievement.

"The medium explains some of the odd effects you will have noticed, for instance the apparent, but only apparent, invisibility of the work. Since the difference between the refractive index of space-time (that is, everything outside the sculpture) and that of nothingness is total, the statue is completely reflective. However, because of the reversal of probability occasioned by the presence of nothing, the reflection is seen on the *opposite side* of the sculpture, so it seems as if the light is simply *passing through* it. You will also notice the lack of dimension to the work. This is because of the effect I mentioned earlier, the lack of dimensions in nothingness, of which the work is composed. It occupies, so to speak, a mathematical point.

"Were we able to go forward in time we would be able more clearly to see the statue, as its stuff is futurity, it is a beckoning onward. However, the future in its strongest sense is nonexistent, and thus the sculpture will, I am afraid, always be just beyond our reach.

"Touch it if you like; go on, don't hesitate. You'll notice the absence of sensation.

"I would appreciate an early decision from our guest of honor."

Remington steps forward and examines the sculpture carefully. There is a silence. At last:

"I fear that I compliment this work less by accepting it as mine than I would by disowning it. Nevertheless"—and he swiftly signs the base with his elaborate signature—"I hereby acknowledge it mine. I feel sure, Lord Chrysanthemum, that this work will have as great an influence on future Martian artists as did the paintings of Apelles and Zeuxis on the Italian Renaissance."

The allusion is apt, for these great Greek classical artists were indeed a seminal force in the Renaissance, though their works were never discovered. There is a ripple of applause which is broken by Gunther, who can contain himself no longer.

"But it's all a hoax! There's nothing there!" He goes up to the sculpture, passes his hand over the base like a magician, turns a questioning expression to the audience. He has a long bony face with large brow arches. "I follow your reasoning, of course, but one wants to see something concrete at the end of it all."

The audience, embarrassed, with a few titters, pretends not to notice him, begins to turn away to examine the other works of art along the walls. Gunther loses his temper.

"Artists! You're nothing but snobs. Give me something real that I can touch or see, not this solemn pretence."

Chrysanthemum smiles maliciously behind his hand. Better than he expected. Poor Gunther is falling into the trap. Now Gunther is not stupid; rather, he is stupidly intelligent. He is an expert on the play-behavior of animals, but unable to play himself. He is himself one of those naive characters that writers like to put into their stories to show how much more sophisticated than that they are, but who say much of what the author believes.

4.

The Reception

THE RECEPTION IS held at the graceful home of the owner of the Gallery. Michael and Snow have managed to calm Gunther and brought him along with them against his protests.

By ill chance they meet Narcissus in the foyer, in a conversational situation that allows no escape. Such is the perfection of their enemy's control that he seems perfectly relaxed; his brown face and golden dress shining with supernatural beauty, a deceptive softness in the mouth and eyes. They are almost remorseful that they must attempt to destroy this beautiful creature. The rivals exchange polite conversation about the exhibition, some small-change gossip. Everyone around them is listening, and pretending not to. There is no confrontation, and they are disappointed.

Within, Narcissus is in turmoil: sick with boredom at the whole affair. His deep-laid plans no longer appeal to him, because of the intervention of the boy Hermes; nevertheless he must fight the course.

Since the first moment at the theatre when he had been suddenly struck by the decent honesty of Michael as at the same time he was enraged on behalf of his sister, Narcissus has been nursing a profound aesthetic strategy. Essentially, there is a quality of freshness in his rival which he wishes to test, appropriate, or despoil.

Anger on behalf of someone else is often enough anger *at* that same person. In the weeks prior to the challenge, Cleopatra had neglected Narcissus because of the demands of her training and rehearsals. Narcissus, almost unconsciously, had resented and envied her. At the moment of the confrontation his anger had burst forth, and his many motives had coalesced into a single theme.

His challenge was at once an impulse, the declaration of a wish to be involved with Michael's life—so much narrower and clearer than his own—and an expression of anger at and independence of his sister. At that moment an idea came to his mind, based on the fact that years before, when Snow was still a young girl, Narcissus had met her and they had fallen in love.

They had been at school in the northern city of Rennet; Narcissus parted from his sister, who was under the care of a dancing-master in the south. He and Cleopatra, because of their scoffing indulgence in the pleasures of the Vision and their insolent and sophisticated behavior— playing truant, acts of mischief on important people, and a sexual licence and inventiveness offensive even to Martian tastes—had been separated as a punishment, and forbidden the use of the Vision for a year. Thus they had no way of seeing each other. Their guardians (both parents had committed suicide when their children were infants) were strict and inflexible.

Thus Narcissus' encounter with the young Snow was almost inevitable. At that time she was full of brightness and hope: thin, white, under the blossoming apple boughs of the school orchard, smelling fresh and clean, her earlobes and nostril-wings glowing with the waxy clarity of youth, her characteristic seriousness charming and exciting in one so young. To her the slightly older free-martin was a vision of sinister beauty and forbidden pleasure; his sophistication and the complex pain she sensed in him made him appear infinitely grown up. He, moreover, needed a confidante, a confederate. Snow's freshness captured him altogether for some weeks.

However, he had gone back to Cleopatra at the first opportunity, leaving Snow despoiled of hope, remembering Narcissus with an exquisite shortness of breath, the seriousness transmuted into a quiet, ashen bitterness, with a new need for safety and the unchanging. Pain is only one of the strategies with which we deal with experience; it had become her whole style. In that mood some three years later she met Michael; and for some odd reason never told him of the affair. Thus when the challenge was issued Snow felt the most devastating and contradictory passions—which Narcissus sensed instantly.

Narcissus knows that his trump card in the conflict with Michael is Snow's secret desire for him, which, he feels sure, has not dimished. Ruthless calculations, perhaps, in terms of an earlier morality: but no more ruthless than the decision to have a baby to be used as a weapon.

Narcissus' plan is to undercut Michael, to bring him into a state of psychological disadvantage, and thus dependence, by renewing the affair with Snow. But the new and frightening passion he has discovered for Hermes has taken away the savor of such an encounter; and, oddly, though he is Cleopatra's rival for the boy, he no longer wishes to punish her by means of an outside attachment of his own. Indeed, he feels a curious friendship for her, a fellow-feeling. He knows the torment of loving the boy, and must sympathize. She, on the other hand, has turned against him altogether, but in a sisterly and vicious manner that betrays the guilty disturbance of her feelings.

The four protagonists face each other in the foyer, smiling, perhaps a trifle too graceful, among nicely worded banalities. After what seems an interminable period—during which Narcissus catches a new element in the relationship of Michael and Snow, a serenity and sharedness that disturbs and intrigues him—the prescribed pleasantries have been observed, and they part and mingle with the other guests.

Meanwhile Chrysanthemum prepares himself for his

revenge on the unfortunate Gunther. Gunther is being protected by his friend Rokujo, who suspects, knowing Chrysanthemum well, that he is planning something. She keeps Gunther in a corner, in conversation with a harmless Professor of Thaumaturgy.

But this strategy plays right into Chrysanthemum's hands. Quickly finding an empty room, he transforms himself by means of the Vision into an exact replica of Gunther. Next, he improves the replica with almost imperceptible touches, caricaturing the lantern jaw, the ill-fittingness of the clothes, the slight sniffle. When all is complete he saunters out into the company, tripping over people's feet, looking dazedly for the bar, ignoring the greetings of his acquaintances. There is a high art in so perfectly imitating the mannerisms of another person that his closest intimates do not suspect, while at the same time ruthlessly parodying his style. Avoiding the room in which he knows Rokujo has barricaded her protégé, he proceeds to make a fool of himself: getting rather drunk, cornering people and telling them about his explorations and experiments, finally denouncing in a loud voice the artist Remington, who is standing just behind him.

"An ass, that'sh what he is. The whole art world sucks, up to him, and all he does is p-play clever tricksh and steal other people's ideas."

At that moment Gunther himself, followed by Rokujo, reappears wondering what the noise and the sudden silence can mean. The timing is perfect: Gunther recognizes "himself"; everybody has turned away in embarrassment; Rokujo has hidden her face;—and Chrysanthemum changes instantly back into himself, and bows to Remington, who acknowledges the subtle compliment.

Some of the people in the room do not realize that there were ever two "Gunthers"; others wonder which is the right one; others are simply confused. In any case, Gunther has been made a complete fool of. Nobody takes his outrage seriously, and the few who see the point of the elaborate aesthetic joke are convulsed with silent laughter.

Rokujo leads him away. She herself has lost face disastrously and now wishes only for a place to hide. She

pities Gunther but now her pity is mixed with contempt.
Even the conceit of pupil and teacher is no defense against
the harshness and gracelessness she has had to suffer.
Michael, seeing his friend in retreat, follows, leaving
Snow by herself.

Narcissus' mood has changed. Stimulated by drink and
by the comedy of Chrysanthemum's impersonation, he
forgets the Tribunal on the morrow and enters what feels
like the phase-state of the sword-master in combat. But
still there is something wrong about it all, some muffling
or obstruction which mars the psychic nakedness he
should possess. And underneath there is the sense of some
greater moment, some terrifying and inviting mistake.

Determined to force the issue and discover the flaw his
intuition has detected, he approaches Snow and asks her
if they can talk in private. She is shocked by this—it is as if
Narcissus had dropped out of that flamboyant decorum
she associates with him—but complies in confusion.

They enter an empty room whose great shot silk screen
of grey and silver is painted in the lower corner with
winter branches and a hugh white moon aureoled by a
subtle dark shadow; and yet the boughs are touched here
and there with blossom—or snow?—in the same matte
white as the moon. As if referring to the screen, Narcissus
recalls their first meeting, in a Haiku:

> *"Since spring made white the branches,*
> *I have oft longed to see that snow again."*

She replies, not knowing what she says, but carried away
by the words:

> *"Alas, that the petals should be melted*
> *And the snow be turned to fruit!"*

Narcissus is disturbed by the paradox, and turns to
normal speech:
  "What does it mean, that the snow be turned to fruit?"
  "I am bound not to reveal it."
  "Nevertheless, you remember our meeting as children."

"Of course. But now it is different. Do you not understand?"

"No."

"Why are you hounding us? All we ask is to live sadly in peace."

Narcissus speaks another poem:

> *"Does the hound control the pattern of the hunt,*
> *Or the scent he follows?"*

The multiple question confuses Snow for a moment, but she replies:

"What scent draws you, Lord Narcissus? Could you not have left me to die of my wounds?"

The image of the carrion-bird or hyena strikes home. Narcissus is tortured by his own insincerity, but presses his painful advantage. It is like touching an open sore. He decides on a frontal attack.

"Come away with me. It's not too late. I have a house in Rennet. Come and live with me there."

Snow has a potent weapon which she does not know how to use, for it is two-edged. But it must be used now, against both her enemy and herself.

"I cannot come, for I carry Michael's child, and there are crimes that no tribunal can excuse."

Narcissus at last understands. The tiny handful of Martian sexual taboos includes mating with a woman who is pregnant by another man. Narcissus is staggered by the power and coolness of Michael's strategy; in sudden anger and despair he turns on his heel and leaves the room.

Now Michael, returning, notices Narcissus' pallor as he steps through the doorway, and in curosity glances into the room of the silk screen. He sees Snow there, in tears, and his heart drops with apprehension.

"What did he do?"

"Nothing."

"What did he do?"

"He asked me to go away with him. I don't know why I . . . he told me he had a house in Rennet . . . I had to tell him about our baby."

Michael goes white with rage. He leaves her at once and pushes through the crowd in pursuit of Narcissus, who is preparing to leave. At the main entranceway, he catches him by the shoulder, spins him around, and palely demands What the devil did he mean with his wife? Narcissus, sick with despair and overcome with the absurity of it all, laughs in his face. Michael, in control no longer, slaps him across the cheek—the ancient gesture of defiance, contempt and challenge.

All around there is a quick gasp of breath. "A duel!" Narcissus is suddenly serious; he looks at his rival in friendly pity.

"*You* cannot fight with me."

"I leave that to your honor; nevertheless I am your servant in this matter whether you will or nill. My seconds will call on you tomorrow morning."

"Reflect, Michael." But Narcissus now senses a breeze of fear in himself, that Michael is serious about this foolish thing: he will endanger both of them. He, Narcissus, has already lost face and is technically an honorable loser at this point in the status conflict. What more does Michael want of him?

He looks again into Michael's face, and sees there, with his feminine intuition, something else beside cold rage: an abandon not unlike his own, a feverish and seductive excitement, a giving way to the improper, a passionate and disordered commotion of the blood. This conversion explains the action of a man who would challenge a killer as effective as Narcissus, and sacrifice his life to stain the honor of his enemy. Narcissus leans forward very gently, and with an unironic tenderness kisses Michael on the cheek; the latter is too surprised to resist.

"Yes, I will be ready for you, Michael; but you do not know what it is you ask." Narcissus' lovely contralto, low and controlled, can be heard in the silence several rooms away. With that he quits the house, leaving on Michael's cheek the impalpable pressure of his princely fragrance.

Word of what has passed spreads quickly. Cleopatra looks about the house for Hermes, does not find him. He

has witnessed everything. Chrysanthemum has found a
pretty young theological student at the party and has
disappeared with him.

Cleopatra returns home, but Hermes is nowhere to be
found, and some of his belongings are missing. (They had
been teleported to the house from his room in New
Babylon.) Narcissus has not yet returned; in a few
minutes, however, she hears his steps outside. Not
wishing to see him, she leaves by a side entrance.

But Narcissus knows that she has been home. Indeed,
he knows her very well, and it is her, and her only, that he
wishes to see. Forgetting Hermes he sets out after his
sister, guessing where she has gone: the great park of
Tehuantepec under the volcano Huacatl in the eastern
sector of the city. It is the place she goes when she is
troubled in mind. Winged, he passes over the city in the
light of the moon.

Under him there are ten thousand rooftops and a million lights; he sails in middle air, blindly, his wingbeats irregular and almost exhausted, though he feels the illusory strength of passion and drunkenness.

At last he finds Cleopatra, walking in the "White"
garden with a sad and dragging step; designed for darkness and the monochrome light of Phobos, the garden
glows with the petals of mutated Janet-flowers, tree-
peonies, white roses, all of them fluorescing slightly in the
ultraviolet blaze of the moon.

He discards his wings and falls into step with her. She
ignores him. He lights her a cigarette, passes it across. It is
one of the most ancient and tender of their gestures, and
she accepts it automatically. Drawing on it, the smoke
goes to her eyes, and she wipes away a tear. Narcissus,
deliberately misinterpreting, speaks to her now.

"Don't cry."

"I'm not."

"I'll give up Hermes."

"You'll never give up Hermes."

"Yes I will."

"That isn't the point anyway," she says. "It isn't you I
want."

This hurts, but the fact that she has said it is signifi-

cant. She cares enough to be angry. It gives them a place
to start from.

"We'll just have to change the basis of our friendship,"
he says. "We can't cope with situations like Hermes. He's
too much for us. We have to give him up."

"Why should I?"

"Yes, why should you." He speaks without spirit now.

"What were you doing with Snow?" she asks.

"Trying to seduce her."

"Why?"

"To catch Michael off balance."

"You're not serious about the feud still, are you?"

"No, but one's got to have something to go on doing."

"Why?"

"Because a story shouldn't get sidetracked by its own
subplot."

"*I'm* a subplot?"

"You know that's not what I meant. Actually the feud
was a pre-Hermes idea. If you only knew how much it *did*
involve you!"

"I don't like you when you beg."

"I'm not asking you to *like* me."

She bursts into laughter now; it is a game like the games
of their childhood, elaborate emotional sparring. Yes,
after all, it would be hard to lose Narcissus. Indeed, part
of the fatal allure of Hermes is the excitement of rivalry.

Actually it is precisely *liking* to which Narcissus is
making his appeal: the fact that nobody in the world is
quite so interesting to Cleopatra, after all, as himself. An
intimate sisterly tenderness rises between them; and their
conversation becomes affectionately spiteful.

"It's just as well you're not asking to be liked."

"When I want your *opinions,* my dear, I'll ask for
them."

"What *do* you want? Mummy love?"

Although nothing more is said about Hermes, some
kind of agreement has been reached; whether of sharing,
or if sharing does not work, renunciation, will never be
known, for events are now determining intentions rather
than vice-versa. However, they sit together at last on a

volcanic crag above the park, in the perpetual warm air of Cleopolis, with only the stars for company, silent, fierce passions now briefly assuaged.

5.

A Gesture Of Independence

SHADRACH, THE DAY after his son's abduction, has dispatched agents to the City to try to bring him back. They are unsuccessful, for Narcissus and Cleopatra command powerful street gangs of *ragazzi,* and are themselves skilled in the use of the Vision to frustrate surveillance. Finally the baron himself comes to Cleopolis, and succeeds at last in establishing a spy channel in the house of his enemies.

There, one evening some time before the events of the last chapter, he witnesses Hermes in voluptuous dalliance with Narcissus, throat to throat, eyes closed in ecstasy. Instantly he falls down in a fit, blood vessels burst in his head, and his heart stops abruptly. Revived by his Idiot Guardian, he dies of apoplexy two or three times more. He survives, but he is a changed man. He returns to New Babylon quieter, colder, as if a spring had shattered in him. Dismissing the bulk of his servants, he diminishes his establishment and tears down those statues of his ancestors whose features remind him of Hermes. He takes up with a local boy, a son of one of the estate's bird-catchers; it is a purely convenient affair, for the desires of the flesh have outlived, for once, the desires of the heart.

Hermes himself, having observed the events at the reception, though he does not fully understand them, is convinced that he is destroying his generous friends; he feels a rush of hatred for himself, and in that mood admits to himself what he must have done to his father. He returns to the house of Narcissus and Cleopatra, and finds it empty (Cleopatra has not yet returned). Picking up some of his most prized possessions, he decides to return and make amends with his father. He has a coat of many colors, a battered old teddy-bear, and a tiny teaching-robot called Jiminy Cricket.

He projects himself into the gardens of New Babylon. At once he is aware of the changes that have been made in the estate. A sense of foreboding passes over him. He creeps up to the windows of his father's suite. In the study he sees Shadrach sitting at his desk, paler and rather healthier looking than before, but with a look of infinite misery on his face. His elbow is on the desk, and his chin is supported by his hand—a posture of carelessness, neglect, and despair.

Hermes' heart bleeds for his father; quickly he retraces his steps, turns at the corner of the main building, and enters through its unattended doors. He does not wish to disturb his father without warning. An old retainer, the butler, whose pompous and affectionate rule had been one of the givens of the boy's childhood, comes into the foyer, hearing the door squeak. For a moment the old look of tender disapproval and indulgence of the boy's mischief crosses his face; but suddenly it goes hard.

"I suppose you want to see your father."

Hermes nods, and the old man leads him to an anteroom and leaves him there. After a few moments he returns and ushers the boy into his father's presence. Shadrach stares at him blankly.

"Father, please, I've come back."

Shadrach makes no reply; the boy throws his arms about his neck and begs forgiveness; but Shadrach does not change his expression, nor does he even attempt to move away. Hermes pulls back and stares in anguish into his father's face. There is still that look of misery that he had noticed from outside, but now he sees something else: the misery is unaware of itself, blank, forlorn. It has in it neither anger nor welcome nor any warmth at all, nor even recognition. The boy detaches himself, and is suddenly more totally afraid than he has ever been before. Still Shadrach does not speak; Hermes retreats, tears beginning to stream down his face, heart beating unbearably, sighing and sighing. He stumbles out through the desolate parlors and into the overgrown gardens of the estate. The moon casts huge shadows away from every shrub and urn, as it sets with perceptible swiftness.

In an instant he is back in the house of Narcissus and Cleopatra, who have left it moments earlier. Finding the place empty—even the servants have retired—he is strick-en anew with loneliness and the desire for a safe home, somewhere he can sit down and no one will injure him or be injured by him. In desperation he calls out for Venus—a dangerous figure for him, associated with adventures for which he is too young, unready, but the only mothering he has known—and she comes at once into his mind.

"What do you want, child?"

"I'm afraid. Please help me."

"Where is Narcissus?"

"I don't know. Everyone has left me. My father doesn't recognize me."

Venus is bored but out of a sense of duty she attempts to comfort the boy.

"They'll come back in the morning."

"No they won't. They'll probably be killed or exiled because of me. It's no wonder they've gone."

"You surely don't imagine, child, that they are altruistically concerned for your welfare? They're not martyrs for your sake, you know. Why don't you realize that they don't *love* you—they love *each other*; they're quite clear about what they're doing, and if they are sacrificing anything, they are doing it for something they *want*."

Hermes is silent, but now a great sob gathers itself in his

chest. Loyally, he denies to himself what Venus is saying; and at the same moment, in the Park, Narcissus and Cleopatra are indeed tacitly betraying him. He breaks, into renewed tears.

Venus is suddenly solicitous. She materializes in the room, beautiful, naked but for a filmy garment, cut to reveal the breasts, that barely reaches her dimpled knees—the costume of the succubus.

"All you want is a little love," she says, kindly. She gathers him to her, he kneeling, dark head between her white paps. But it is the wrong kind of love. Hermes cannot respond, is aware of an aching lack. Aphrodite now does something quite unusual: she enters the boy's mind as at the same time she remains in the flesh. With subtle force she opens the arteries of the boy's passion. But it is unnatural, unnatural. Hermes is terrified: he is being totally submerged. At last the slow rage of his pioneer ancestors rises in him; the human will cannot be ultimately abused.

"Get out of my mind."

Venus is shaken by the child's wrath. In pain, she quits his mind like a guilty thing.

"You are trying to steal me. Go away!"

He advances on her fleshly presence, the forces of the Vision surging through his body, prepared for some supernatural act of violence. He draws back his hand to strike her; she cringes, and he gives her a moment's pause.

"Yes, you are probably right about Narcissus and Cleopatra. I am a fool, a foolish child, a silly boy. But I am a Person too, and a Blood, and I will swallow no more."

He strikes at her, the act of sacrilege nothing to him now; as he does so she dematerializes, distraught, dishevelled, a young nymph caught at a forbidden game.

Now Hermes becomes sombre. His face shows years he has not lived. He is beginning to know what he must do. They have used him; and he is still in love with them. The only house he has is theirs.

His eye falls on the very ancient gramophone at the side of the room, a toy from Old Earth that has fascinated him. He picks up a record which Narcissus has been playing and has not put away (the servants are forbidden to touch them). It is Gustav Mahler's *Das Lied von der Erde,* written shortly after the death of two of the composer's children, himself under a death sentence from a fatal disorder of the heart. Absently, as he weighs his choices, he lays the record on the turntable and sets the antique diamond on the permaplastic. The first ironic and bitter chords issue from hidden louvres:

> *"Schön winkt der Wein im gold'nen Pokale*
> *Doch trinkt noch nicht, erst sing'ich euch ein Lied!*
> *Das Lied von Kummer*
> *Soll auflachen in die Seele euch klingen . . ."*

Chrysanthemum's translation is set in the ancient Anglo-Saxon alliterative meter:

> Gay gleams the wine in golden goblet,
> But stay your drinking while I sing you a song,
> A sorrowsong in the soul shall
> Linger with longtrouble's longlaughter ringing.

The song winds on, with its slow withering, its call for the cup and the lute, its voluptuous romantic cynicism; and above all its terrible refrain *Dunkel ist das Leben, ist der Tod*—"dark is life, and dark is death." For modern Martians the song is an elegant flirting with a primitive terror: orginally a delicate and sententious Confucian Chinese poem, it took on heavier romantic-Teutonic overtones in its translation into German centuries later; and now, in the context of Mars, it has become something else again.

> *Cold carecold, when carecold comes close*
> *Then goes to waste the gaygarden of the soul,*
> *Winters the joy away, withers the song.*
> *Dark is life, and dark is death.*

> *Hall's hall-lord! your hoard holds*

Great plenty of golden wine!
And I hold here this harp for my own.
To draw the harpstring, drain the cup—
Such are the things that sort well together:
Brightbeaker of wine at the best time now
Counts more to me than kingdoms of the world.
Dark is life, and dark is death.

The airheaven's everblue; always the Earth
Steadfast stands fast and flowers in the spring.
But lean, O manlife, life is not long—
Not for a hundred years happily may we taste
The vanishing, fading vanities of the world.

Look in the moonlight! Lurking in the graves
Wildghastly gangles a grim form!
An ape it is! Hear him! How horrible he howls!
Screaming and shrilling in the sweet air of life.
Bend to your wine now, benchmates, now it is
time!
Empty your golden goblets to the grounds!
Dark is life, and dark is death.

But the boy is no longer there to hear. He has left his
coat of many colors on the floor. Halfway between the
veranda and the pool he has dropped his Jiminy Cricket.
Lying soaked among the rushes of the pool, across from
the little pavilion, is his teddy-bear.

Dawn is coming: a double dawn, Phobos rising in the
West, Sol in the East. Before them come the Harbingers—
Venus, or Lucifer, and Terra, the Morning Star, the
Homestar wheeling up over the horizon, with an already
disappearing speck in the golden haze that may be Mer-
cury, that protean messenger, Hermes, the quicksilver
star.

Narcissus and Cleopatra are flying home in the green
bright air of morning; they do not notice the white
shadow in the pool; when they enter they hear the
repeated and meaningless syllable of the spent record, see
the coat of colors on the floor, follow the pathetic trail to

the pool's edge, and find the boy drowned in the middle waters, a reproach beyond measure, every eyelash clearly visible as if preserved in crystal.

Suicide on Mars is the one action which commands automatic respect. As such, it is aesthetically crude, though effective. It eschews the creating of an illusion of value by means of mutually sustaining relationships, judgments, and definitions, which is the Martian forte; and chooses instead the sensational but undeniable assertion of the value of life in terms of its true opposite, death. Suicides devastate their targets; and Hermes' is particularly well chosen, for besides revenging the boy's betrayal by Narcissus and Cleopatra, it also takes aim at all their enemies in Cleopolis who by their malicious gossip had subjected Hermes to an unbearable personal pressure, equivalent to witchcraft. Thus the suicide is at once an accusation against his friends, and a gesture of loyalty toward them. Beyond this, moreover, the suicide strikes at a goddess as well. It comes as a surprise to all, for Hermes was not credited with the resources to be a true actor in the game, but an extra, so to speak, brought in for decoration.

I have killed off my Hermes. To make this move bearable, he will be revived if you like by Venus many years later when all this has blown over, with the gift of immortality, to be the cupbearer of Olympus and the special favorite of Cytherea; and he will live happily ever after, surrounded by super-feminine nurture. So much for tragedy. Anything can be reversed. The boy's act is only fictionally final: it is real in its artistic meaning, not in its physical consequences. So, after all, suicide itself is as trivial as any other act, and the value given it by Martian convention is indeed nothing more than a convention. My apologies for this reversal, but it was necessary. I must insist, in my Mars, on the purely contextual nature of value. (Mendel disagrees, but he does not understand my work.)

6.
The Tribunal

MARTIANS LIMIT THEMSELVES not just for the sake of artistic challenge, but also for the sake of explicitness. Were they to live in the state of pure subjectivity or madness, they would be rejecting the very language with which they can know each other and themselves. The "outside world" is that with which we explain ourselves to ourselves; it is social and linguistic in its essence; it is synonymous with the intersubjective.

Ritual is, among other things, the language of language, intersubjectivity raised to a high power. When it creates something new out of nothing, it is art. And ritual is a stringent limitation, a confinement to arbitrary and grotesque conventions, a spiritual binding of the feet. It is thus the essence of the explicit.

A tribunal is such a limiting, such an explicitness. Narcissus has not enough time to prepare himself. He is bone-tired emotionally and physically, and despite a psychomorphic is weeping still when he enters the courtroom, barely three hours after the death of his betrayed sweetheart, Hermes, the beloved child.

It is a building characteristic of the severest and most

domestic vein in Martian architecture. Rather like the Phoenix theatre at Hellas in shape, it is plainly constructed of high cedarwood, unpainted, in perfect proportion; the lines of beams beat a lofty and restrained rhythm, the curves of the tiled roof are austere and graceful, the space within seems to float and contain rather than to oppress. It is obviously massive, but carries itself lightly and with an unobtrusive sense of balance.

All this is appropriate to is legal function. The place is full and quiet. Narcissus, despite the tears running uncontrollably down his face, can see many of his acquaintance. Cleopatra sits near the back, her face pale, not looking at her brother-lover. As is the custom the accused enters by the main doors, through which the general public has also been admitted. Before him are the three seats of justice: the left one, empty, signifying the verdict of the future; the right one, occupied by one of the pioneers of Mars, whom Narcissus does not recognize (actually Master Peter Grimstead, a close friend of Raphael Mendel's), and the center one, held, to Narcissus' surprise, by the goddess Athena, grey eyed and clothed in grey. The highest goddesses do not usually adjudicate in such matters as a simple accidental murder. The case is attracting divine attention, then.

From the point of view of the audience Narcissus is a fatally attractive figure. He is wearing a fresh white and gold kimono with a faint purple pattern of flowers; he is surrounded with a kingly fragrance; but it is clear that he has not slept, for his golden face is darkened with shadows; his long black hair, gathered in the top-knot of the Samurai, falls down his back and shoulders. At intervals he covers his face with a fold of the kimono, and wipes away the unbidden tears.

Even in his present state Narcissus is evidently dangerous, a master-player in the game of life. Some say that he may well be Topcock, the noblest, that is the most aesthetically subtle, person on Mars.

The accusation of murder is read; the legal formalities completed; Athena bows her head, looks up, and asks, what Narcissus has to say.

"Let me confront him who is said to be my victim," he replies.

"Gunther, if it is he you mean, cannot be present today."

Indeed, as Chrysanthemum had forecast, the shame of the previous night has caused Gunther to leave Cleopolis altogether, though it has taken Rokujo's urgent pleading to bring about this result. (Rokujo did not accompany him; she has promised to follow, but could not miss the tribunal; and she is at last tiring of his insensitivity.)

"Do you deny the charges, then?"

"No, but it is your business, not mine, to establish a judgment on this matter."

"What was your reason for killing Gunther?" asks, Master Grimstead.

"Jealousy, rage, nostalgia. I did not especially intend to kill him."

"That's immaterial. Killing is a trivial offence. But this is a case of Crude Contact," says Athena, who is more *au fait* with current law than the Terraformer.

"If it is any help," Narcissus says ironically, "The blow with which I killed him was a *butterfly-wing*; for those who know the art, this is one of the most elegant and difficult of the killing blows."

"It is to be expected, Lord Narcissus," replies Athena with a cool glance, "that you would do whatever it is you do with some grace. But it is *what* you have done, not *how,* which is in question."

"You yourself, Madam, stipulated that this was a case of Crude Contact, not of murder."

"You are arguing against a legal definition," says Master Grimstead, asserting his expertise. "Crude Contact is any violent laying of hands on another without his or her consent. You do not deny that this describes your action?"

"No."

"You understand the penalty for such a crime?"

"Demotion, yes."

"What is your defence?"

"I leave it in your hands to elicit it."

There is a silence. This is an unusual legal device; Athena and Grimstead confer with each other and with the Vision.

"Why is Gunther not present?" asks Athena.

"I must call a witness," replies Narcissus.

"Do so."

He calls to the stand one of the guests at last night's party, who testifies to the humiliation of Gunther. Then he calls Chrysanthemum, who, pendular and hung-over, waddles dolefully forward.

"Why did you make a fool of Gunther?" asks Athena.

"We were seconding our friend Narcissus in his status-conflict."

"What has a status-conflict to do with all this?"

"Naturally, dear lady, this whole business didn't just *materialize* out of the *blue*. Narcissus is in conflict with Michael; Gunther is Michael's closest friend."

Athena turns to Narcissus.

"So it is your claim that the status-conflict justifies Crude Contact with Gunther?"

"I did not make that claim. All I said was that I did it out of rage, jealousy, and nostalgia."

"So what is the point of your defence?"

"A work of art, madam, is as you know a creation whose parts are sometimes hidden from one another. A status-conflict, which is the highest of all arts, is not so much a series of planned and intended events, but an *opportunity* for beautiful and passionate action. The Trojan War, which was the archetypal status-conflict, was a model in this kind. Who could have foreseen the wrath of Achilles when Agamemnon and Menelaus first set sail?"

The court is swayed by this, but Athena smiles. "I know a little about that war myself. However, what you have done is to commit a crude and unaesthetic act in the pursuit of a higher goal. Even granting this generous formulation, and a favorable ambiguity of the words 'in the pursuit of,' what reason can you give why the ugliness should be forgiven?"

"Is not ugliness, madam, merely unreclaimed beauty?" exclaims Narcissus, weeping anew at the memory of his dead boy-lover. "Can it not be the masterstroke of the daring artist, to turn ugliness to beauty? Is not the ugly the space which beauty must conquer, without which beauty would be merely order?"

"You are convincing, but your rhetoric is empty," says Master Grimstead. "A moment ago you were proclaiming the glories of aesthetic unconsciousness. Now you are defending yourself on the basis of a highly self-conscious, not to say contrived, aesthetic."

"Master Grimstead, are you judging the whole status-conflict (which is not yet complete), or this one action which is before us?" asks Narcissus sharply. To snub a Terraformer is dangerous, typical of Narcissus' scared, crazy, arrogant courage. "For if you do the former, you judge also my opponent, one of whom is the victim. A work of art which stands an aesthetic on its head owes many of its virtues and all of its flaws to what is opposes."

"Let us take up your parenthetical remark about the conflict not being complete," says Athena, trying to soothe the offended Grimstead. She is beginning to like Narcissus, though her prime loyalty is to Michael. She realizes how dangerous is the freemartin, how partial she must be if her protégé is to triumph. "What is the next step in this conflict?"

"Michael's seconds called on me this morning, but owing to unforseen circumstances I was unable to answer them at once. They wished, of course, to know what weapons and what site I had chosen."

"A lapse. Surely you are not afraid of Michael, that you delay in giving him his answer? What are the 'unforeseen circumstances'?"

At this, Narcissus cannot speak; and Cleopatra comes forward to speak for him. She tells the story of Hermes' suicide, briefly and passionlessly. Most of the audience does not know of this, and when she has finished there is a shocked and uneasy silence.

"Clearly the whole affair has gone further already than the strict scope of this tribunal," says Athena, attempting to restore some balance to the case. She confers with Master Grimstead, turns back to the courtroom. "It is the opinion of this court that the crime of which the defendant is accused is not an isolated piece of hooliganism, and that the defendant himself is not merely a ruffian. However, the structure of which this action was a part is not by any means proven, to the satisfaction of this court, to be one which satisfies our most basic canons of taste.

"The somewhat speculative argument has been put forward that in the process of creating *new* canons of taste the old must sometimes be violated. This construction has merit as an *a posteriori* critique of an existing major work of art, but cannot be used prospectively as a justification of any act of mayhem on the basis of its novelty. And since, as the defendant implies, the status-conflict is not yet complete, we cannot make an absolute judgment at this time."

"However, we do not dismiss the case," Master Grimstead goes on, as the Goddess falls silent. "The verdict is guilty, but we suspend the sentence until the outcome of the status-conflict is known. Its effect is conditional on the outcome of that conflict. In other words, if you lose the conflict, you will lose not only face, but also rank. It is incumbent on you to make this conflict not merely an interesting experiment but a major creative act."

Such is the verdict of the past. Athena concurs, and the ritual questioning of the third, empty, seat does not contradict them.

Athena sums up: "In rendering this verdict the court was not uninfluenced by considerations of compassion with respect to the defendant's recent bereavement, though the whole matter appears to us to have been ill judged, impulsive, and wild. But if that is an integral part of your style, we cannot complain.

"However, let us warn you that there are heavier sentences than demotion. You run, it seems to us, the gravest risk in this affair, of falling into an *ipso facto* state of madness; and this court will legally ratify that state, and officially withdraw the society of this planet from you, if you transgress the limits which define the mutual understanding of persons in our culture. You may say what you like, so to speak; but your syntax must be correct. Do you have anything to say?"

"Only this, Madam. There is a sense of the word 'meaning' which insists that the only meaningful statement is a statement which in some way violates its own code or medium. I take 'code' to mean simply that which the hearer *expects* of the speaker (and what better definition could there be, in absolute terms?); obviously nothing has been communicated if the speaker merely performs in all respects according to the hearer's expectations. There can be no ultimate separation of content from code; content is an anomaly of code.

"However, my Lady, I shall endeavor with my best efforts to fulfill the spirit of your injunctions; and I accept, my Lord," (bowing to Master Peter Grimstead) "the sentence which you have so graciously mitigated."

So saying, he bows once more, turns, and glitteringly leaves the courtroom. His manner is just short of arrogant: it would be arrogant had he not the grace to carry it off.

As he leaves he remembers the expression on Cleopatra's face as she testified to the suicide of Hermes: it was utterly dead, a terrifying face. He looks for her in the audience, but she is gone. Nor is she at home when he returns with Chrysanthemum; instead, he finds there Michael's two seconds, whom he had earlier asked to wait until the end of the morning session at court.

They are not well known to him; one is a cousin of the Baron Shadrach, who has changed into formal mourning for Hermes. The original strategy of using a relative of the boy as a second, which was to suggest the shame Narcissus has brought on the house of Shadrach, has now borne unexpected fruit, for the suggestion is now that Narcissus was to blame for the child's death. The implication brings out the sharpest and quickest side of Narcissus' personality: he is icy, polite, and incurious with the seconds, and asks them to take the matter up with Chrysanthemum, who has agreed to act as his second. The relative of Hermes, who is named Yuen, insists on speaking with Narcissus in person, however, and so with an ironic smile the latter waits in the doorway of the room, with his hands on his hips, for his guest to deliver himself.

"We must have some reply to bring back to your opponent. We do not wish to have to inform him that the Lord Narcissus is delaying in a matter of honor.

Narcissus ignores the implication. "I have already indicated my second."

"But he cannot decide for you what the weapons and mode of combat will be."

This is the crucial issue, for Narcissus is clearly Michael's superior in any of the martial arts. Part of Michael's desperate strategy is to cause Narcissus to lose face by making him choose a weapon in which he is obviously superior.

"Michael may have the choice, as far as I am concerned," says Narcissus, avoiding the trap and forcing his opponents' insistence and tactics to reveal themselves.

"It is your prerogative, however."

"One that I waive."

"Michael insists."

"Then really, gentlemen, I am helpless. If I must choose, then it shall be a Cockfight."

There is a hiss of indrawn breath; the ritual of the Cockfight is not usually employed for ordinary duels; normally Cockfights only take place between two Cocks or aristocrats, by mutual consent, with the result that the loser, if he does not die, automatically suffers loss of rank. It is a sort of violent blackball. The last Cockfight was over a hundred years ago: it is so terrible a ritual that it is seldom invoked. For the Cocks are human beings, in the brilliant feathers of their dueling wings, and their weapons are long steel spurs at ankle and wrist: it is the most fatal form of duel, physically, and it expresses a total and unmitigated hatred on both sides. Narcissus has re-escalated the conflict, and has put Michael once again on the defensive. It is a brilliant stroke, for it nullifies the sentence of the court that morning: losing the Cockfight would carry with it the same penalty whether the court had ordered it or not.

The ritual is a modification of the ancient Balinese game of cockfighting. The men of Bali, ordinarily rather passive, graceful, and even girlish in behavior, used the cockfight to express their sociosexual potency and test it against one another. The same pun between male fowl and the male genital is found in Balinese as in English and Martian.

A Balinese cockfight took place in the center of the village, on a designated day. The whole village would attend; in the middle of a circle of people the birds would tear each other to bloody rags in seconds with razor-sharp steel spurs bound to their feets. Any given cockfight divided the community into two factions, and the members of one faction wagered against the members of the other according to an intricate and stylized method for determining the odds. An elaborate and formulaic set of moods and behaviors accompanied every phase of the ritual. The winner was the winner not only in terms of his own wager, but also in terms of symbolic sexual potency, face, and social recognition. A loser was temporarily a psychosocical nobody. The anthropologist who investigated the ritual was struck by the way in which the owner of a cock treated the bird as an external projection of his own selfhood, fondling it with a narcissistic and languid dreaminess, provoking its fighting spirit, squatting with it between his knees and thrusting it forward suddenly again and again.

Many of the psychic and social implications of the Martian Cockfight resemble closely those of its original. Much of the etiquette remains the same: the apparent indifference of the principals, the refusal to make explicit the social conflicts and factionalization that the cockfight represents, the avoidance of each other's eyes.

Narcissus' offer of this form of combat carries with it sexual implications, for Cockfighting is primarily a male preserve. Narcissus, as a hermaphrodite, is, so to speak, offering sexual odds, for he has no formal training in the art. It is the one area where Michael may well have more skill than Narcissus, at least in the specific techniques of it that can be isolated from those of flying and knife-fighting. Narcissus is being sexually unconventional in proposing such a form of combat; yet again, he is cleaving to his own aesthetic style, of daring, arrogance, almost bad taste.

Michael's seconds, after a few moments of silence, attempt to dissuade Narcissus from the course he has chosen. But he acts as though he does not understand the seriousness of his proposal, and brushes aside their objections. He is exhausted, manic.

"I leave the time of our rendezvous to Lord Michael," he says. "As for the place, may I suggest the Great Canyon of Coprates."

Another shock. The weather conditions of the Canyon are the most violent on the planet; flying there would be suicidal for anyone who was not an expert. Again, Narcissus waves aside the protests of his guests. Once or twice in the past Cockfights have been held in the Canyon between inveterate enemies: battles which left no survivors, and which were the stuff of poetry and story for years afterward. Thus there is precedent for Narcissus' suggestion, but at the same time he is inviting distinguished and risky comparisons, and seems in danger of pretentiousness. Still, a good artist can use pretensions themselves as one of his materials.

"If you have no more to communicate, gentlemen, then I am sure there is no need for us to detain you any longer," says Narcissus; and the seconds are ushered out by Chrysanthemum, who has silently enjoyed their discomfiture. However, when he returns to Narcissus he is grave.

"Brilliantly done, my dear, but don't you think you're going too far? It all sounds frightfully dangerous. You don't expect Michael to collapse under the strain, surely? He's too stupid."

"No. I'm quite serious. By the way, have you seen Cleopatra?"

7.

The House of the Broken Wall

CLEOPATRA LEAVES THE courtroom before the tribunal is over, in a deadness of feeling that she has never before experienced. She feels as if she is carrying some large dead object inside her, like a strangled and drowned fetus, or like the knowledge of a disaster to come that she cannot quite remember. In the tribunal she felt the same admiration for her brother that she experienced when together they roamed the planet as children, uncontrolled, brilliant, sophisticated, frightened by their own wantonness; but this time the dead torso of Hermes comes between her and her brother; it is as if their wickedness were *proved* by the suicide, as if they were no longer playing a game, or as if in a game someone had been horribly injured. Narcissus, as we have seen, has only been thrust farther into his own gay and desperate arrogance; but Cleopatra has been wounded in some deep way, and even the thought of her brother makes her feel physically nauseated, as well as faintingly afraid on his behalf.

Certainly she cannot bear to be in his presence. She tries various parts of the City: they are all tainted. She returns briefly to Eleuthera; it is full summer now, the place is empty, smells of sun-warmed wood, but is too full of her brother's character and fragrance; at last she goes to the house in Rennet, telling nobody of her purpose, and takes up residence there alone.

It is late autumn in this northern latitude. The small city lies in shallow hills, lightly wooded; the brilliant orange of early Fall is past, and now the woods are bare or wear a handsome integument of brown, maroon, and purple, tipped with silver-grey.

The house is in the outskirts of the town, near a temple of Freya, in a slightly rundown district where the ways are muddy and the gardens unkempt. It is a large, rambling structure of stone and wood, with broken statuary, choked ponds, wild and unweeded flowerbeds, and an outer wall of drystone that has fallen down in several places. At night under the cold moon (flying along near the horizon), the dried stalks of rosebay willow-herb and docks, and the light heads of teazels, glimmer iridescently; darker patches of rhododendron look like crouching invaders. The house is cold, with half-empty rooms and clocks in hallways.

Cleopatra wanders through the rooms restlessly, her long chin vulpine, her eyes bright as fever. She wears a great gown of brown and purple, her hair is unbound and uncombed and flows over her shoulders. She fears that by some witchcraft she has unconsciously been the agent of Hermes' death, and explores again and again with the delicate weapons of her mind the world of the uncanny that lies so close behind the sunlit surfaces of the will. She relives in one way and another, technological and empathetic, the last agony of the boy, his appalling altruism, his simplicity, his ultimate insight. She is hindered, however, by the goddess, from finding out Venus' part in the affair; and the missing information gives the mystery an even darker and more unnatural cast.

Autumn deepens gradually into winter. Cleopatra's mood loses its frenzy and wildness, becomes more elegiac. She makes no attempt to contact her brother, though the sense of loss is more and more poignant. She is cared for by the homely and solicitous Mrs. Bottomly, who lives down the street in a well-kept frame house.

One day the sky dawns a dirty white, with the hint of a darker shadow across one half of the horizon. The air is very cold. Untrimmed dead roses hang by the whitewashed outbuildings; dead chyrsanthemums, almost choked with weeds, loll in the garden paths. There is a smoky smell in the air. Cleopatra wanders shivering in the terraces until she is seen by Mrs. Bottomly and scolded for her negligence.

"Now then, my lady, you naughty girl, you'll catch your death. Come on in for mercy's sake. What'll Master Narcissus think of me if I let you freeze out here." With a look at the sky: "There'll be snow, I shouldn't wonder. In your summer wrap too!" Indeed, Cleopatra is wearing little more than a thin green silk gown, bound about the waist with a white *obi*.

Later that afternoon it does indeed begin to snow: at first, a minute prismatic dust of crystals which glitters almost imperceptibly in the early lamplight, later a downward rush of icy flakes; at last, the slow, dreamy descent (or as if the ghostly outbuildings themselves were floating upward) of hugh bales of white, a foot or two across, held together by an impalpable structure, lit to yellow at the windows. On Mars the accumulation of snow crystals is much slower than on Earth, as the lower gravity makes available a longer time for a flake to rise and fall through the clouds, gathering material from their icy breath. Therefore it is not unusual to find snowflakes as much as three feet across, but so delicate they are scarcely more than a frozen concatenation of vapor.

Rapidly the snow rises to the windows, and above. The house is utterly silent. Mrs. Bottomly has left some hot dishes of food for her charge in the big kitchen (a meal which goes uneaten) and has returned home. All is dim and muffled. Crazy masts and crenellations of snow have built themselves on posts and branches, the city bears a gentle and insensible mask.

She plays a piece of music from her brother's favorite song-cycle: they have no gramophone in Rennet, so the music is reproduced by direct vibration of the air. Its title is *The Lonely One in Autumn:*

> *Mists of Fall drift bluely on the water;*
> *The grass stands frozen in its whitish rime;*
> *As if, in thought, an artist were to scatter*
> *A dust of jade on summer's leaving time.*
>
> *The flowers' scent is flown; a colder wind*
> *Buckles the stems. The faded golden petal*
> *Of the Lotus closes in the pond.*
> *My heart is tired. The lamp-flame will not settle;*
>
> *It beckons me to sleep. I come to you,*
> *My trusted resting-place, yes, give me rest,*
> *I need new strength. My heart's autumnal guest,*
> *These lonely days, outstays its time; and you,*
>
> *The Sun of love, will you no longer shine*
> *And with your warm face dry the tears on mine?*

The reader may well feel that Cleopatra, by working herself up with this sort of thing, is fashioning tragedy into sentimentality; there may even be a sense that she is enjoying what she is doing. In the words of a great poet, discussing Cleopatra's namesake,

". . . we cannot but perceive that the passion itself springs out of the habitual craving of a licentious nature, and that it is supported and reinforced by voluntary stimulus and sought-for associations, instead of blossoming out of spontaneous emotion."

Permit me to quote the comments of an obscure twentieth-century critic on the subject of Coleridge's protests:

"Of course the idea of self-creation, of self-stimulus, would shock a Romantic: we should be 'wisely passive' before Nature. But here, I think, Cleopatra may be right and Coleridge wrong. Coleridge's genius penetrates to the heart of Cleopatra—he is aware of her licentious (etymologically 'free') nature, her 'voluntary' (i.e. self-directed) self-stimulus; his choice of the word 'spon-

taneous,' from Wordsworth, is almost dazzlingly il-
luminating; it is not his inability to remain content with
half-knowledge that is at fault, but the inappropriate
moral construction he gives to his insight. 'Spontaneous
emotion' is a broken reed, as the author of the *Dejection
Ode* should have known: the innocence and directness he
wants cannot be achieved by a retreat from knowledge
and self-awareness into a childish ignorance, but must be
sought at the very heart of self-awareness, knowledge,
'voluntary stimulus.' If we are really to find an existential
freedom, it will not be on the path we have already
traversed: not in instinctive acts of self-preservation in an
environment hostile to survival, the panacea of the twentieth-century novelist; not in a Romantic 'spontaneity' of
emotion—mere misdirected libido—; not even in reason
and objectivity: but only in the imaginative hypertrophy
of our own self-awareness so that we do not only know
ourselves, Socratically, but *create* ourselves and each
other, imaginatively, from moment to moment. Perhaps
such freedom is not a good thing: but it is achievable only
in the way I have described."

This critique contains the germ of an idea which I see at
the heart of my Mars. Cleopatra is indeed voluntarily
stimulating herself with the pathos of the situation; this is
the whole point of the stresses of a status-conflict. An idea
of tragedy which necessarily implies the absence of self-
awareness is a limited and inadequate one.

Again she summons music from the air: another piece
by Gustav Mahler, to the words of the German late Romantic poet Friedrich Rückert:

> I've altogether lost the way of the world
> Where once much wasted time I led;
> It's been so long since last on it I called,
> Indeed, it may well think I'm dead.
>
> And so it's surely not my place to ask
> Whether it holds me live or dead;
> I cannot surely take the world to task
> For dead to it I am indeed;

Dead to the turmoil of the world I rest
In a still country I'm at home;
Alive here only, in my heaven-nest
In this my love, in this my poem.

8.

The Boy in the Bed-Chamber

ONE DAY WHILE the snow is still thick on the ground Cleopatra, wandering through the muffled rooms whose ceilings are lit white by the snow, happens on a sturdy young man lighting a fire in a grate. She comes up behind him silently and watches while he burns his large, clownish hands and curses under his breath in a strong dialect. Suddenly he feels her perfume steal over him—he is not insensitive—and starts guiltily, looking up with honest blue eyes.

"Oh, ma'am, you gave me a shock."

"Who are you?"

"Matthew, ma'am."

"I see, Mrs. Bottomly's son. She's told me a great deal about you." He blushes to his fair eyebrows. "Where is your mother?"

"She couldn't come, my Lady. She had to go to one of her meetings, so she sent me to do for you, ma'am. She didn't tell you because she didn't want to disturb you, you being so downcast and wrapped up in yourself, like . . ." He breaks off, blushing again. Mrs. Bottomly is a spiritualist, and attends séances in which the souls of departed relatives really and truly return, giving messages and advice.

Cleopatra smiles at him and tousles his hair. "You poor boy, you don't have to be afraid of me. I won't eat you."

He is not a pretty boy, but he has a clumsy charm, muscular and dutiful, with a broad, pleasant face and a smell of snow about him.

Some days later she sees him again, out by the woodshed, carrying large baulks of wood. When he enters the house she asks him to come and talk to her.

"What about, ma'am? I don't know anything about anything. What could *I* say to *you*?"

"Just tell me about your friends, your relatives, your school. What do you do in winter?"

"Oh, we go sledging, and we fly a bit too, though it's cold; and we bundle, too," he says, shyly.

"What's bundling, for heaven's sake?"

"Well, when we're courting, a boy will take his girl out in the hills in winter and stay out there for two or three days. It's the custom."

"Isn't it terribly cold?"

"That's where the bundling come in, ma'am. We wrap up in a big warmsuit, see, and bury ourselves half with snow."

"But why? Can't you do it at home?"

"There's things you don't like to do with your parents in the house. And then it brings us luck. 'Bundle and never part,' we say; it means if you've bundled with the girl you marry, you'll have a happy marriage."

"How charming. What about freemartins?"

"Oh, they do it too, with us or with the girls."

"Can you go bundling with anyone?"

"If both people want to."

"Could you do it with me?"

"Oh, ma'am!"

"Really, Matthew. I'm not joking. Could you do it with me?"

Over the last months she has become paler, and with the lack of exercise and Mrs. Bottomly's substantial fare, a little flabby. She is wearing a red silk wrap which pulls

into little wrinkles about the softness of her bosom and
buttocks. She is like an Odalisque, extravagantly delicious, and she has not satisfied her physical desires for
many weeks.

Matthew is overcome. "What about Master Narcissus?" he stammers, looking for a means of escape, but
unable to keep his eyes from the opening of Cleopatra's
gown, where the silk sash, carelessly tied, is loosening
momentarily.

"If he finds out he'll be delighted with you for looking
after his sister so kindly and politely," she says, relentless.

"But . . ."

"Don't you like me, Matthew?"

"Oh, I *do,* ma'am, it's just that I don't know if I'll do
right for you, if you see what I mean."

"Let's try, then, shall we? Then if it's all right you can
take me bundling."

She leads him trembling to an upstairs room with a
great bed, covered with a brocaded red silk bedspread.
There she unbuttons his coarse brown shirt, revealing a
hard, stocky torso; she runs her hand down the front of
his breeches. He is almost unable to breathe; his heart
beats thickly. She helps him out of his remaining clothes.
It is a little cold, and he shivers. "Poor thing," she says,
and comes to him. The wrap slips open to reveal her
matchless beauty, delicate but voluptuous; she seals
herself against his body, and now, impatience itself, he
thrusts her down violently on the bed while she gasps with
faintness and surprise. The paroxysm is brief; afterward
he lies on the bed looking up at her with a dazed expression as she kneels above him.

"You see, you were fine," she says after a while. "Now
let's try it more slowly."

When it is all over Cleopatra becomes a little distant.
Matthew, at a loss, pulls on his clothes, and in an absent
and comic gesture, dusts his hands together like a work-
man. Cleopatra laughs. He is hurt.

"Aren't you going bundling with me, then?"

"Of course I am, you silly boy, but not now."

Next day Mrs. Bottomly appears, full of sly winks and

generalized expressions of thanks for "everything you've done for my boy." She hopes "he was found satisfactory" and exclaims about "the honor to the family." Cleopatra, amused and annoyed, finally asks her, "What on earth do you mean?" at which she blushes furiously and exclaims, "Oh ma'am!"

Matthew and his mother are natural-born human beings, not androids. They represent a large class on the planet: those who, unoriginal in their lives but with a strong inheritance of folk culture, find their fulfillment in the service of the Bloods. They are by no means underprivileged. Mrs. Bottomly has an immense country mansion, designed by herself with the help of the Vision along the lines of Twentieth-century Hollywood Gothic, a fashion that was in vogue when she was a girl, out in the hills to the North. The planetary planners have given the place an unusual spatial polarization, so that the traveler would be most unlikely to have the bad luck of coming across it, explaining this tactfully to Mrs. Bottomly as being in the interests of privacy. For some time she lived there, waited on hand and foot by artificial servants provided by the Vision; but at last she became bored and returned to the city where lived her friends in the psychic circle and the aristocrats who provided the essential sources of gossip. Mr. Bottomly had long since disappeared; having ambitions for a change in rank, he had decided on a change of identity and body, and migrated to Cleopolis. There, without talent, and failing to achieve the advancement he coveted, he committed suicide.

Some days afterward Matthew by prearrangement calls on Cleopatra with a sledge loaded with equipment, and extra winter clothes for his mistress. They trudge out into the white hills, their breath making ghosts in the air. After a few miles they come to a wooded slope where Matthew decides to stop. It is quiet and wild. Streamers of powdery snow slip from the branches. They eat a warm lunch from self-heating containers, and then push their way through the woods to the hilltop. It is a beautiful place. The sky is white, though darker than the snow; and below them is a tumbled wilderness of rounded hills, and a little lake whose green ice has been swept clean of snow by the wind. Brown needles of grass in thin clumps poke out through the whiteness, where they have not been nibbled by the hungry deer; here and there can be seen the prints of other animals, with one bright yellow stain of urine where a caribou relieved itself.

Matthew is pleased, for he has brought a hunting-bow, and has promised to teach Cleopatra the skill of it (Narcissus has never got around to teaching her himself, though he is a master of the art, and she has often begged him to).

They spend the afternoon sledging, breathless, red-faced, and with spiracles of ice in the nostrils. In the evening they eat a hearty meal of snowshoe rabbit, shot by Matthew to Cleopatra's dismay and edification, and cooked by him over an open woodfire. Afterward he sings her the simple folksongs of the region, to the sharp chords of the guitar. She has become quite entranced and docile, and the turbulence of the last months recedes a little.

At night they curl up together inside a double warm-suit. Like hibernating animals they perserve their life-warmth in a waste of snow. The next day passes in much the same fashion; they snowball each other (the white missiles tracing a flat Martian trajectory in the grey snow-sky), they skate, and afterward they cut a circular hole in the lake ice and draw forth fat and lively fish—lake-trout, pickerel, and Martian puppyfish.

They spend the next day or two at similar pursuits; but the time comes to leave, suggesting itself by invisible persuasions. They pack up and return to town; as they enter the suburbs their easy chatter becomes more formal and strangerhood settles between them once more.

The night after their return Cleopatra goes to bed feeling a complete absence of motive, a state too flat to be called misery. She thinks of calling Matthew to keep her company: but that has already been done, used up. She falls asleep without difficulty, being physically tired and healthy; but wakes again an hour or so after midnight with a spasm of terror, despair, and unutterable sadness.

It is very dark. She can hear a sound, like a wounded

animal or a human cough. The ceiling seems to be a mile away, covered with dark designs. Suddenly she notices a strange, familiar smell that she cannot quite recognize, an acid, metallic, yet organic smell, a little like blood or seawater. In utter fear she makes the room blaze with light. It is the same room, yet different. She cannot see anything out of the ordinary, but the sound persists, muffled yet so loud it shakes her, in the heartlessly brilliant light, a sound which she at once recognizes now as weeping—a heartbroken, inconsolable sobbing which gives no sign of abatement. And now she recognizes the smell, too, which has become unbearably strong. It is the smell of tears, tears dried by the fever of the skin and moistened anew, the raw inner smell of human feeling, obscene, unconcealed. Still she can see nothing but the ordinary furniture, which, however, seems to have taken on a sinister configuration. She rolls toward the edge of the bed: but the invisible source of the sound forestalls her—and at last she knows the hoarse voice that is sobbing so terrifyingly before her. It is the voice of Hermes. She swoons at that; as she does so she realizes with a rock-bottom sick satisfaction that now she will be entirely at the mercy of the thing in her room.

Yet when she recovers, the sound and the smell have disappeared, and the room, dark once more, contains the familiar night dust and clothes odors, the quiet of a winter dawn. But she is still nauseated with fear, and spends the rest of the night in the kitchen, in front of the stove, with a cup of cocoa.

In the morning she asks Mrs. Bottomly if she can join the spiritualist circle, and is accepted with surprise and delight. "It is an honor, ma'am." The next meeting is not for some days, and Cleopatra can scarcely contain herself until then. She sleeps in Mrs. Bottomly's house, in an old bed that had belonged to Mr. Bottomly. Matthew approaches her once but she looks at him as if he were a ghost, and he leaves her alone from then on.

The séance takes place in an underground room, much like a cave or vault, under the house of one of Mrs. Bottomly's friends. It is dimly lit with braziers: the heady, slightly nauseating fume of white-hot charcoal fills the air. There are three or four local ladies, a young man, and two hermaphrodites, both dressed to display a female orientation. One is middle-aged, and the other is barely adolescent, pimply, pale, and clumsy; she has a tendency towards albinoism and her slightly crazed eyes glow pinkly. The latter turns out to be the medium. There is something seedy and socially crippled about the gathering: spiritualism here as on old Earth carries a taint of unsoundness, enthusiasm, overconsciousness, personal weakness. Most of the company is dissatisfied with their social position but not talented enough to rise above it. Cleopatra conceals her fear and contempt; the group's attitude to her is a mixture of awe and an insolent assumption of equality, together with suspicion—perhaps there is something wrong or unrespectable about her if she would come to such a gathering.

After a few preliminaries they link hands; the medium enters her trance. In this state she possesses the capacity to enter the Vision and constrain it through a paralyzing psychic feedback into yielding the secrets it guards. Thus she can force it to reveal the subconscious activities of the personality-patterns of the dead, which remain stored forever with total accuracy in its memory circuits. After a few trivial messages the medium speaks to Cleopatra.

"Someone is trying to get through. Shall I let him?"

"Yes."

At once there is a loud clatter. The tray full of teacups which is waiting on the side suddenly comes alive; the cups and saucers fly through the air with terrible violence, shattering themselves on the walls. Cleopatra's forehead is cut with one of the shards. Next there is the sound of a great wind, and suddenly the room is full of a blowing flame like the inside of a blast furnace. Nobody is harmed, but some loose threads and hairs burn briefly, giving an unpleasant smell. Then it becomes dark, and there is the sobbing that Cleopatra had heard that night, and the smell of tears. Cleopatra is petrified with terror. She feels her hair, like one organism, stir and rise upon her head; and clings like a child to Mrs. Bottomly, who is next to her.

The medium speaks:

"It is Hermes. He does not wish to speak to you, but he has permitted me to tell you that he is displeased that you have deserted Narcissus; and especially that you have tried to avoid your destiny. He feels that he has separated you from your brother."

"I'll go back to him. Is there any more?"

"No . . . wait, there is something, that I can't quite make out . . . he says that your child is even now being carried in the womb . . . that, sterile, you are nonetheless fruitful . . . that you must bring up the child as the son of your brother, in memory of Hermes . . . that you must betray Narcissus once more before he passes away . . . that he will go where he cannot be followed."

Some of this reminds Cleopatra oddly of the prophecy of Gabriel—it seems so long ago—on his island in the Sporades. She still does not know what it means.

Nevertheless she obeys Hermes' desire, and the next day prepares to return to Cleopolis.

9.

The Black Flower

AFTER THE FUNERAL OF HERMES, Narcissus, realizing that his sister must have her privacy, makes no attempt to find her. He continues to live in the house in Cleopolis, but he withdraws more and more from society. He is back in practice again; with his old flying instructor he is beginning to master the art of Cockfighting. Using longer and longer spurs he has become increasingly adept at ripping the flying-dummy to shreds. The duel has been set some time ahead, in the month of Harmony, the northern spring equinox, when the weather conditions of the Canyon are least violent.

The funeral had been turbulent and painful: but now Narcissus has discovered a serenity or clarity which arises out of loss, a regularity of life beyond the extremes of passion.

Michael and Snow, too, continue to live in Cleopolis, though their friend Gunther, fully aware at last of the shame of his humiliation, has retired to his odd little house, full of chronometers and ships in bottles, on the Great Northern Canal. Snow has lost the brief gaiety of the early months of her pregnancy. The encounter with Narcissus has renewed all her ancient feelings for him, her pity and fear of his brilliant destructiveness, his fatal beauty. Of course she must conceal all this from Michael; counterfeiting the complacency of her state she draws on resources that cannot be renewed.

Michael, like his rival, is in training. Though he senses that all is not well with his wife, he avoids thinking about it and devotes himself to self-preparation. Physically he is stronger than Narcissus, and his instructor has advised him to capitalize on this fact. Although he never achieves real gracefulness, he becomes increasingly efficient. Often he consults Athena, who has become his divine confidante; and she accompanies him invisibly in his aerial maneuvers over the city. He has lost his old apprehension, despite the shock of Narcissus' choice of combat; and is now committing himself to the rôle of hero, insensitive, a little crazy. Snow finds no help there: she wanders among the blossoming trees of their garden, more and more heavily pregnant, a little sick from the perfume, thinking of Narcissus with both hatred and love. She has no illusions about his feelings for her: but the loss of illusions has never had much real effect upon human desire.

Venus, without a host to carry her to Narcissus, is able to visit him once as a succubus without arousing his suspicions; but the visit, the first time she has tasted him truly in the flesh, inflames her still more. She is almost ready now to reveal herself to him and risk the anger of Olympus by explicitly taking a human lover; she paces her mansion, feared by her servants. At last an expedient suggests itself to her.

Rokujo, now alienated altogether from Gunther, has been at Hermes' funeral, drawn there against all her training, not to triumph over her dead rival, but attracted by the sweet and sickly smell of guilt. The ceremony takes place at the Crematorium on an island in the center of Lake Tehuantepec; the island is connected to the rest of the park by a long causeway of beautifully laid and

mortised stone without mortar, along which the
pallbearers and mourners walk swiftly in the misty morning sunshine, their figures reflected in the slow, indiffer-
ent ripples of the lake. From the death temple there comes
the deep, almost tangible booming of the bell, struck by
the saffron-robed priests with a padded battering-ram.
Rokujo follows the cortège at a distance, in a correct
white kimono, almost stumbling in the tight-skirted gait
of the geisha, her face hidden with her fan.

Rokujo is still some way from the low summit of the
island when the cedar pyre bursts into flames. In the mild
light the fire is livid and harsh; as she approaches, the heat
of it glows her cheeks and makes her catch her breath.
After the pyre dies down the mourners turn one by one
and leave the island; Narcissus comes last, passing
Rokujo without giving any sign of acknowledgment.
When he is gone she casts herself to the ground in grief
and despair, and, sobbing, begs the goddess Amaterasu to
take her spirit; for she is still in love with Narcissus, and
the shame of it is more than she can bear. Nevertheless,
her fear of death is such that she cannot bring herself to
the resolution of suicide: she realizes she is essentially a
creature of this world.

It is Rokujo's desperation, not unobserved by Aphrodite, that serves as the goddess' means of access to
Narcissus. It is three months since the funeral. Rokujo is
in her apartment, which she has not left in all that time.
Her maid Aoi has tended her, compelling her to eat the
little rice cakes which are the only nourishment she will
accept. One evening—one of those heartlessly lovely
desert evenings of Cleopolis, a band of orange at the
horizon, saffron bars of light upon the walls—Aoi is
trimming up her mistress' coiffure when there is a sudden
aura of solemnity, and a new light blazes in the darkest
corner of the room, a white supernatural glow. Aoi turns
her body toward the light, shudders suddenly as if with
fear, and falls as if poleaxed. The light increases so that
even the sun is dimmed—it is like the rising of Phobos on
a misty afternoon—and takes form in the shape of the

goddess, dressed in white and looking both wanton and worthy of veneration. She radiates about her the full aura of her power, an undefined sexual excitement that affects even Rokujo, flushing her cheeks and quickening her heartbeat.

Nonetheless she confronts the goddess bravely:

"What have you done to my servant?"

"She is only in a swoon. She will wake and remember nothing."

"What do you want of me? Surely you must kow that I wish only to be left alone. What should I want of the goddess of Love?"

"You are bitter, my child; but do not underestimate the expedients of divinity. I have come to offer you what you most deeply desire."

"That is impossible."

"Remember that the one you love is of a hot spirit, very lecherous, and that he has not felt the touch of love for many months. He must surely visit a house of pleasure, and there, if you are desperate enough, and without pride, a meeting may be arranged."

There is a pause. Then:

"I will do anything you ask."

"I shall afflict him with longing tomorrow night, and when he comes to Cherry Blossom Street to find a woman of pleasure you shall meet him. I shall alter your appearance, so that you will not be recognized. And we must use a different apartment, or he will be suspicious."

"Why are you doing this for me, Lady? What have I done to deserve this generosity? Or is it something that I have not yet done?"

"As you have guessed, it is the latter. But I ask one thing only; that I may share your body when you encounter Narcissus."

Rokujo is shocked and surprised by this request.

"But why, Lady?"

"Even the goddess of Love is not immune to desire."

"Why should I help you to enjoy the one I love?"

"Why should *I* help *you* to enjoy him? We are helpless without each other. We must make the best of our plight."

"Very well, then." Both women sigh at that; there is suddenly a girlish and conspiratorial atmosphere in the room.

When Aoi recovers, Venus has disappeared.

"What happened, madam?"

"You fell asleep, darling."

"You seem different."

"I am. I have come to a decision." She tells her servant that she is going to attempt a bed-trick but does not mention the goddess. The servant girl is almost as excited as her mistress and joins in the planning. Narcissus' doom is sealed; a most perfidious plot is about to close around him.

The following evening Narcissus is struck with a sudden and at first indefinable desire. He has been thinking all day about Cleopatra; in their many quarrels she has never stayed away so long. He misses her, feels incomplete without her; remembers the sisterly and catty tenderness of their encounters. Restlessly he paces the house, till at last, on impulse, and against the advice of his flying-master, he puts on his wings and makes for Cherry Blossom Street.

There he walks under the lanterns for almost an hour, among the scents of flowers and a multitiude of lovely courtesans, male, hermaphrodite, and female. He is dissatisfied and wants none of them. At last he sees a woman who seems vaguely familiar in her bearing. She is attended by a maid. His attention is curiously drawn to her, as if little hooks had caught between them. She is not beautiful; she wears a plain dark red kimono of heavy silk, is plump and has a rather fat face. Still, there is a quality about her of attractive evil, a suggestiveness like the play of iridescence on something that has rotted, or the glow of dangerous radioactivity. Aphrodite, begotten by Zeus on the sea foam, has done her work well.

Narcissus approaches her. He notices that her eyebrows are unpleasantly thick, and meet across the middle of her forehead. She is *ugly*! As he comes closer the woman retreats; he pursues; the maid, who is elegant and beautiful but oddly flat in tone beside her mistress, comes back to talk to him.

"My mistress is not what you think her to be."

"Then why is she here in Cherry Blossom Street?"

"No reason. She may walk where she pleases."

"Let me talk to her."

"No."

"I shall use force."

Without a word Aoi yields the way, and Narcissus approaches the dark lady. He speaks a poem, choosing as a pretext a hanging basket of purple blossoms in an alleyway:

> *Is it an illusion*
> *that the black flower*
> *has the most heady perfume?*

She replies:

> *This flower's not like the others.*
> *Twinned and not itself, it's not for plucking.*

For a moment, obsessed now, Narcissus thinks she means that she is pregnant; his mind flies to Snow's rejection of him. But the image is of a genetically mutated flower, not of a fertilized one.

> *Like the flower, your words are dark,*
> *divided, unplucked, and not themselves.*

"It was not my intention to explain myself to you," she replies, dropping into ordinary speech. "What do you want of me?"

"I'm afraid in this setting it must be obvious."

"How strange you are. There are so many prettier blossoms to choose. I'm not sure I like your motives."

"I beg of you, lady. I am helpless. If you do not do what I ask, I may do something foolish."

"Well, I suppose we can't have that."

In dreamlike surprise Narcissus realizes that she is

giving in to his request. And so it proves. In a house in a part of the city he does not know he is initiated into terrifying and bewitching rites; he must call on energies beyond the human to remain in the realm of such perversion; it is a saturnalia of ugliness, a brutal, cannibalistic time. Aphrodite is at her full strength; and through Rokujo's changed and yet familiar body the great goddess works her skill, accumulated over five hundred years of sensuality. Even Rokujo herself is frightened, and wishes to withdraw from what is happening; but the goddess is too powerful, and the thing must run its course.

In his new obsession Narcissus dismisses his flying-instructor and gives up his Cockfighting practice, his custom of ink-drawing, and his peace of mind. He begs Rokujo (who has taken the name Murasaki, which means "purple," in honor of the dark flower to which Narcissus first compared her) to come and live with him in his house; and she obeys. Still under the control of Venus, altered in appearance and lent by her a diabolic attraction, she obeys Narcissus' perverted will.

As time goes by Narcissus realizes that Murasaki reminds him irresistibly of someone he knows. He denies this knowledge, but in their lovemaking, if it can be called "love," there is a quality of experience and abandon that he has experienced elsewhere. At last he can refuse it no longer—Murasaki reminds him of *Hermes*! It is an aspect of Hermes that always puzzled Narcissus, an agedness in feeling that came out only in sexual play and nowhere else. Murasaki has exactly the same quality. One day he mentions this fact to her:

"It disturbs me deeply, but you remind me of someone." Murasaki catches her breath. "Yes; my dead lover Hermes."

Murasaki shudders at this, and then suddenly pales. Her body is responding to two sets of reactions. On Rokujo's part, there is guilt, jealousy and relief: guilt, for she still feels responsible for Hermes' death; jealousy, for now she feels as if she is her own rival for Narcissus, where she had half-hoped that he would remember through this alien body his old love for Rokujo herself; relief, at not being found out. On Venus' part there is a simpler reaction: apprehension that Narcissus has penetrated her secret, and a more lively fear that Rokujo will guess from this that her body was not the first to be used for access to Narcissus. If Rokujo were to find out, she would surely expel Venus from her body forever.

Nevertheless, Rokujo remains unaware of Hermes' secret, and Narcissus interprets his own feelings as an expression of his guilt for Hermes' death. The relationship changes somewhat; Aphrodite withdraws herself slightly from participation in it, for fear of exposure.

About two months later Cleopatra returns in secret to the city. She goes to an apartment she keeps in the suburbs and dresses herself as if for a celebration. It is her birthday. She feels as though she were beginning her life anew. Over her now pale gold body she throws a great mantle of intricate grey lace; tying up her hair, she covers her head with a cap of white-gold lace, like a helmet of artificial hair, with tassels that hang down over her long cheeks. She is heavily made up in a fashion resembling that of the women's puberty ritual in equatorial Mars.

In the cool of the day she arrives at the entrance to the gardens of her house. Because it is her house as well as Narcissus', the privacy mechanisms do not respond to her presence. She passes through the aromatic shrubs, exuding clouds of giant bees; a gold light on everything, for Phobos is below the horizon; as she emerges from the obscurity of a huge magnolia she sees Narcissus himself bending over before the weathered cedar of the west wall of the house. She is about to run forward and greet him when someone she does not know comes out of the house. It is Murasaki. Cleopatra shrinks back.

She has never seen an uglier woman in her life. She is pouchy, with coarse black hair, a misshapen figure, a dirty, musty feeling about her. Despite the evening heat, Cleopatra shivers. Narcissus, who has been picking flowers, turns to Murasaki with a hangdog look.

"Flowers for you, my dear," he says. He sounds like a husband.

Cleopatra is horrified. Of course she had half-expected her brother to have found some woman or young man, or even another freemartin; but there is a quality—one could not call it *evil*—a quality of insidious vileness about this situation. At that moment the sun sinks, and Phobos rises: the golden glow disappears, and the scene is lit with ghastly blue. For a few seconds all three are apparently paralyzed: Narcissus holding out the flowers; Murasaki, with one hand in her hair, the other about to accept them; Cleopatra, unseen, in pale gray, her arms wrapped about herself.

Murasaki speaks: "Thank you Cissy. I'll put them in water. What shall we do tonight?"

Cleopatra almost faints. The nickname was private between her and her brother. Narcissus and Murasaki hear a gasp behind the tree, but by the time they investigate, Cleopatra has disappeared.

Back at her apartment, overcome by the passions of the last days, Cleopatra sinks onto a divan and lies there dazed, breathing shallowly. At last a great sob forces its way out of her, and she weeps openly for an hour. Gradually a new mood creeps over her: a hardness and bitterness, a steeliness that she shares with her brother, that is half-abandon.

In the next weeks she returns to her profession as an actress. She plays Electra, Antigone, Ophelia, with shocking irony and cynicism. She is a great success: Narcissus hears of it and goes to the theatre to see her. He has never seen her like that: she gives mad Ophelia an emphasis that suggests entirely new interpretations of the play. Afterward he tries to see her in her dressing room, but is denied entrance by the stagehands; and when he visits her at her apartment, her maid refuses to allow him in.

Shortly afterward the allies of Michael and Snow get wind of what has happened. One day Yuen, the cousin of Baron Shadrach who is acting as Michael's second, comes to call on her and is not refused; she is invited to dinner with Michael and Snow, who is now heavily pregnant;

and soon she has become part of the faction opposed to
her brother, is seen in the inns and coffee-houses they
frequent, is written up in their gossip columns. The
defection is highly damaging to Narcissus: virtually the
only Blood in the city who still supports him is Chrysanthemum. They are isolated; Chrysanthemum takes it
philosophically, and Narcissus, besotted with his "purple
flower," does not care. And so the time of the Cockfight
approaches, and Narcissus is not prepared.

BOOK III

1.
The Canyon

THE GREAT CANYON OF COPRATES is a series of immense cracks or ravines in the Martian sursface. To quote from Gunther's account of it in his *Introduction to Martian Morphology:*

"The existence of the Canyon was first revealed by the early Mariner 9 photographs in 1973, Old Earth Time. It is a major landform about four thousand kilometers long, one hundred kilometers across, and six kilometers deep; lying on, or a little to the south of, the equator, and roughly parallel to it. Actually the name 'Coprates' is not quite accurate: much of the Canyon lies in the area which used to be known as Tithonius Lacus.

"The west end of the Canyon is a wilderness of cracks, horst-blocks, and depressions originating in the foothills of the volcanic Tharsis Ridge. Following the Canyon eastward, we find that the system consolidates itself into a series of huge trenches that continue for about two thousand kilometers; then the Canyon turns northward, crosses the equator, and loses itself in an area of channel deposits on the southern shores of what is now the Northern Ocean.

"About two hundred million years ago the planet, previously dormant, began to develop an indigenous geological and climatic history, as radioactive elements in the planet's core began to release their energy. Actually Mars is in many ways a very 'young' planet; or perhaps it is better described as a 'late developer.' The great volcanoes sprang into being; certain layers of the mantle heated up sufficiently so that, with the assistance of the sun, the permafrost was melted. Under the Tharsis Ridge was a mass of hot magma, which supplied the infant volcanoes. The heat in the rock, combined with the warm equatorial latitude, caused catastrophic changes in the planet's crust. Millions of cubic kilometers of frozen gas and water locked up in the rocks were melted. The gas joined the new atmosphere; the water began to flow under the ground, eastward down the slope. These were not rivers, let it be understood; the effect was more like what can be observed when water-bearing sand and gravel, which have been frozen, begin to thaw, producing subsidence, slumping, and cracking, braiding and deposition. Henry David Thoreau observed such effects:

"'Few phenomena gave me more delight than to observe the forms which thawing sand and clay assume in flowing down the sides of a deep cut on the railroad through which I passed on the way to the village, a phenomenon not very common on so large a scale, though the number of freshly exposed banks of the right material must have been greatly multiplied since railroads were invented. The material was sand of every degree of fineness and of various rich colors, commonly mixed with a little clay. When the frost comes out in the spring, and even in a thawing day in winter, the sand begins to flow down the slopes like lava, sometimes bursting out through the snow and overflowing it where no sand was to be seen before. Innumerable little streams overlap and interlace one with another, exhibiting a sort of hybrid product, which obeys halfway the law of currents, and halfway that of vegetation. As it flows it takes the form of sappy leaves or vines, making heaps of pulpy sprays a foot or more in depth, and resembling, as you look down on them, the laciniated, lobed, and imbricated thalluses of some lichens; or you are reminded of coral, of leopards' paws or birds' feet, of brains or lungs or bowels, and excrements of all kinds. It is a truly *grotesque* vegetation, whose forms and color we see imitated in bronze, a sort of architectural foliage more ancient and typical than acanthus, chicory, ivy, vine, or any vegetable leaves; destined perhaps, under some circumstances, to become a puzzle to future geologists.'

"This highly active period in Mars' geological history provided the basis on which the Terraformers were to set to work. Already there were sizable amounts of gas and vapor locked up in the north and south polar icecaps, which had been released by outgassing from Nix Olympica and the Tharsis volcanoes. These icecaps displayed a characteristic laminar structure, as a result of the displacements of the planet's rotational axis due to the new disturbances of the planetary mantle. As the spin axis shifted, the laminated plates formed concentrically about each successive position of the poles.

"Hence the great Canyon in Coprates is not an isolated geological freak, but an important variation of the main theme of Mars' morphological history. The tectonics of the Canyon are the tectonics of the planet itself."

Since the Terraforming Period the Canyon has been transformed again, mainly as a result of changes in the weather. To quote Gunther again, this time from *The Coprates Canyon: A General Study*:

"Terraforming, in its early stages, produced conditions approximating that of the hot Tharsis area *all over the planet*. It was only with great care that such major features as Nix Olympica and the Canyon itself were not obliterated in the general chaos. With the kindling of Phobos temperatures rose all over the planet, and vast quantities of water were released, especially in the mountainous tropical area at the western end of the Canyon. Torrents foamed down the huge ravines, eroding them still deeper and wider, depositing extensive alluvial fans to the northeast.

"As the weather settled down a curious and unexpected

climatic effect began to make itself felt. The highlands
around the Canyon remained relatively cool and dry; but
the Canyon itself seemed to concentrate within itself the
typically hot and wet equatorial weather. On the other
hemisphere of Mars the gradation from tropical through
subtropical to temperate climates is much gentler. Thus it
is that Cleopolis has relatively mild weather, while the
Canyon, only a hundred kilometers north, is hot, humid,
and stormy.

"The climatology of the Canyon makes a fascinating
study in itself. To begin with, the entire airmass tends to
flow in the opposite direction from the planet's rotation
from west to east. Within this general westward motion
there are powerful and violent convection currents rising
from the hot damp floor of the Canyon into the cooler
regions above, where extensive cumulo-nimbus clouds
are formed and the moisture is precipitated. Vast
amounts of static electricity are generated, to be dis-
charged in almost continuous thunderstorms; meanwhile the air drawn down the sides of the Canyon, to
replace the rising airmass in the center, often reaches
hurricane force.

"At the bottom of the Canyon the great river
Ouroboros rages, fed by cataracts which plunge
thousands of meters down the Canyon walls, and which
have carved their own canyons back from the main
trench.

"As one would expect, the Canyon floor is thick with
vegetation: rainforest, with a highly complex ecology.
Several new species have evolved to deal with the unusual
weather conditions: Xiorns, Muorns, Lambdaorns,
Piorns; Egg-Trees, Lungs, Giant Cabbages, Treeferns,
Flying Timber, Milks, and Barrels. Because of the limited
light combined with the low gravity, the funguses and
fungoids have had an evolutionary advantage, and the
explorer is always encountering new multicolored
puffballs, some with a degree of mobility and primitive
sense organs. Huge tree-ears, toadstools, poisonous and
hallucinogenic mushrooms, phalluses, and spores as big
as insects abound.

"As for higher forms of life, the Canyon's gallery-forests and swamps are the domain of the reptile. Through a combination of genetic engineering and natural devolution the ancient dinosaurs of Earth have reappeared, but with increased size because of the lower than Earthly gravity. There are Neobrachiosaurs weighing many hundreds of tons, and Neotyrannosaurs with teeth the length of a tall man. Because of the high winds the Pterosaurs have evolved into sturdy, short-winged forms resembling the manta-rays; they are deadly, with shovel-shaped heads and razor-sharp bills.

"Not many people live in the Canyon: there are a few tribes of Mystics, albino death-worshippers who experience dying over and over again and have developed an incomprehensible doctrine of terror as the only true contact with Being. There are also some isolated Mad people; like the Sporades, this is one of the areas they particularly choose for their exile. There are usually some tourists, big-game hunters and the like; but the human component of this ecology is relatively insignificant."

Gunther is wrong, of course, in this last formulation; actually the Canyon is as highly artificial as a minuet or a tankful of tropical fish; but he may be excused his scientific bias. Certainly, on the face of it, Narcissus has chosen, or has been forced into, a scenario that has all the heroic, existential, and aesthetically serious elements of Michael's *Weltanschauung*; but in a profounder sense the Canyon nicely expresses the perversity, waywardness, complexity, and unsoundness of Narcissus. However, the superficial can often be more important than the profound.

The actual site of the duel is the flat top of a gigantic mesa which rises out of the boiling turbulence of the Canyon floor into the clearer air above. Here on this three-acre tableland the weather is much like that of Cleopolis, only a little warmer and windier. Thick clumps of fine gold-and-green grass cover the ground, with an occasional arbutus and euphorbia. There is a fresh smell, as of herbs. The place is neutral, a trifle tedious. In its center is shallow valley a hundred meters across, which is an excellent place to sleep.

The morning before the Cockfight Snow, now past term, awakes crying bitterly from a bad dream. Michael, who has noticed his wife's unhappiness these last months but in his odd calmness and readiness has been unmoved by it, asks her to tell the dream.

"I dreamt that the baby was not yours, but Narcissus's. We were climbing the mountain, and when we got to the top, and I broke my leg, you went off without me. Narcissus came and took me to the mansion of the goddesses. We made love, and conceived the child. Then I dreamt that I was very hungry, and I was eating and eating as if I had a hole inside me. I was eating whole chickens like larks, crunching up the bones. Then I dreamt that you and Narcissus were fighting in a horrible green place, with no way out and the sound of drums beating. I was very frightened, but also, in another part of my mind, pleased. Then Narcissus hit you so that his arm went right through you and out the other side, and you died. I had a terrible wave of grief, it forced me to wake up.

"I think I know what the dream means, but I don't want to."

Michael is silent. The nightmare affects him as if it were his own; and he too is reluctant to touch it. "It's probably just one of your cravings, and anxiety about tomorrow," he says falsely.

"I suppose so," she agrees hopelessly.

The morning of the duel itself is bright and clear. Two small knots of people are gathered on the plateau, wearing the customary black. A little wind rustles in the tussocks. The sky above is very blue, with a few strands of cirrus pinkish-yellow in the morning light. For once the Canyon itself is clear of cloud: an immense pool of hazy air, kilometers deep, the floor too far down even for vertigo to have any meaning. It looks very peaceful: gallery after gallery, shelf after shelf of green, the silver thread of Ouroboros winding through it; occasional buttes, mesas, and pinnacles struggle up into the sharper air, casting vast shadows along the ravine, their bases covered with vegetation. Where the sun's rays have not yet penetrated, the jungle is a dark indigo; banks of mist are still rising from the forest, plumes and whorls of it lit to fiery orange by the sun; in the shadow the fog is the color of the sky. A peaceful green hell; around midday it will be a sunlit chaos full of mindless murder and the terrible gaiety of the lower species: a vision for a Douanier Rousseau or a drugged and hysterical Arthur Rimbaud.

2.

The First Day

BEFORE THE DUEL there is a ceremonial attempt at reconciliation. Yuen comes over to the "injured" party, which consists of Chrysanthemum, two servants, and Narcissus. Yuen's mediation in the quarrel is dismissed, but a counteroffer is proposed.

"It has come to our ears," says Chrysanthemum, who is wearing the traditional top hat and morning-coat, "that the challenged party's wife is at present entering the first stages of labor. Let us propose a postponement; we recognize the claims of humanity, after all, and wish to do nothing to separate a man from his wife at such a time."

Yuen replies: "The onset of labor was two weeks past the expected term. Nevertheless my principal desires to finish this business at once, if his opponent is still willing. He wishes me to communicate to you that there will be time afterward for him to see his child."

There is laughter at this; Yuen departs, and the principals are brought together for the last time. They draw lots as to which sides of the pinnacle they will be assigned; they must, according to the ground rules drawn up and agreed to by Yuen and Chrysanthemum, leave the pinnacle at the same moment, on opposite sides, north and south. (Because of the prevailing east wind, the east-west axis was deemed to give one combatant an unfair advantage.) Narcissus, pale and breathing hard, takes the long straw and is given the southern position. Michael is stolid, expressionless.

Now the duelist strip for combat. When they are completely naked the differences between their physiques can clearly be seen. Michael is massively muscled about the shoulders and thighs: he has been in constant practice and the betting in Cleopolis has been overwhelmingly in his favor. His body is like a useful instrument, integrated, compact, insensitive. He has become an object, existential, like a stone or a tree, taking its place under the sun with other structures, whether of flesh or steel. He is like a sculpture in which all the doubts and self-consciousness of the sculptor have been lost, only the moment of crystalline act remaining.

By contrast Narcissus' body, gone very slightly to fat, is the embodiment of the irremediable glory and weakness of total self-awareness. He is shivering slightly in the cool morning air; his breasts with their rosy nipples, the slight womanliness of his hips and loins, carry that hint of an unhealthy intimacy and knowledge that the hermaphrodite's body always suggests. He is pale with a flush at the throat. His hair, in raven and rainbow curls, clusters to his nape and neck. His beauty strikes the onlookers with terror and pity; it catches the morning sun like a pale gold flame. Yet in the smallest movement Narcissus displays the subordination of flesh to will, the balance or metastability of the dancer or professional fighter: all infused with fatal knowledge, he (or she) is a fallen archangel, a satire of Being that counters mere fact with a self-destructive beauty.

Now their seconds bind on their spurs, each thirty centimeters long, slivers of titanium-steel sharpened and polished to the consistency of semitransparent stone or flint, with slightly curved edges like razors, weighing a few grams apiece and as thin as flensing knives. They have sturdy butts at right angles to the blade, by which they are fastened to the wrist and ankle.

Next they put on their dueling-wings. Michael's are black, with a soft anodized glitter and a rustle of sable foil; Narcissus' are characteristically of all colors, some glowing, some flashing, some matte; there is an airy tinkle or chime, a crawling of points of light, a seething on the ground about him.

Clumsy now they both approach their respective edges, with the odd wading gait of the fully accoutered duelist. By this time most of the mist has cleared, and the dreamy depths below are open in detail to the fresh light. Everything is lucid, tiny. In the middle distance below them one or two minute incipient clouds, with sharp and perfect edges and distant unconnected shadows, have formed: these will later become storm clouds of unguessable fury. Narcissus, like a mythical bird, stands on the edge and looks awhile. He feels a very faint tremor of vertigo, of nausea.

Now the aura of the goddesses begins to grow about the combatants. It has been agreed that each may enlist the limited help of his divine patroness; this expedient provides them with superhuman powers of vision, foresight, and endurance but does not ultimately affect the outcome of the struggle. Superior mind, strength, skill, and spirit on the part of one of the principals will still result in victory. Further, the help of goddesses creates a finer spectacle: and the combined Press of the planet is invisibly present, with its recording devices, its ace reporters, and its air of meretricious excitement.

Michael has chosen Athena as his patroness; Narcissus Aphrodite. Above Michael the Aegis begins to form, faintly, like a stormcloud or a shield; electrical discharges seethe and go out like glowworms in the air, leaving a faint odor of ozone. Meanwhile Narcissus himself begins to fill with pure white light, which grows swiftly until it is too bright to see and the armorlike wings with all their colors seem to have become translucent. In a moment the light dies down. Both now dismiss their Idiot Guardians for the duration of the fight.

There is a sharp report; the judge has fired the first

warning gun, according to ancient ritual. A light arrangement of smoke flits across the plateau, with a choking smell of fire. The silence that follows is more intense. A few seconds go by. Another shot goes off. Michael tenses on the brink, his toes clasping like a diver's. Narcissus on the other hand is suddenly distracted. He has noticed a tiny red flower growing at the cliff edge, whose background is twenty kilometers of jungle. He drops to one knee to pluck it, disengaging his right hand from its wing, and as he does so the final gunshot goes off. Michael disappears over the edge. Narcissus rises to his feet dreamily, holding the flower. Suddenly he becomes alert; weighs the situation for a moment; and plunges into the immense gulf of air below him.

At first he is simply falling, the wind rushing past his ears and batting his hair behind him. Having achieved flying air-speed, he gradually brings his control surfaces to bear and levels off in a long zoom. The cliff is already a kilometer away. Now he begins to fly steadily away from the pinnacle, rising slightly but making no attempt to gain height quickly. He knows he can cover distance quicker than Michael, though Michael is distinctly stronger and can gain height more swiftly; and Narcissus has lost a crucial three or four seconds in the takeoff.

Height in this game is an essential factor. The combatant who is above can dictate the action; he has accumulated a gravitational capital which he can spend when he likes. Moreover, he can impose a continuous levy of effort on his opponent, who must take pains not to put himself in a vulnerable position. Further, the "lower" antagonist has a disadvantage of visibility; a human being flies face downward, and it is an effort to keep an eye on an object above him.

Indeed, Michael has immediately made it his business to gain height. He has veered almost immediately to the eastern end of the pinnacle, where the prevailing wind is forced upward in a continuously rising column of air. His strategy was to contest this advantage immediately with his rival; Narcissus' ceding of it was beyond his most optimistic hopes. He has, moreover, a futher advantage.

A flyer who approaches the edges of the Canyon is in danger of being caught in the powerful down-draughts that pour down the sides to replace the rising air in its center. Thus Narcissus cannot afford to go too far.

What Michael does not realize is that Narcissus is heading directly for one of the growing clouds that have begun to form. Those clouds are the visible signs of thermals, powerful rising air currents generated by patches of warmer ground that heat the air above them and cause it to become lighter than the colder air surrounding it. Clouds form where this rising air cools with decompression and the water vapor dissolved in it condenses into droplets. On Mars a phenomenon known as "stacking" takes place: a whole series of small cumulus clouds will form one above the other, as the rising air crosses different pressure and temperature zones. As Narcissus approaches the rising air a new cloud begins to form above the first. His gamble has paid off.

Michael, seeing what has happened, and realizing that his own rising air current has given him as much height as it can, turns to pursue his enemy. In a steep glide he rushes down upon Narcissus: it is almost a stoop, like the attacking charge of a gerfalcon. Both combatants now call on their supreme energies, and as they close the aura of the goddesses surrounds them more and more: a strange vigor and clarity of eyesight suffuses them, and they breathe more deeply, as if they were drinking the air as well as inhaling it. Indeed, without the goddesses' help neither would have been capable of the intricate calculations that these maneuvers demand, and both would already have lost sight of each other. Of course neither combatant is permitted to use the Vision directly: each must rely on the help of his patroness.

Suddenly Narcissus begins to rise swiftly, with a blow of air beneath him that almost pulls off his wings. At that moment Michael arrives, traveling at over a hundred and fifty kilometers per hour. He rakes across Narcissus' back; but Narcissus at the last moment spills air from his wings and the spur of Michael's right ankle merely slices across the secondary feathers of Narcissus' left wing.

Fragments of torn foil glitter as they fall from the conflict. But Michael has overshot the thermal and Narcissus takes his opportunity. Diving steeply he catches his enemy and with a wrist-spur lays open a long shallow welt on Michael's back. Michael screams, then is silent. Narcissus recovers from his dive, re-enters the thermal, and begins to rise in towering circles. However, he notices that he has lost a good deal of lift. One of the hair-like tendons which keep the primary feathers in position has been cut by Michael's attack, and one of his primaries is as a result providing less lift. By shifting his fingers he is able to correct the deficiency, but now he is deprived of considerable maneuverability. He circles upward for a while, followed by Michael, who stays carefully behind him so as to make a surprise attack impossible.

It is now afternoon, and the day is getting hotter. Above both combatants the cloud has grown to gigantic proportions and has turned to purple, the characteristic shade of the Martian nimbus cloud. There are already faint crackles and bumpings in the air from internal discharges, tapping at their naked ears, midway between earth and heaven. The air is very humid, and has taken on the slightly fetid grassy smell of the jungle below.

Narcissus is already tired, being out of training, and his loss of maneuverability robs him of his greatest asset. Nevertheless he will not play a waiting game; he squanders his advantage in a sudden dive. At that moment the long-expected storm breaks out; the air is full of enormous hailstones and the raw, immediate smashing of thunder, as myriad bolts of lightning make contact between the upper and lower cloud. Above and below there are yet other clouds "stacked" down to the valley floor and up to the stratosphere. It is a series of huge batteries discharging.

Narcissus glows with the white light of Venus. Like a thunderbolt himself, he drops a thousand feet in seconds, the whole world of hail around him lit to its depths by lightning. Michael sees him coming, turns tightly and deliberately stalls. For a few seconds he is almost on his back, his spurs directed at his enemy: a trick taught him by his flying-master. But he is now falling freely: as the antagonists encounter each other, in a savage flutter of wings, they plunge into the lower cloud, to be lost to sight.

There they are separated by buffeting winds and lose all knowledge of where they are. The dim light is greenish: they are in the birthplace of thunder and lightning. Narcissus has sustained a slight wound across the breast and another on the thigh. Michael is deeply gored in the flank.

When they emerge from the cloud they are twenty or thirty kilometers apart. They are both exhausted. According to the rules temporary truces are permitted so that both sides may recuperate; such a respite is suggested by the judge and agreed to by both combatants. They return, limping through the air, to the plateau, as evening begins to fall. It is agreed that they will be permitted to heal their wounds and repair their equipment that night, and resume the combat next day. Like loving brothers they approach each other and tenderly each divests the other of his wings, performing the office of servant; they unbind each others' spurs, still caked with the blood of him who serves his enemy, and apply a healing salve to each other's wounds.

Gay tents have been set up on the grassy swale in the midst of the plateau. From their conical tops flutter the emblems of their houses: the snake and phoenix of Narcissus and the rods and lions of Michael. Between them a trestle table has been set up: here the antagonists sit across from each other, with no others present save the servants who bring them food. They feast lightly on the delicacies that have been prepared by Chrysanthemum's excellent cook. With great gentleness Michael and Narcissus offer each other the choicest morsels. The storm has ceased and a blue evening, lit by the racing brilliance of Phobos, settles down with a line of bright purple in the western horizon. Candleflames in fine glass jars flutter among the viands. The faces of the antagonists glow with the warm light, serious, very young, intent on their meal. When they have finished they embrace and retire to their tents.

The salves that have been applied contain growth and repair hormones that close their wounds almost at once. By morning there will only be scars and a faint itch to bear witness to the bitter pains of the previous day. Before retiring Narcissus repairs the delicate fabric of his wings, imping in new secondary feathers and reconnecting the primary tendon that had been broken, annealing it with a tiny laser torch.

3.
The Second Day

THE NEXT DAY dawns hotter than the first: there is a faint mist or miasma over the Canyon, an almost unbearable humidity. The air has the quality of human flesh, smothering and overclose.

This time the duelists begin to spar almost at once. As on the previous day Michael has planned his moves meticulously, Narcissus relies on his immediate sense of the situation. As soon as he leaves the brink Michael turns and crosses the plateau, gaining height vigorously, in an attempt to use his superior strength and catch his enemy unawares from behind. Narcissus, seeing what has happened, turns to meet his opponent, and they clash above the judge and seconds. Though Narcissus is at a disadvantage, he wards off the attack with a few minor cuts on his belly. The conflict is cut short by their descent almost to the ground; they break off the fight and glide away from each other, seeking rising air.

Today they do not find it. The air is oddly dead, and though clouds begin to form, they do so in the depths of the Canyon. After a time Narcissus becomes bored and begins to pursue his opponent, trying to drive him into a

disadvantageous position. Michael, surprised, gains
height and then drops upon Narcissus once more. This
time Narcissus receives a deeper wound, in the small of
the back; but he has driven Michael against the side of a
mesa, where he has no escape. Narcissus now rips open
one of Michael's rear wings, depriving his enemy of a
large fraction of his power. Michael can do nothing but
dive. He does so, pursued by Narcissus, angry as a harpy.

They enter the clouds and continue to fall, by previous
agreement using the powers of the goddesses to keep track
of each other. The air is still and stifling. At last they
emerge from the base of the cloudmass with the jungle
only a hundred meters below. Seeing them, a group of
hunting pterodactyls rises toward them, screaming
hoarsely.

Now the enemies become allies. Together Michael and
Narcissus stoop upon the ghastly, skull-like reptiles. In
moments two of them are falling like broken bags of
blood, their horrible membranes fluttering in the wind of
their descent. The others scatter in terror.

But Narcissus has lost his immediate advantage. He
now begins to gain height, circling and looking for a
chance to destroy his crippled antagonist. At that moment a sudden flaw of wind bends the treetops, which
whiten as the huge leaves display their furry undersides.
Something is happening. Michael takes his opportunity
and flies with the wind. Narcissus follows. The wind
grows to hurricane force. The grey vapor begins to shred,
revealing a higher level of nimbus clouds above them.
There is a roaring. Before them is a small tornado, tearing
up trees as if they were playthings. Now both combatants
circle the vortex, rising swiftly and exerting their
maximum effort to avoid being sucked in.

The tornado pulls them up into the belly of an immense
thundercloud. They are hurled hither and thither, but all
the time Narcissus is closing on his enemy, At last he sees
his chance. Both have emerged from the cloud into an odd
dark antechamber of the storm, a clear space lit periodically by the stupefying forks of the lightning. Narcissus is
above. Glowing whitely he stoops upon his dazed oppon-

ent, and strikes him a deep and sudden blow in the back
with his ankle-spur. The blade penetrates into Michael's
lung, and he drops away, only the power of the goddess
sustaining him, in shocking pain, seeking only refuge.

Narcissus follows; but as if in revenge the stormcloud
above him, which has assumed the shape of a shield,
shoots forth a bolt of lightning, one of whose blinding
tines transfixes Narcissus, spreadeagled on his wings, in
an unbearable flash of light and energy. Now he is
stunned, his mind wiped clean by the forces he has
sustained. He sinks toward the forest, only the barest
flicker of consciousness guiding him to the haven of a
little hillock above the raging waters of the Ouroboros.

Michael, it appears, has sought the same spot. Like
blind beasts they crawl together, and with his last strength
each unburdens the other of his wings and spurs. Naked,
burned, and deeply wounded they lie in each other's arms.

At last Athena and Aphrodite take pity on their
charges, infusing them with a little strength and clarity of
mind, supplying them with food and drink, and salve for
their wounds. The place is gloomy, a small rocky space
overlooking the endless jungles that stretch away into the
mist. It is almost dark. Using the Vision they call up a tent,
and sit in it together on cushions, drinking wine and sharing the last of the provisions brought by their patron-
esses. They set up a force-field about them to protect them
from the nightmarish creatures of the Canyon.

Both Narcissus and Michael feel a curious sense of
freedom, as if all their lives were over and nothing were
left but the immediate situation. Narcissus has recovered
from the wanton and formless spells of Murasaki as if
they were a dream. Michael feels released from the con-
straints of his marriage, his chosen style, his political
stance; he has forgotten his parents, his wife, even his own
approaching paternity which is now only a few moments
away, although he does not know it.

Snow has had a hard labor. Refusing help, and in a
more and more desperate state, she has been struggling
with an unborn who is too large for her. She wants it to be

born but has ceased to care whether she herself lives or dies. In a darkened room, attended only by servants and refusing any human or metaphysical aid, she strives without joy, as she has done so many times in her life. Now that the combat between her lover and her husband has begun, there is no escape for her that combines honor with happiness: she cannot get the image of Narcissus out of her mind, yet it is Michael's baby with whom she is suffering; even suicide is impossible, for this will reveal to Michael that all this time she had been in love with his enemy. Thus her pain is welcome to her, and as she feels her strength ebbing away, she sees the way to freedom.

At last, many hours after the first contractions, the baby's head crowns: it is covered with black hair.

At that moment, in the tent by the Ouroboros, Michael and Narcissus, cleansed of the soil and blood of the day, and in a kind of ecstasy, are joined in a total embrace. If Narcissus had not become addicted to the Vision in the womb, he would have been a woman and not a hermaphrodite; and now I must change the pronoun, for Narcissus here returns to the female side of her nature, and her maleness now only completes and fulfills her. Like a mother she fondles the torn body of her enemy, a kind of charity; and as Snow, a hundred kilometers away, gives birth to the child whose life will be her death, Michael spends himself on the soft body of her lover Narcissus.

4.
Cleopatra and Murasaki

YUEN, WHO IS, since the decline of Shadrach, the most prominent member of the clan, and therefore charged to avenge the dishonor and death of Hermes, has other interests than simply those implicit in acting as Michael's second. He has been watching the duel carefully, and has noticed the increasing tenderness between the duelists; and furthermore, he views with alarm the fact that Narcissus seems to have the advantage of Michael, and will probably kill him on the third day.

Excusing to himself the great breach of manners by the demands of honor, he has observed, by means of the Vision, what happened in the tent. He feels sure he can use this information; and next morning he presents himself to Cleopatra, on the pretext of informing her of the course of the fight. The harm that his story may do her is not absent from his mind: she is, after all, partly to blame for Hermes' death, according to his analysis.

·"My apologies, madam, for disturbing you so early in the morning." (Cleopatra is dressed in a simple golden nightgown, and her hair, brushed but uncoiffed, pours over her shoulders and down her back.)

"I am not disturbed," she replies. She does not trust Yuen, because she knows of his duty to the dead Hermes. Nevertheless they are obstensibly on the same side, and she hears him out.

"The news, madam, is not good, unless your loyalty is still to your brother."

"Not at all." She smiles bitterly.

"Michael has been badly wounded, and his wings have been damaged. Of course this damage will have been repaired overnight, but it does not augur well for today. If you have any desire to be avenged for Narcissus' desertion of you, you should bend your greatest efforts toward helping Michael."

"What can I do?"

"Most important, you can go to that woman he keeps—what's her name?—Murasaki—and find out what you can about her. Perhaps she knows something with which we can damage the poise and confidence of your . . . brother, I was going to say, but of course he is your enemy."

"As you say, my enemy. Is that all you have to say?"

"For the present, yes."

"Why should I dishonor myself by spying on my brother because your great champion cannot fend for himself? It's true that I do not owe much love to Narcissus, but really, really, it is too much to ask. Master Yuen, you might have considered to whom you are speaking."

"A pity, my lady, that you should find it necessary to take that attitude—"

"Don't attempt to bully me!"

"—for now I must say what I had promised myself not to say. Your brother has betrayed you again—this time with Michael himself. He brings dishonor on both houses, and especially upon you."

Cleopatra starts to laugh; a change comes over her, and suddenly she gasps and falls in a faint. Yuen bends to assist her; as he does so Cleopatra stirs and half-opens her brown eyes. She murmurs: "Cissy, you bad thing. What are you doing now? They want me to help them kill you. Must I do it?" Then, more strongly: "Yes, I must. It's the

least you'd expect from me. Why do we have to fight,
though? I wish . . ." She breaks off, rises to a kneeling
position. "Yes, Yuen, I will do what you ask. But stay out
of my way. The next time I see you, I will kill you, I
promise. Go away now."

Yuen has never seen Cleopatra like this. He backs
away, afraid; but his work has been done. Cleopatra must
do what he has asked, as Yuen well knows. Her public
stance of rejecting her brother and joining the opposed
faction is being tested: any hesitation would be a sign of
the aesthetic weakness of her position. But there are
deeper reasons: she is fighting a personal battle with her
brother, and only an absolute opposition will adequately
express the love she still bears him. And finally, Cleopatra
cannot resist the temptation to gloat over her rival, who
has been betrayed in turn.

As soon as Yuen is gone, Cleopatra prepares herself to
meet Murasaki. She puts on her most magnificent robes,
of white and purple and gold; her handmaidens put up her
hair and crown her with a tiara of amethysts. She is
carried to her own house, where Murasaki has taken up
residence, in a litter borne by four brothers (not androids,
but true human beings); around her is a full entourage of
courtiers, mounted ceremonial guards, and ladies in waiting. She has called on the full resources of her rank and
clan; Cleopolis does not see a procession like this from
one month's end to another.

When she arrives she is kept waiting for a few moments
in the dusty street with its straggling marigolds and
patches of nasturtiums, which are a weed in Cleopolis,
while her gentlemen go in to demand an audience. Almost
at once one of Cleopatra's old servants, now Murasaki's,
ushers her into an antechamber where she alights from
her palanquin, dismisses her servants, and awaits her
rival.

At last Murasaki, who has been profoundly shaken by
this visit, appears with her servant Aoi.

Aoi speaks for her mistress:

"What is your will, madam? For what reason have you
honored this house once more with your presence?"

"I did not come here to speak with your servant," says Cleopatra to Murasaki. The latter beckons with her head, and Aoi disappears.

Murasaki does not speak, but stands expectantly; at this range Cleopatra can half-understand the appeal that she makes to her brother's desires. Ugly she is indeed, with a mottled and dewlapped face and rounded shoulders; but there is a suggestive fullness in the lips and depth of bosom, and her hair is beautiful; the eyes, lowered now in a resistant and stubborn humility, though coarse, are long lashed and curl sensually at the corners.

At last Cleopatra speaks. "I have come to speak to you about my brother."

"My regrets, madam. What have I to say of him? He is a spirit of his own; he does what he wishes. Perhaps it would be better to address yourself to him in person."

"Do not play games with me. I am not in a mood to be trifled with. Look at me when you speak to me!" The tone of command is irresistible: Murasaki raises her oddly familiar eyes. "I demean myself by this visit; nevertheless, my apologies for any personal inconvenience it may cause you." This last is almost contemptuous. She continues.

"First I must ask you, Who are you?"

"I cannot answer, madam."

"Why not?"

Murasaki blurts it out: "It is a question of the confidence of a goddess."

"I take the responsibility for that upon myself. Who are you?"

Murasaki is silent. She is afraid of this woman, once her mistress, her lover. She knows of her potential for violence and fears it. Cleopatra takes a step forward, her head perfectly balanced, her arms a little spread, the small fists clenched.

"Narcissus has been unfaithful to you with Michael. Don't you see what that means? He has broken your spell. Whatever goddess it is who is helping you, and for whatever reason, you have lost him in any case. *Tell me who you are!*"

Murasaki, in tears, begins to change before Cleopatra's

eyes. The forms and masses of her body shift oddly, as if her flesh were a community of animals rather than a single organism; she sobs; under her simple gown she seems to lose substance, straighten, grow graceful. Her face, half-turned, seethes like the indistinct trouble at the misty surface of a boiling vessel, and begins to take on its true features. Both women stand there speechless.

"Rokujo! What have you done?" cries Cleopatra.

"Madam, I could do nothing else. It was love that drove me. Surely you must understand." There is another pause.

"Poor girl," says Cleopatra, stroking her hair. "What lengths you went to, to keep him." She continues:

"But I am not finished. Who is the goddess who assisted you in this matter?"

"Venus, my lady."

"Why?"

"She, too, desired Narcissus. In return for being his mistress, I permitted her to share my body. It was her spells that bewitched him though, not mine."

"Where was your pride?"

"There is no pride in love, madam: you know that, for you came here today against your pride, for the love of the same person."

"How did you guess that? I told myself it was for revenge."

"It was not a guess."

"But you have lost him now. What are you going to do?"

"I will wait to serve him once again as his courtesan. That would be enough, if he would have me. Please help me. Perhaps he can defeat Michael. Perhaps all can be as it was, before any of these things happened."

As a courtesan, Rokujo would not, in Martian society, count as a rival to Cleopatra; in fact courtesans are often the close friends, and even the lovers, of their clients' spouses. Cleopatra's feelings toward "Murasaki" have changed altogether; of course what Rokujo has done is an act of madness according to Martian law, as is any deep violation of a chosen role: she is "out of character." But

Cleopatra, like her brother, pays little attention to the law.

"He must be told. His honor is at stake. Still, I shall do what I can to intercede for you."

"What about the goddess? Will she give him up?"

"That is between her and Narcissus. He must choose. Nevertheless I fear the result of that choice. It is dangerous to tamper with the designs of Olympus."

And so it is decided. At once Cleopatra makes contact through the Vision with her brother, who is already high in the air above the Canyon, in the last stages of his battle with Michael.

5.
The Third Day

THE CONFLICT THAT morning has been relatively uneventful. Embracing lovingly, Michael and Narcissus assist each other into their wings and spurs. It is a clear, bright morning like the first, the forest glittering with dew, the greatest trees, rising two or three hundred feet above the others, clothed in a grey mantle of spiderwebs and mist, lit to pale blue on one side by Phobos, orange on the other by the sun.

They rise into the dawn above the bright misty waters of the Ouroboros. Both know that today one of them must die, but neither wishes to initiate the last bloody encounter. Instead, they strive for height, using different thermals about five kilometers apart. The two suns glitter on the metal of their wings. It is this peaceful scene, full of incipient violence, that Frederick Remington will choose for his epic painting of the duel of Michael and Narcissus, completed years later and in the light of succeeding events.

When the combatants rise above the edges of the Canyon their mood changes. Michael, the stronger climber, is somewhat above Narcissus. He makes a pass at his enemy, but misses. Both continue to rise, until noon finds them as high as it is possible to breathe, many kilometers above the Canyon floor. Below them a huge panorama spreads itself, warped grotesquely by the planet's curvature like a view from a fisheye lens. Clouds have begun to form in the valley.

At that moment of noon Narcissus hears in his mind the words of Cleopatra, telling him of the masquerade of Rokujo and the complicity of Venus. Far above the world, in an abstraction of blue sky, he barely understands her words at first, so remote are the spheres of existence that here intersect. Gradually he begins to comprehend; he feels vaguely the intensity of Cleopatra's passion, and at last the new situation comes into focus. So Murasaki was really Rokujo. How could he not have known? He remembers that moment of odd familiarity when he realized that Murasaki reminded him of Hermes.

In a flash a monstrous suggestion occurs to him. Was Hermes, too, the host and victim of the goddess, no less the instrument of her desire? The moment he asks the question he is convinced of it. Cleopatra, reading this new thought in her brother's mind, falls away in horror. The inference is overwhelming. What Aphrodite has so carefully concealed has come to light. He feels the goddess struggle in his mind; she is afraid, and the divine terror makes him smile.

A curious impersonality comes over him, a detachment, even amusement. Everything is indeed arbitrary. Nothing remains, all is subject to reinterpretation. He has lost his honor, and is a fool, and it makes no difference. His mind is set like a clock. He dismisses Venus from his brain and body with a kind of gentleness. Now he is naked of all the powers with which she has provided him. Cleopatra, understanding dimly what he intends to do, clamors desperately in his mind. He shuts her out. At this height he can barely breathe, and without the help of the goddess his sight is dimmed and his muscles feeble.

Nonetheless, because of Michael's earlier mistake, Narcissus has a few hundred meters in hand. Below him his enemy circles in the sun. Narcissus turns on a wingtip and drops like a stone. Michael, warned by Athena, rises to face his antagonist; and in the last moment evades him. Now Michael stoops on Narcissus, made clumsy by the loss of his divine assistant, and unable to escape. The heel spurs rip through Narcissus' wings in an explosion of color; metal feathers tinkle and release; Narcissus, bereft of support, begins his long fall. Head first, the rear wings intact but useless, and with the torn fragments of his fore wings fluttering at wrist and elbow, both arms ripped to the bone and paralyzed, in free fall he tumbles from the great height he has achieved.

The descent seems to take hours: down through the pure sky he falls, his face impassive, his arms waving in the wind. Down through the highest clouds, brushed by the cool mist; down past the tallest pinnacles, down through a series of storms, falling like a bolt from heaven, he drops from the zenith like a shooting star; down through the crowns of the highest trees he plunges, into the twilight of the forest, where at last his fall is stayed, and his body, white and beautiful, lies broken on the jungle floor.

But he is not yet dead. A spark of life persists, and he looks around, unable otherwise to move, to see what sort of world he has fallen into. His eyes adjust to the gloom, and he sees that he is in a kind of chamber, floored by a pinkish mould, walled in by the immense trunks of Xiorns and Lambdaorns, furnished in the weird pastel colors of a multitude of funguses—umbrellas, ears, balls, cushions, and phalluses. There is a thick, pale smell of mushrooms, dry and rubbery or damp and slick. As he watches, a puffball collapses with a sigh. Its dumpy body dimpling as it releases its cloud of greyish spores.

There is an interruption. A tiny dinosaur—Oviraptor or Struthiomimus—enters the chamber suddenly, stops, peers at the still body of Narcissus, runs up to him and investigates inquisitively, and then, in response to a slight movement of the head, scuttles away on its long legs. Narcissus tries to chuckle.

Above there is a crashing. Michael, who had dived after Narcissus when he began to fall, is searching for his lover-antagonist. There is no time to be lost. Narcissus closes his eyes and enters the Vision.

A few moments later Michael drops beside him. Looking at the beautiful crushed body, he begins to weep, falls to his knees beside it. Chrysanthemum is the next to arrive. He sees what has happened and he, too, for the first time in centuries, sheds tears of grief, his huge belly shaking with the sobs.

There is a rustle among the almost-sentient funguses, and a group of Mystic tribesmen appear around them. They are tiny people, darker than is common, almost naked, with amulets and beads about their bodies. They are not unfriendly: they have been drawn by an intuitive sense of the expenditure of psychic energy. They are shepherds of a sort, tending the stranger species of fungus for the psychedelic juices they secrete. Finally a pair of philosopher-aestheticians, accompanied by Frederick Remington, arrive on the scene. They make a curious tableau. Remington sets up his easel.

But Cleopatra does not come yet. She has been called away from Rokujo's side very suddenly by a summons from Snow. Snow is dying, and wishes to look at her rival a last time. Setting aside her anxiety for her brother, Cleopatra appears at Snow's bedside. Snow is barely breathing, and her complexion has taken on a frightening bluish cast. She does not wish to live anymore, though in her arms is her son, a big healthy baby with a full head of hair.

"You have come," says Snow faintly.

"As you see. What do you desire of me?"

"I wanted to see you before I die. Yes, you *are* like him, as everyone says."

"What is this! I do not understand."

Snow replies in a haiku:

> "*Before the white flower that now dies*
> *Was plucked, your brother stole her perfume.*"

Now Cleopatra's spirit almost quails. "Why are you telling me this?"

Snow is about to reply when a change passes over her face. With a part of herself she has been following the conflict in the Canyon: it is at this moment that Narcissus' wings are broken by the spurs of his enemy.

"Narcissus has fallen!" she cries. She attempts to sit up, and the baby begins to cry. Cleopatra sends forth her mind's eye, and perceives Narcissus lying broken on the forest floor. "Cissy!" she screams; and almost swoons, but yet again seizes hold of herself. "I must go now. Your husband has the victory."

"No . . . Wait." With a supreme effort Snow clings to the garments of Cleopatra.

"The baby must be called Narcissus. You shall rear him as if he were your own; and you shall teach him that his father is his dead namesake Narcissus, and that I, his unhappy mother, bore him unfaithful to her husband, and died in the shame of it. This duty I lay on you, that shall have no child but for this. And you must tell my husband that the child was dead when it was born, and keep the child a secret from him; for indeed the only love of his mother was the one for whom he was named."

Now Cleopatra at last understands the prophecy of Gabriel on the island of the great temple, and the strange words of Hermes' ghost in the underground room at Rennet. As she leans forward to kiss the mother, Snow gives a long sigh and is still. The baby, which had quieted in the last moments, begins to cry again, beating the dead breast of his mother with a tiny fist. Very gently Cleopatra draws aside the arms of Snow, picks up the infant, who is quiet at once, and resettles the dead arms across the dead breast. Holding the baby with one arm, she closes Snow's eyes and draws up a silk spread over the face.

The servants and maids are stunned. Cleopatra turns to them. "You heard your mistress' last words. Let none of you disobey her. Now you must prepare a double funeral, for it must be known abroad that the baby is to join the mother in the pyre. Let all be done quickly, that the father may not return and find out the truth. It may be said that Snow wished for a swift funeral, and that she desired her husband not to see her or the child in death." Such is the force of Cleopatra's presence that all is done as she commands. And so the son of Michael has become the son of Narcissus; and the revenge of Aphrodite, plotted by her long ago in the mansions of the goddesses when Michael repulsed her desires, is complete. Michael has been forced to destroy his new beloved, and must, unwitting, see his own child raised in the house of his mortal enemy.

Cleopatra is the last to arrive by the body of her brother. She has entrusted the child to her handmaidens. She does not weep; she shows the actress' poise, and all her heroines are in her bearing: Medea, Electra, Antigone, and her namesake Cleopatra.

6.

The Dark Angel

NARCISSUS HAS SLIPPED into the Vision moments before his body is discovered. As he does so, the excruciating physical pain of his smashed limbs disappears, to be replaced by the cool, neutral, slightly echoic mental space of the Vision's threshold. Here an infinite potentiality offers itself: lying ready are powers of action, vision, knowledge, and logic beyond the grasp of the ancient gods of humankind. Here Narcissus rests awhile, as a sense of great light grows around and within his identity. Little shades and flickers of his past life run across the flanks of his quiescent self, like tiny fish across the dim bulk of a sleeping whale. The experience is synaesthetic, and as always a trifle frightening. Madness is so close, so seductive: on every side there are opportunities, deep slopes of feedback, drunkenness, ecstasy from which there is no return.

Now Narcissus probes deeper, and the light grows. He is heading for the heart of the Visison, for that mysterious coordination that renders its every operation and state consistent and logically inevitable.

As he does so he detects an annoying distraction

"behind" him: his body is beginning to die, and his natural brain is disintegrating, its cells, deprived of oxygen, destroying themselves as they release their last packets of energy. Impatiently, and with the gesture of a person who corrects a minor oversight, Narcissus separates himself entirely from his body, taking with him a perfect record of his physical and emotional identity, so perfect that it will continue to develop, according to its own logic, within the spaces of the Vision itself. He shuts the gates of the world behind him, collects his remaining energies. It is as if he has closed the door on a draught or a distracting noise. At the same time he feels oddly and painlessly truncated. A wave of nostalgia passes over him, for a certain day of the world, a summer, woody, sunlit episode in the treehouse on Eleuthera. He puts this feeling behind him, and penetrates deeper still.

And now he begins to enter realms that are forbidden on pain of madness, realms which he has half-investigated before but from which he had always drawn back in prudence and fear. Each has a triple structure: the point of entry, the place itself, and the point of departure. They are like flavors, of cut wood, strawberries, mown grass, frying, or sherbet; or like the quality of certain relationships, with a brother when you were a child, with a loving aunt, with a woman who catches your eye across a street on a sunny day. They are also powers, of altering the logic of geometric structure, of affecting the actual course of past history, of pure gravitational sculpture.

As Narcissus presses forward, he encounters here and there the errant spirits of other uneasy travelers: from human cultures of which he has no comprehension, from nonhuman cultures whose presence is felt only as an experience for which there are no names; and even one or two familiar faces. At one point he thinks he catches a glimpse of Hermes, and flees from the place in terror.

And he enters the myriad elysiums and hells of the dead: religious paradises bathed in the beatific vision; pagan and humanistic agoras where Socrates debates forever, as in the Raphael *School of Athens*; baroque and romantic heavens and self-punishing infernos, with alabaster saints with upturned eyes and a damned soul, hiding his face in his hands but peering through the fingers in fascination at the gulfs below him; he passes through a complete Zen problem, here in its concrete mental form; and voluptuous and abandoned scenes of carnal delight, perversion, huge airy bubbles, animals with human genital organs, fountains of nectar, arbors of vines.

In none of these does Narcissus find place and refuge for his restlessness. He pushes deeper in, the light almost unbearable, against the repeated warnings of his solicitous Idiot Guardian, which has followed him faithfully this far. At last he leaves even this last familiar form behind, entering the final regions of light and madness.

As he does so an intolerable pressure mounts and mounts; it is as if he were being crushed to a point, and the light cannot be borne. But he bears it; his fierce personality, accepting the challenge with panache, willingly squanders its resources in the effort of resistance. Against these satanic rigors, this black-hole brilliance, he sets the untested energies of his pride; his self is warped almost into unrecognizability by tidal forces of the will that threaten to rip him apart, but he presses on.

The great computer has seldom experienced anything of this sort. It must draw on cosmic powers to sustain the encounter: on a thousand worlds there is a flicker like a defective light fixture as suns are briefly drained of their strength to supply the deficit.

At last Narcissus reaches the center, and there he finally collapses. But even now a shred of self remains, that remembers the smell of spring mornings, the crackle of a cat's fur, the little jokes of Cleopatra; but these are dim, a million years ago.

And time ceases: at once all history, past and future, is present to him: he is the still point, the heart of the mandala, the mystical rose, the embryo of the world. He is effectively and theologically God Himself. He sleeps, as if for a billion years, though not a second passes. In his sleep he dreams of a whole cluster of new universes (which instantly become fact). But they are only variants or recombinations of the already existent.

And at last he comes back to himself and knows that he is bored, grotesquely and elaborately bored. He is the center of everything and knows all; it is as if he stands in the sun and can see nothing but his own light reflected back to him, shadowless, in a perpetual noon: he knows all, for he does all. And with a sudden spasm of nausea, he rejects it all.

In a lightless flash he implodes, leaving around his vanished center a shell of psychic radiation, blasted outward at the limit speed of actuality, generating his own time in the process. Or it might be more correct to say that the convulsion he has initiated in the core of godhead generates an expanding wave whose front he rides, rejected, into the outer regions of non-existence. He is translated from center to circumference. Having experienced pure Being, he has denied it: what remains is only process, only a continuous act of fiction by which he creates himself anew from moment to moment, and destroys himself as he does so, for whatever he *is* is what he rejects. He is a chattering spirit driven out into the void, an improvisation of language, a pure generativeness, a radical novelty.

More than this, he has become an element of the edge of the real universe. The quality of the present moment from now on is subtly changed: time works in a slightly different fashion. Everything everywhere that happens, takes place in a wilder and more arbitrary way. Causality is attenuated, experience is at once richer and more difficult to get hold of. The universe tends more readily now to spawn independent subsystems, which persist and contradict the canonical reality with more vigor than heretofore.

The change is noted in several histories of the period, but no explanation is given. In Chrysanthemum's account of the whole affair written some years later, he correctly identifies the change with the fall of Narcissus: but this explanation is generally taken to be fanciful, typical of its author's habitual hyperbole.

Epilogue

SHORTLY AFTER THE events that have just been described, Rokujo, aware now that she was not the first to be possessed by Aphrodite, and of her odd kinship with her dead rival Hermes; unable to live without Narcissus, and blaming herself for his death, takes her own life. She is found in her apartment hanging from a roofbeam by a long scarf of yellow silk, her face distorted by her mode of death into something that oddly resembles her avatar Murasaki.

Her simple funeral takes place on the very island in Lake Tehuantepec where she had witnessed the cremation of Hermes. As part of the ceremony Aoi, weeping and dressed in mourning white, reads her mistress' last poem, found near her body after the suicide:

> *These nights those many deaths call me to go,*
> *A call that nothing in me can deny:*
> *It's my profession to be weak, and so*
> *Despite delays and coquetries, I die.*
>
> *They cannot beckon me with half the force*
> *That my own weakness calls on me to die:*
> *I feel it in my breasts, my womb, my source,*

As in first love, that first unslaking sigh.

My masquerades have all been torn away,
My games and poetries were all a lie;
It pleased the jealous goddess to betray
My love, my lover, and myself; but I

Leave her with this one question: Goddess, why
Like Adonis, must your lovers die?

Venus herself, in her mansion in the crater of Nix Olympica, has no reply. The goddess has been overcome with bitter remorse: she confines herself to her room where, unable to stand the sight of her own body, she has wrapped herself in silks and sits huddled in a divan. Her servants cannot tempt her with celestial viands; she will not sleep or eat, and she does not care for company. A serving-eunuch who was too insistently comforting had his head broken by her in a rage, with a priceless vase that came to hand.

However, this mood does not last long. The habit of centuries, the craving and inertia of that ancient and voracious personality, cannot be diverted by an episode of mere months. Before long Venus has secretly consoled herself with a visit to a pretty boy in New Bristol; and within a few weeks she is quarreling vigorously with the other goddesses, meddling as before in the lives of men, and making the springtime wilder, lovelier, and more dangerous.

But some effects remain. She refuses to speak to Athena (who was never her favorite colleague) for some decades; and the memory of Narcissus leaves her sometimes pensive and respectful. She avoids Cleopatra like the plague, and does not interfere with the affairs of that family again for many years.

*   *   *

Gunther attends Rokujo's funeral, and, without comprehending why, is compelled to weep and dash himself to the ground before the flames. He develops in the succeeding months a new interest in poetry, and though he never becomes very good at it, he does become more adept at understanding allusions and synecdoche. He embarks on an enormous and unsuccessful work on human psychology, in twenty-five volumes, which is essentially an attempt to define scientifically the meaning of the term "aesthetic."

Michael, now Topcock of the planet, must suffer his triumph alone. Shortly before Rokujo's funeral the double cremation of Snow and her son has taken place: in accordance with his wife's last desires he makes no attempt to view the bodies, and so an empty coffin, pathetically small, burns beside Snow's.

He decides that he must go on living, and he does so in torment of mind, clinging steadfastly to the style that has destroyed his heart and gained for him the warlordship of Mars. His face, over the years, takes on a grey and rocky look; he begs for accidental death but it will not come. In the series of portraits of him that Remington executed over the years, we can see the grief settling in, getting a grip on aspect after aspect of his personality. He becomes deeply respected for his suffering, and is consulted on aesthetic questions for his advice. He replies tonelessly and without irony, as is his duty.

Snow's baby, the second Narcissus, grows up in secret on the island of Eleuthera. Cleopatra surprises herself with her gifts as a mother; she has had hormone treatments to make her lactate, and sits on the sunlit terrace among the trees with the baby at her golden breast, her hair and suntanned shoulders shining in the light.

The baby is supernaturally beautiful, with a face like Buddha's at first, becoming elfin in a year or two, and rounding out to a delicate strength by the time he is five or six. Oddly enough he resembles Narcissus more than his true father Michael: his small mouth with close, pearly white teeth, is the image of his dead foster-father's.

He is an intelligent, lazy, and mischievous child: he

learns to fly very early, and uses the Vision precociously. The platforms of the house thump with the running brown heels.

Cleopatra is oddly happy. She still acts and dances occasionally in the theatre at Hellas, but her main preoccupation is the boy Narcissus; she coaches him in mime, fighting, and poetry. True to Snow's last desires she raises him in the belief that Narcissus was his true father, and fields the intelligent questions (for the child is also sexually precocious) about Narcissus' hermaphroditic sterility, with learned scientific explanations.

Occasionally Uncle Chrysanthemum comes to visit, which is always a red-letter-day for the boy. Chrysanthemum draws him pictures and teaches him scatological poetry; blowing like a whale he carries his little nephew on his back and throws him, screaming, again and again into the air. Chrysanthemum is fatter and sadder, but has not changed otherwise. He has taken up with a vulgar and debased young student who gratifies his every vile desire, accumulated over years of experiment.

Sometimes during the northern winter Cleopatra takes the boy to the house at Rennet for the winter sports, where Matthew, delighted with his small companion, instructs him in archery, fishing, tracking, and the mysteries of skis. Besides these adventures the boy has "inherited" a habit of his foster-parents: traveling in secret from place to place on the planet by means of the Vision, delighting the dissolutes of the city by asking them informed questions, stealing small articles from the shops, and eavesdropping on lovers' banal conversations. One of his favourite haunts is the Great Southern Canal, where he rides the barges and feluccas, and jabbers with the boatmen. Everywhere he goes he is admired for his radiant grace and beauty.

When he is fourteen Cleopatra tells him of the death of Narcissus at Michael's hand. He has already heard the story in various forms, but this is the first time he is sure of what happened.

Upon learning of his "father's" death he vows vengeance. In the sunny glades of the School of Martial

Arts he hones himself into a refined killer, nor does he neglect the disciplines of history, philosophy, and oratory. Some years later, a movement begins among the southern cities to contest the Warlordship of Michael. Mars has been quiescent for some time, and everyone is impatient for a new conflict to generate the suffering and beauty that alone make life worth living. Instead of a duel, Narcissus the younger, who turns out to be the secret leader of the movement, initiates a full-scale war against Michael and his supporters. In the Battle of the Syrtis Major Narcissus' forces defeat Michael's and Narcissus faces his true father for the first and last time. There is an epic fight between the two in which Narcissus, wounded across the face, half-blinded, and his beauty ruined, brings his father to his knees and strikes off his head with the sword of Narcissus the Elder.

All these things are according to the prophecy of Gabriel; and one day Narcissus himself visits the ancient fortune teller. Confusing future with past, Gabriel lets drop some remarks that bear a strange emphasis. Narcissus presses him for an explanation; is refused; takes the old hermaphrodite by his beard and threatens him with violence; and at last finds out the truth about his father. In a later play about this episode, done in the Greek style, the playwright has Narcissus *laugh* at his mistake, and at that moment his left eye, which has been damaged by Michael's sword, suddenly regains its function of sight. Actually there was no correlation between the healing of Narcissus' optic nerve and the revelation of the truth, although they occurred within a few months of one another. Nevertheless, it is true that Narcissus laughed.

As soon as he returns home he seeks out Cleopatra and acccuses her of her lies. He is about to kill her with his sword when she begs leave to tell him a story, as she had often done when he was a child. The story she tells explains the death and last wishes of his mother Snow. As she tells the tale a strange emotion passes over Narcissus, and he sees the woman he had thought to be his mother with new eyes. That day he and Cleopatra become lovers, an affair whose strange course is the subject of many songs and poems.

And so I leave the story: it has got away from me into the green and geometric jungles of myth, where everything is structure and all self and particularity is lost. Here plot is self-generating and automatic, like the operation of an algorithm, or the opening of a blossom, or the song of the nightingale. And so the human lament is metamorphosed into the abstraction of number, the melodies of a bird, the pathetic elegance of a freshly blown flower.

SCIENCE FICTION BESTSELLERS
FROM BERKLEY!

Frank Herbert